GUILTY WATERS

GUILTY WATERS

Priscilla Masters

This first world edition published 2014
in Great Britain and 2015 in the USA by
SEVERN HOUSE PUBLISHERS LTD of
19 Cedar Road, Sutton, Surrey, England, SM2 5DA.
Trade paperback edition first published 2015 in Great
Britain and the USA by SEVERN HOUSE PUBLISHERS LTD.

British Library Cataloguing in Publication Data

Masters, Priscilla author.
  Guilty waters. – (Joanna Piercy series)
  1. Piercy, Joanna (Fictitious character)–Fiction.
  2. Missing persons–Investigation–Fiction.
  3. Women detectives–England–Staffordshire–Fiction.
  4. Detective and mystery stories.
  I. Title II. Series
  823.9'2-dc23

ISBN-13: 978-0-7278-8461-9 (cased)
ISBN-13: 978-1-84751-564-3 (trade paper)
ISBN-13: 978-1-78010-612-0 (e-book)

Typeset by Palimpsest Book Production Ltd.,
Falkirk, Stirlingshire, Scotland.

By the old Moulmein Pagoda, lookin' lazy at the sea,
There's a Burma girl a-settin', and I know she thinks o' me;
For the wind is in the palm-trees, and the temple-bells they say:
'Come you back, you British soldier; come you back to
    Mandalay!'
Come you back to Mandalay,
Where the old Flotilla lay:
Can't you 'ear their paddles chunkin' from Rangoon to Mandalay?
On the road to Mandalay,
Where the flyin'-fishes play,
An' the dawn comes up like thunder outer China 'crost the Bay!

'Er petticoat was yaller an' 'er little cap was green,
An' 'er name was Supi-yaw-lat – jes' the same as Theebaw's
    Queen,
An' I seed her first a-smokin' of a whackin' white cheroot,
An' a-wastin' Christian kisses on an 'eathen idol's foot:
Bloomin' idol made o' mud
Wot they called the Great Gawd Budd
Plucky lot she cared for idols when I kissed 'er where she stud!
On the road to Mandalay . . .

Excerpt from 'Mandalay',
Barrack-Room Ballads and Other Verses,
Rudyard Kipling, 1892

ONE

Sunday, 19 May, 2014

H e spotted the picture at a car boot fair on a rainy day
in May. Amongst the piles of outgrown toys and racks
of clothes, bric-a-brac spread out randomly on plastic
sheets, Barker spotted a framed print leaning against a trestle
table looking straight at him, seduction in her eyes. As though
pulled on a string he moved towards the exoticism which
beckoned him across the muddy field. Pushing a few people
out of his way he strode towards her, quickening his pace as
he grew nearer. It was her. He knew her. He recognized her.

It was Supi-yaw-lat. The girl from the poem – the very
poem he had named Mandalay after. Right down to the ground.
Petticoat yaller. Little cap green. Well, she'd left that off today
to show her lovely thick black hair.

He picked it up and studied it closer, almost smelling her
exotic perfume – oleander, patchouli, musk. He liked everything about her, from the shining, embroidered gold of her
exotic costume to the pensive look on her face. Her foreign
features, full red lips, dark, dark hair. She looked . . . Barker
put his head on one side. Burmese, of course. She had to be.
There was only one strange thing about her that jarred: her
skin colour. It was a sort of unhealthy blue/green. It was not
realistic. What had the artist been thinking of to distort such
a beautiful face? Why had he painted her skin tone that strange,
dead colour, as though she was not from Burma but from
somewhere else, maybe another planet? Barker narrowed his
eyes. It was the only thing that annoyed him.

But he still had to have her, to take her home, as it were,
to live with him. He held the picture at arm's length and
studied her closer.

'It's a bargain that,' the vendor put in, standing far too close
behind him, trying to push the sale with his smoky breath.

'Most popular picture of the sixties.' He had a slight cockney accent which made him appear a bit of a spiv, a wide boy. A cheat. Barker turned to look at him, took in the mean, grabbing little eyes, the thin mouth, the hands wafting him towards a purchase. And the man rattled on: 'Practically an icon of the sixties.' When Barker said nothing in response he continued with his spiel, walking around him to stand next to the picture. 'That's more than fifty years ago, of course. Now she's practically an antique.' He glanced slyly at Barker. 'Maybe I should put a nought on the end of the price.'

Barker stiffened. He wasn't paying a hundred pounds for her.

The vendor looked affectionately at his picture. 'Know what they called her?'

Barker shook his head, mesmerized by the dark invite in the girl's slanting eyes, so dark they were unreadable, and contrasting almost glaringly with the gleaming richness of the yellow shawl that half-covered the red dress.

The guy laughed through tobacco-stained teeth. 'The real title is *Miss Wong* but they call her the kitsch Mona Lisa.' He giggled and Barker eyed him, puzzled. What was funny about that? It was . . . insulting. He looked curiously at the woman. She didn't seem kitsch to him, although she *was* a sort of inviting, exotic Mona Lisa. He felt almost protective towards her. He wanted to defend her against that horrid description – *kitsch*.

The vendor's mouth was open wide and he was still laughing, which made Barker want to punch him. He bunched up his fists but kept his arms rigidly by his side. He was not really the fighting sort.

The vendor hadn't finished with him yet. 'Want to know something else, mate?'

Barker's hostility was compounded. This man was certainly *not* his mate.

The dealer picked up the girl and held her at arm's length, his hands gripping the frame so hard his knuckles showed through, knobs of blue/white bone. He put his face close to Barker so he could smell his breath. 'It's the most reproduced painting in the whole world.'

Barker eyed the girl with suspicion. He wasn't sure he was pleased she had put herself around quite so much. He frowned. It sounded . . . well . . . cheap. The dealer saw the frown and continued hastily, studying both the picture and his potential customer hard, trying to find the right words to complete the sale. 'Yeah. She's popular, Miss Wong.'

Barker's face tightened. 'Oh, no,' he said clearly and with dignity. 'Her name is Supi-yaw-lat.'

The vendor gaped at him. Was this guy for real? Was he even sane?

But Barker knew she was not Miss Wong. That wasn't her name at all. He knew exactly who she was. And now he had identified her, when he looked at her he felt conspiratorial. Oh, what fun, what adventures they would have together, he and Supi-yaw-lat. What sights they would see together! There was only one thing he didn't know. 'Who painted her?'

A couple had approached the stall, which was little more than a flimsy plastic gazebo to shelter potential customers from the gusts of rain, and were peering over his shoulder at the picture. Barker panicked. What if they liked her too? What if they knew the poem and her real name?

The vendor was losing interest in him and was eyeing up the couple, sizing up their purchasing potential and comparing them favourably with the weirdo in front of him. He didn't even look at Barker when he answered the question. 'Don't know, mate. There's some sort of name in the corner. Looks Russian or somethin'.'

Barker felt resentful. People did this to him all the time: got bored with him, turned their attention to someone else. Anyone else was better to speak to than Barker.

The vendor was talking quickly to the couple now. Trying to sell the girl to them.

'Frame's nice too, ain't it?'

The frame was, in fact, horrible. Chipped white gloss paint on a narrow, mass-produced sliver of wood. Cheap as chips, Barker thought. Cheaper even. And an insult to her. He would have painted the frame gold.

He eyed up the vendor, wondering how much he would have to pay for Supi-yaw-lat. The vendor was short and plump with a lazy, lardy face. He was wearing ill-fitting jeans looped below a beer belly and a thin brown fleece that was slipping off his shoulders and he shrugged back up when he thought about it. He had pale brown eyes, almost the same colour as the fleece. His hair was sparse, grey and wispy and he had very bad teeth, a missing incisor and a mean look to him, as though he would squeeze every penny out of Barker. 'It's just a print,' he said dismissively, tossing the words over his shoulder, 'but a very famous one.'

Barker nodded again, sure that she would rather come home with him than stay here on this seedy stall, on this muddy field crowded with tat. He was already apologizing to her for what he was about to do. But sometimes bad things had to be done. She had a role but she wasn't his yet. He fingered his purse and peered ostentatiously at the label – £10, it read. And now he had a quandary. At car boot fairs it was his policy always to bargain. It was expected of you. That was what people came to car boot fairs for – to bargain away as though you were in a souk. Arguing over the pounds and the pence was part of the fun. But she was watching him. He couldn't bargain right in front of her, treating her no better than if she was on parade at a slave market. He pulled his purse out of his pocket and took out a ten-pound note, looking at it reluctantly as he handed it over, feeling the loss as keenly as a bereavement. Barker worked hard for his money. He disliked waste and tried to justify every penny he spent.

The man grabbed the tenner. 'Wanna bag?'

Barker shook his head. 'No, thanks.'

'You be careful,' the man said, pocketing the money and widening his grin to display almost all of his gaps and horribly stained teeth. 'She has a way with men.'

Barker didn't reply. Supi-yaw-lat was safely tucked underneath his arm as he strode across the field, back towards his car. She was his. He put her carefully, face up, in the boot. 'I'm so sorry,' he said to her as she watched him suspiciously. 'I'll try not to hurt you too much.'

In her face he had already read forgiveness.

TWO

Barker was home in less than half an hour.

Home was a large, Victorian house within sight of Rudyard Lake, today rain-spattered and grey. The house had originally belonged to his mother and father, but his father had died years ago, leaving him alone with his mother. It had seemed too big a house for the two of them and money was tight, but neither had wanted to abandon it so Barker's mother, Dora, had hit on the bright idea of opening it up as a guest house. That had been ten years ago, when they had rebranded Laurel Lodge as Mandalay and marketed it using Kipling's image both as their logo and their icon. The thick moustache and rimless glasses looked good on their business cards and even better on the website Barker had perfected five years ago.

Of course, they had needed to carry out some alterations over the years. Tastes in décor had changed radically. People these days expected en suite bathrooms, the highest standards of cleanliness and a good breakfast to send them on their way. But this had been no problem to either Barker or his mother, and they had made a tidy profit until his mother had had a stroke three years ago and died shortly after, leaving Barker to do all the cleaning himself plus all the cooking – breakfasts only, mind – as well as keeping Mandalay in reasonable condition. He also did all the laundry and acknowledged it had been a struggle, but all in all it was a very satisfactory business. Many of the people who stayed were Kipling fans who appreciated the relaxed atmosphere and prints of colonial India as well as the framed printouts of his better known poems. 'If' was always going to be popular and featured in four of the rooms, but 'Mandalay' was Barker's favourite. Most occupants were either couples or climbers. Holiday makers mostly, and a few families, though he didn't encourage children. Truth was he didn't like them.

At the moment he had a young couple from Berkshire and a teacher from Holland, who appeared to be travelling around the country on her own in a small red Citroen. She spoke such excellent English that Barker found it hard to believe she was Dutch. However, luckily, both the young couple and the Dutch girl were out for the day and not due back until this evening. At the moment he had Mandalay to himself. Himself and Supi-yaw-lat.

He opened the front door to the empty house then, returning to his car, he lifted Supi out of the boot, carried her inside and placed her, face up, on the kitchen table. He felt guilty as she eyed him with her two slanting eyes. She must be wondering what he was about to do to her. He evaded her gaze and trotted out to his garden shed, returning with a Stanley knife then carefully, very carefully, oh so carefully, apologies bubbling out of his mouth like water from a spring, he cut around the outline of her left eye, the blade slicing easily through the backboard. Then he picked the picture up, turned it around and put his own eye to the hole. Now he and Supi-yaw-lat could watch their own peep show together. He took her upstairs into the small twin-bed room, next to the box room, and hung her on the wall that stood between them. With a gimlet, he marked the spot where he needed to drill a hole through from the other side. Ten minutes later? Job done.

He stood back. There was one problem that worried him. His own eyes were blue, whereas his lady's eyes were dark. Very dark – almost a black hole in her oriental face. It was possible that his eye, peering through, would look too bright. He would just have to hope that no one noticed.

Ever.

THREE

Four months later
Saturday, 7 September, 10 a.m.

On the outskirts of Paris, in the suburb of Vincennes, Madame Cécile Bellange was looking at the mantelpiece on which stood a very fine Japy Frères boulle clock. A postcard was propped against it. For the umpteenth time since she had put it there she picked it up and studied the picture. It looked such a nice place, a pretty lake, a few boats sailing. A train in the background. People in the foreground all looking happy. She smiled. Happy families. Children, dogs, all running around, throwing balls, enjoying themselves. The English at play at a lake called Rudyard. She turned the postcard over and read the back. Again.

Maman, it read, *c'est beau ici. Les gens sont très sympathiques et nous avons trouvé un endroit propre agréable où séjourner. Se détendre. Il n'est pas trop cher. Nous avons encore de l'argent de côté. Vous nous verrez, quand nous aurons dépensé tout notre argent. J'ai découvert le letterboxing. Je t'embrasse, Annabelle* XXXXXX

It was clear the girls were having a good time, Annabelle talking about how beautiful it was there, how friendly the people were and how they'd found a clean, nice place to stay which wasn't too expensive. They still had money left, and Cécile would see them when it ran out. Her daughter had discovered letterboxing. She had signed off by sending her love.

Madame Bellange frowned. The postmark on the card was July. Now it was September. Since then, nothing. Not a word, written or telephoned. She had rung Annabelle's mobile many times, leaving messages, but had heard nothing back, and now she was worried. Her ex-husband, Armand, was not concerned. He was too busy with his new *amour*, Juliette, and had told her (nastily, she thought) that she was over-possessive of Annabelle, that she should learn to treat her as a normal seventeen-year-old and that the girl was simply enjoying what all young women should – a little bit of freedom. She had slammed the phone down on him after shouting that both Annabelle and Dorothée should be starting their college courses next week. Madame Bellange's face hardened. She had been to the National Police, whom she still thought of as the Sûreté. They had not been interested. 'Two teenage girls,' they'd said scornfully, 'hitchhiking around England. What do you expect? A letter every day?' And they had laughed.

'But Dorothée's mother has heard nothing either,' Cécile had insisted.

They'd shrugged. 'And is *she* worried?'

'Not like I,' Madame Bellange had said with dignity, and repeated, 'but next week they are due back at college.'

'Then they'll be back. You'll see,' the police had said, still exchanging amused glances between themselves.

Madame Bellange had grown angry. 'But their mobile phones . . .' she'd insisted.

'Run out of credit, I expect,' the policeman had said, touching his moustache to hide his amusement, which was turning towards impatience.

'Or maybe lost,' the other one had suggested. 'I have an eighteen-year-old daughter, madame. She has lost four mobile phones – so far. And she never has any credit.'

'Girls,' the other one had chimed in.

'Both of them?'

This had provoked a shrug and Madame Bellange had been even more annoyed then because the balding Sûreté man had winked at his colleague. *Winked.* Without trying to hide it. They were making fun of her, she realized.

She went home.

But the walls of the flat seemed to press in on her; accuse her of neglect. Annabelle's lilac bedroom, completely cleaned, curtains, duvet, bedding all washed, ironed and sprinkled with lavender water, seemed to emphasize how long it had been since her daughter had inhabited it. It didn't even smell of her any more.

She moved back to the lounge, picked up the postcard again and looked even closer at the picture on the front. The people looked so happy. It seemed like an innocent, pretty, old-fashioned sort of place. The girls would surely have been safe here. That was where she should start her search.

If no one would help her she'd find them herself. She would show them all, Armand included. She would take the Eurostar, hire a car and drive up to this place in Staffordshire. She would find the girls. She would return with them. For a second she wondered whether to speak to Dorothée's parents again but, like her and Armand, the girl's parents were also separated and Madame Caron was a career woman who had hardly noticed Dorothée's escape to Britain, while Monsieur Caron was 'not well', so everyone said. Cécile Bellange suspected *not well* was a euphemism for *alcoholic*, as it apparently affected his ability to function in any job and worry about his daughter, who had not been heard of for two months. Two whole months. And so it was up to her. She would drive to this lake Rudyard. She stared at the postcard. 'I will find you, *ma chérie*,' she whispered, kissing the card. 'Wait for me and I will come and bring you home. As the Sûreté will not help me, I will find you with the help of the British police.'

She closed her eyes and pictured her daughter, small and slight, always laughing, funny and sweet. Dark eyes, long, shining, straight brown hair. Her little girl.

The British police, in the form of Detective Inspector Joanna Piercy, had listened to the weather forecast that morning. Coincidentally, by eleven o'clock, on the same morning as Madame Bellange was looking at the postcard, in shorts and hiking boots and a picnic basket in front of them, Joanna and her husband of nine months, pathologist Matthew Levin, were sitting on the bank, looking down on Rudyard Lake. For a moment they were dazzled by the golden sparkle of the sun, feeling its warmth on their faces and listening to the whispers of the leaves in the trees as the breeze kept the temperatures in the mid-seventies, perfect for hiking and picnics. While Joanna had been showering that morning, Matthew had packed some rolls and a flask of coffee and they were eating *eau sauvage.* 'Fantastic,' Joanna said, biting into the bread roll filled with ham, tomatoes, beetroot, cream cheese and an eye-watering dollop of Colman's English mustard. 'Blimey, Matt,' she said, panting. 'You didn't spare the mustard, did you?'

He simply laughed and put his arm around her. 'Certainly not,' he said. 'Can't stand ham without mustard. It's tasteless. Don't be such a wimp, Jo.' He wiped a crumb away from the side of her mouth. 'It is lovely up here,' he said, looking down at the Boathouse and the sparkling lake. 'Simply beautiful.' He gave her a light kiss on her mouth. 'I'm glad you suggested it.'

As they watched, the small train steamed its way along the side of the lake accompanied by whoops from excited children and a *whooh whooh* in response from the train. Joanna nestled into Matthew's arms and for a few moments they were silent. The air hung heavy between them, full of things better left unsaid. Joanna knew she had been ducking away from them for long enough. It was time to face their demons. In this idyllic setting, Matthew content, herself the same – for a change – it seemed the right time and place. They had been married for almost nine months. A gestation period. She couldn't avoid unpleasant subjects any longer.

'Matthew,' she began tentatively.

Always intuitive to her moods, she felt him tense beside her. He brushed her hair with his lips and was silent for a long moment, neither encouraging nor discouraging her from continuing. She could feel his heart pounding against her cheek. Then he said, very quietly, 'I'm all ears, Jo.'

And she didn't know how to proceed. Instead she focused on the gleaming body of water, which gave her an answer. 'Rudyard,' she said softly. 'Would you call *your* son Rudyard?'

Matthew froze. So did she.

Then, 'What exactly are you saying?' Each syllable was uttered quietly and carefully.

'You know what I'm saying, Matt,' she said, without looking at him.

It was enough. His arm tightened around her.

Martin and James Stuart were champion climbers and letter-boxers. They stashed their notes everywhere, in crevices and cracks, in rocks and trees, at the back of caves, beneath stones and on top of cairns, collecting stamps and leaving hints and accounts of their visits. They had begun, years ago, on Dartmoor, walking to the most remote areas, climbing hills, boating to the middle of islands, finding other messages and hints in return. It was their main obsession. That and climbing. Every time they were off together they roamed the countryside and today was no exception. The perfect day, actually, for stashing messages and recovering others, taking risks and climbing crab-like up the Roaches, joining a few other climbers taking advantage of the perfect weather. They had a few days off together and the Roaches was one of the nearest good climbing sites to their Birmingham base. So, like Joanna and Matthew, they had packed a substantial picnic and were at the moment a few miles north-east of Leek, on the Roaches, a craggy outcrop popular with climbers as it sported more than fifty different challenges. The scene was watched by the Winking Man, another rocky outcrop in the profile of a man's face, except the nose was a little damaged. The strange thing about this natural phenomenon was that a shard of rock behind a hole gave the impression that the man was winking at you as you passed on the high, remote Buxton to Leek road. The area's wild ruggedness was so popular with walkers, hikers and indeed letterboxers, that it was often difficult to find a parking place, the road narrow with gullies at the side. The illusion of being in the great wilderness was sullied a little by the large signs warning visitors to put their valuables out of sight as it was also popular with car thieves.

Martin and James were atop the Winking Man's head on Ramshaw Rocks, savouring both the breeze and the vast panorama with the sense of power that a good climb gives. James poked around in the crevices, ever hopeful. 'Hey,' he said, finding the rusting tin. He opened it, took the stamp out of the paper it was folded in and found himself looking at the King of the Roaches, a bearded figure with a crown on top. He inked the stamp with the inkpad he always carried and stamped his notebook, then picked out the photograph and read the back, grinning broadly. 'Bingo. "Two French girls on a voyage of discovery."' He eyed his brother. 'Well?' he said.

Martin craned over and read. '"Come and find us. We will give you a welcome at the poet's lake, love Annabelle Bellange and Dorothée Caron". Lovely. What say you?'

'Gorgeous,' James said, looking at the photo of the two attractive, smiling girls. 'But it's months old,' he pointed out, always the pessimist, looking at the date scribbled in the corner of the photo. 'They won't still be there.' He hesitated. 'I take it the poet's lake is Rudyard?'

Hands on hips, his brother stood up on the rocks, a powerful, muscular figure silhouetted against the bright blue of the sky. He looked like a conqueror, an Alexander the Great. 'Has to be,' he said. 'And they'll be long gone by now, but if they're still marauding round nearby we can probably get an address out of the visitor's book at wherever they were staying. Or maybe they'll have left us another message somewhere round there. Come on, James. It's worth a try. It'll be a bit of fun anyway. Since you split up with Kay you've been like a frustrated elephant.'

His brother looked affronted. 'I have not.'

But Martin wasn't capitulating. 'Oh, yes you have,' he teased. And then, 'Careful . . .' as his brother inched closer to him and he glanced down at the long drop. 'You don't want me over the edge.'

But his brother's temper had flared, the way if often did these days if Martin tried to tackle the subject of James post-Kay. 'What about you when we were out clubbing the other night?' he retorted angrily. 'I don't think any of the girls were safe with you spreading yourself around.' He thumped his brother's shoulder harder than was necessary. 'If Camilla found out about you there'd be no wedding, I can tell you. She wouldn't be impressed with you draping yourself all over that Swedish girl. It was bordering on obscene. And she didn't like it.'

'I was drunk,' his brother said, embarrassed. He couldn't remember much about that night, no matter how hard he tried. Perhaps it was for the best, though he felt that James was deliberately exaggerating, sticking the knife in.

On top of the rock the two brothers glared at each other, as they had done ever since Martin, the younger by ten months,

had been born. Life had been one great competition ever since,
the younger child catching up with his brother in walking,
talking, running, climbing and finally overtaking, although
he'd remained the shorter of the two. They were endlessly
competitive in everything they did, which naturally led to
frequent confrontations and sometimes dangerous situations
– this had the potential to escalate into one. And then, quite
spontaneously, as suddenly as it had sprung up, the squall was
over. They grinned at each other, slapped each other's backs.

'OK,' James said. 'It might be worth just checking out the
B&B in Rudyard. We'll go tonight. Have a drink at the hotel
there. See if we can find out more about Annabelle and
Dorothée. If they're still around we can chase them up. Track
them down. Offer them a lift if they're still on their hitchhiking
holiday.' He scanned the moorland scene. 'Maybe we'll hit
lucky.'

FOUR

They had continued with the walk hand in hand, Matthew stopping every few steps to study Jo's face, a frown puckering his normally neutral features. 'Are you sure about this, Jo?'

She turned to face him, for once not backing away from awkward topics. 'I've been thinking about it since before we were married,' she said. 'It's inevitable.' She touched the golden hairs on his arm and looked into his face. 'How can I deny you the chance of being a father again?'

How indeed? he was wondering. She could hear the doubt in his voice. He kicked a stone. 'But what about you? Won't you resent it?'

She couldn't look at him now. 'It'll be a—'

'Sacrifice?' he put in perceptively.

'I was thinking more a change,' she lied.

'And work?'

She had to be honest. 'I shan't want to take much time off.'

'There are practical considerations, then.' It was typical of Matthew to cut straight to the bone. She nodded. They walked a little further, in silence now, their thoughts diverging. Matthew was excited at the prospect of a son. A child, he corrected himself, but the idea of a son made him more than happy. At his side, Joanna was contemplating the future with dread. The word sacrifice *had* been the correct one. As usual, Matthew had put his finger right on the painful, throbbing pulse.

Then she turned to look at him. His hair was catching the sunlight. It had been the first thing she had noticed about him – his tawny tousled hair as he had bent over his work, performing a post-mortem on an elderly woman who had been bludgeoned to death. He had looked up, perhaps sensing her nausea and revulsion at the work his hands were doing as he explored the damage caused by each blow. And as he had watched her, his green eyes had lit up with fun, or mischief, or happiness. Possibly even sympathy for her state. In his eyes there was something that made the light dance, like will-o'-the-wisps or the strange and ethereal Northern lights. But those same eyes could also look stormy or angry or simply sad. And there was a tinge of that sadness in them as he returned her stare. She knew he wished she could have been more excited at the prospect of trying for a child together as one, bonded by their wedding vows.

She returned to the past.

The day they'd met, she'd noticed his full mouth and the memory of what she'd thought when she'd noted its shape still made her blush. The chin shaped so square and determinedly uncompromising had been the last thing she'd thought about the pathologist – before the nausea had taken over and she had puked up in the sink, furthering his merriment. But it was that last feature, his chin, which dominated his character. That stubborn streak.

He had started to walk ahead but now he turned. 'What are you thinking, Jo?'

She tried to laugh it off as she shook her head. 'Nothing, really.'

'Nothing?' he queried, still with that searching, curious study of her. And when she did not answer he continued with the conversation. 'When were you thinking of . . .' his mouth twitched, '. . . starting this new venture?'

She shrugged. 'I don't know,' she said. 'I'm not pregnant yet.'

Matthew grinned, his eyes shining green. 'Well, babies have to be made, you know?'

She entered into the silliness of it to disguise her discomfort. 'Really?'

'Aha. And no time like . . .'

'Don't even think about it,' she warned, looking around her at the sunny-day crowds.

'No one's looking,' he put in.

'Matthew, if you think I'm being arrested on the charge of indecent behaviour you've . . .'

He *was* joking. His face leaked nothing but fun and happiness, which made her feel apprehensive.

'Would you be disappointed if it was another . . .'

But even the word, *another*, brought its ghosts. 'I wonder how Eloise will take it,' he mused, and she could have supplied the answer.

Not well. Eloise, her tricky stepdaughter, now a medical student, took *nothing* well in which Joanna Piercy was involved. She still blamed her for her parents' marital breakup.

They walked on, crossing the dam head, heading towards the visitor centre – a stone boathouse. Dinghies for hire were pulled up on the shore and the man was doing brisk business. They stopped at the ice-cream stall where a fresh-faced youth was observing them.

'What can I get you?'

'Two ninety-nines, please,' Matthew said.

The youth grinned. 'Right away, sir,' he said, practically touching his cap. He had an appealing face, cheeky, naive and engaging, a girl's rosy-cheeked complexion with large, cow-brown eyes. He extruded the ice cream into two cones, stuck a Cadbury's flake in each, handed one to Joanna and the other to Matthew, and winked at them.

'Enjoy,' he said.

His manner was so pleasant that they thanked him, turned away and sat on the seat overlooking the lake, watching a couple ineptly spin a rowing boat around and around to the accompaniment of giggles from the shore and an angry exchange in the vessel. The girl stood up, almost capsizing the boat. Sails billowed as the yachts tacked up and down the lake in a fresh breeze, a couple of near collisions resulting in shrieks and squeals which bounced over the water towards them. Dogs barked, children shouted. There was the sound of splashing.

'The English at play on a beautiful late summer's day,' Matthew murmured, biting into his flake and licking right around the cone with a tongue as long as a lizard's.

'Perfect,' Joanna said, doing the same. When they'd finished their ice creams she nestled into him on the wooden seat. 'Just perfect.' But Matthew was gazing across the water, his eyes unfocused, his attention somewhere else. 'You OK?'

He turned to face her. 'I'm just worried,' he said. 'Motherhood. It isn't what you really want, is it, Jo?'

She couldn't lie. 'No.'

'I'm just worried that you'll resent the sacrifice. Hold it against me if things don't work out. Every time the child cries or is sick or disturbs our night's sleep. It's what they do, you know, babies.'

She couldn't find an answer. The boy from the ice-cream stall was watching them with interest and curiosity. She gave him an abstracted smile but somehow the pretty lakeside scene, although the late-afternoon sun was still hot, had left them both feeling chilled.

Martin and James had finished their climbs, changed into shorts and sweatshirts in the car and were now heading for Rudyard Lake, singing with their heads out of the window.

'*Parlez-vous.*'

'Mademoiselle from Armentières . . .'

'*Parlez-vous.*'

'Mademoiselle from Armentieres . . .'

'*Parlez-vous.*'

'Inky pinky *parlez-vous.*'

After a long, cold spring and a disappointing June and early July, then a couple of weeks' hot weather before returning to sunshine mixed with rain and showers and fanned by a cool breeze, the Indian summer was going to everyone's heads, and they sped along quickly.

They would catch a beer at the Rudyard Hotel, sit around the lake, maybe take a canoe out for an hour or so and enjoy the early evening sunshine. They drove through Leek, congested as always, the heat, unfamiliar to moorlanders, making drivers fractious and impatient. Horns blew in frustration at the slow-moving traffic. The trouble was it wasn't only the resident population that clogged up the town: day trippers, climbers, cyclists and walkers were all present, not to mention the mass evacuation from the Potteries – the Peak District attracted them all and the small town struggled to carry the traffic. Once through the streets, which smelt strongly of hot diesel and engine oil, they took the Macclesfield road out, passing the football ground on their left and, in a mile or two, turning towards the lake. They drove under the bridge where the little steam train was chuffing along like something out of a 1950s *Boy's Own Annual*, turned right at the small roundabout and parked in the hotel car park. Then they headed straight for the bar.

'We can ask about the French girls,' Martin suggested. 'They might have paid the hotel a visit while they were here.'

'I doubt it,' James said gloomily, and his brother gave him a soft punch on his arm.

'Don't be such a bloody pessimist,' he said.

Matthew and Joanna had finished their ice creams.

On the upper floor of the visitor centre there was an art exhibition. Anthony Podesta. Joanna had a bit of a conscience about the local artists who trudged around the moorlands, often seeking out the very same views – the Roaches, Hen Cloud and, of course, Rudyard Lake and the picturesque Boathouse, the lovely Victorian stone cottage, available for holiday rent, which projected right out into the lake. It must take them hours of painstaking work, quite apart from the necessary talent. And then they seemed to tote their wares around the county only for people either to misunderstand, insult and only occasionally buy. They must feel disheartened.

'Let's take a look, Matt,' Joanna said impulsively. She wanted to buy a picture to mark this significant day when she had made such a commitment and left, for ever, her single, selfish person behind. She had worries, little demons of her own. She was a committed cop and feared that motherhood would simply bore her. The future looked worrying – the combination of her job with its uncertain hours and sometimes uncertain days and nights, and the unpredictability of parenthood indicated a choppy future. And first she had to conceive. But somehow she did not think that would be a problem.

She and Matthew walked slowly through the gallery, stopping in front of each painting to study it. *Mow Cop Folly*, *Staffordshire Moors*, *River Dane*, *Loaf and Cheese (the Roaches)*, *Hen Cloud*, *Last Snow on the Moor* and *Early Morning, Dam End, Rudyard*. They both stopped at this last one.

Afterwards she would always associate this picture with

this decision, the momentous day in her life, this place. *Early Morning, Dam End, Rudyard.* It was all so right. The quiet, cool water, the slightest tinge of orange that bathed the very top of the trees, the boats lazily pulled up to the water's edge. They both looked at it, then at each other. The price was £390; the artist watched them curiously, wondering whether they would be tempted. Matthew put his head close to hers, his eyes very soft. 'We're going to need a bigger house,' he said.

She smiled and touched his cheek with her forefinger. Buying the picture put an official stamp on their decision.

At the Rudyard Hotel James and Martin were doing their best to elicit information without appearing too nosey or prurient. Martin was acting as casually as he knew how. And the story they gave was that they already knew the girls and had arranged to meet them again at some point during their stay in England, but had lost their contact details.

In this Martin, though younger, was the leader. He took a wary sip of Rudyard Ruby, one of the local ales, then smiled and took a larger slurp. His brother did likewise. The beer was good.

The barmaid, a petite girl in her early twenties, warmed to the sight of the brothers. Both were great physical specimens, probably in their late twenties or early thirties, with friendly faces and broad grins. She wasn't quite so friendly when they made it plain they were hoping to meet up with a couple of French girls that they knew. 'I haven't met any French girls over here,' she said coldly.

'It might have been a month or two ago,' Martin said, trying his best. 'A few weeks, anyway.' They needed to try harder. The brothers exchanged glances.

'They're a bit of a pain, really,' James said confidingly, hoping to get her cooperation. 'But we promised to look 'em up when we went climbing again.' He gave the girl his most disarming smile. 'And, you know?' He shrugged. 'A promise is a promise.'

She thawed a little at that.

Martin took up the reins. 'I bet a gorgeous chick' – his brother winced at the word chick – 'like you,' he continued, 'has already got a boyfriend.' It wasn't even a question, just a statement.

'I have, actually.' The girl had fallen for his flattery. The '*but*' she added almost floated in off the wind.

'Pity, that.' Martin wasn't as good at this so his brother ignored him.

'What's your name, love?' As a chat-up line it was pathetic but as an ice-breaking-information-gatherer it worked.

'Sarah,' she said, biting her bottom lip in a self-consciously coy gesture. 'Sarah Gratton.'

'And do you live here?'

She nodded happily. 'Practically opposite,' she said. 'Rudyard born and bred.'

'It's a nice place,' Martin put in.

His brother nudged him in the ribs.

'Anyway, you've got a bloke,' James said reluctantly, 'so . . . are you sure you didn't serve these French girls? A hundred per cent?'

The girl pressed her lips together. The brothers looked at each other. They'd cast their fly. Now it was time to see if they'd caught their fish.

'There was a couple of girls here,' Sarah Gratton said, as if the words were being dragged out of her, 'but it was a couple of months ago, like you said. Back in July. They'll have moved on by now. Maybe even gone back to Europe.'

'Were they staying here?'

She shook her head. 'No, not here.'

'Camping?'

'No – staying at Barker's place.'

'Barker's place?'

'He runs a sort of B&B-cum-hotel on the road that goes up to Biddulph Moor. Mandalay, it's called.'

'Sounds a bit exotic, that,' James said.

'Yeah. He took it from a poem or something. That's what people say, anyway. Four or five bedrooms, he's got. He's not expensive.' Her smile widened. 'People tell me his breakfasts are very good.' Sarah leaned across the bar. '*I* wouldn't stay there, though,' she said confidingly.

'Why not?'

'Because he gives me the creeps, that's why.' She challenged them with a mocking stare, hands on hips. 'Tell you what, why don't *you* go over there? *You'd* be all right. You're blokes. And you might get your girls' home addresses or find out where they went next.'

Her smile was bland, her expression guileless, but there was no doubt that they'd dropped in her estimation with their keenness to find the girls, and they'd get no more out of her, whatever she knew. They drank up and got halfway through the door before her Parthian shot reached them. 'If you were supposed to be meeting up with them again, why didn't they give you their mobile numbers?'

'We lost them,' Martin said shortly, making a swift exit.

FIVE

Monday, 9 September, 8.30 a.m.

Madame Bellange looked around her at St Pancras station and took a while to adjust. So, she thought. This is England. She wasn't over-impressed. The hustle and the bustle around her and the unfamiliar English language confused her. Also the terminal was surprisingly cold and a metallic smell hung in the air. But she was here now, in the same country as her daughter and Dorothée and she had already planned her route. She would take the train from Euston station to Stoke-on-Trent and from there she would hire a car and drive to this lake. She would take a look, then drive to the nearest police station and enlist their help to find her daughter and her friend. She planned to tell Annabelle off for not keeping her up to date on their movements. She had been good up until the middle of July. And then neglectful.

Cécile Bellange smiled to herself as she pictured the scene. Lecture over, she would embrace her daughter and bring her home. Back to France. She had looked at all the maps and at Google Earth to get her bearings. The nearest police station to Rudyard Lake was in a town called Leek. That was where she would head.

Monday, 9 September, 8.45 a.m.

Joanna cycled in to the station that morning, feeling a warm wind of change blow through her hair. Where would she be in *one* year's time? Pregnant? *Five* years' time? Kissing a little boy off to school? Neither picture seemed realistic.

As her legs worked the hills she chewed on her lip. What on earth was she letting herself in for?

The bike ride helped her mood but it seemed too short. She

still felt fidgety and agitated. Before her mind had time to settle she was turning into the police station and locking her bike to the railings. Even the quick shower and change into tight black jeans and a red shirt didn't help. She still felt out of sorts. Out of control, more likely, she thought.

DS Korpanski breezed in at nine, looking particularly beefy in a pair of beige cargo pants and a blue short-sleeved, open-necked Polo shirt. In his usual good spirits, he grinned at her. 'Morning, Jo. Nice weekend?'

'Yeah,' she answered shortly, turning away and pretending she couldn't feel the bore of his pinprick pupils drilling into her back.

'Oh,' he grunted, and stood still and silent, giving her a chance to enlarge before settling down to his desk and switching on his computer. He waited, frowning to himself, wondering, then was up on his feet. 'Coffee?'

'Yeah,' she said again.

At the door he hesitated, leaning against its edge. 'Anything you want to talk about?'

'No.'

'Right. I'll get the coffee then.'

When he'd gone she dropped her head into her hands. Last night there had been a choppy sea between herself and Matthew, a treacherous sound.

'I shan't want to take more than a couple of months off,' she'd said, not looking at her husband of less than a year.

'Oh,' he'd said, his voice suddenly heavily sarcastic. 'Don't worry, Jo, I wouldn't expect you to become a house-mum and lavish care and attention on our child.'

She'd winced at *our child*. 'I'm not even pregnant yet,' she'd said, not looking at him.

'No,' he'd almost shouted.

And she never would be if this hostility and resentment took hold. So much left unsaid. So much bitterness and anger, so many things she dare not say. She'd felt suddenly angry. Had he wanted more from her than simply to produce? For her to give up her career, stop being a cop – being herself? Then he should have said.

The doubts had wormed in and out of her skull. Maybe she

was the wrong woman for him after all. And for the first time
in her entire life she wondered and doubted his commitment
to her. What if, as he had with Jane, his ex-wife, Matthew
found someone else? What was it *really* like to be a single
parent in sole charge of a baby?

Bloody awful, she thought. It must be bloody awful. She drew
in a long, deep breath.

Mike was back with the coffee quick as a bee and she
managed a thank-you smile though she still felt pig-sick.
She took a couple of tentative sips then swivelled her chair
around. 'How long was Fran off when Jocelyn and Ricky
were born?'

He raised his eyebrows, his eyes fixed on her face. 'Three
years,' he said. 'She didn't go back to being a nurse until
Jossie was three years old and at nursery school. And then
she worked as a school nurse and didn't work at all during
the school holidays.'

His eyes were so black you couldn't distinguish between
his iris and pupil. But in spite of this they were also very
expressive.

Detective Sergeant Mike Korpanski looked carefully at his
colleague. Her shoulders were bowed. She looked bleak. He'd
never seen her like this. Angry? Yes, plenty. Frustrated? Plenty
of that too. Impatient? His mouth twitched. All the time.
Amused? Oh, yes. Anxious? A time or two. In the years they'd
worked together he'd thought he'd seen every single possible
emotion in her. But this one? Defeated? No. This person was
a stranger. An unwelcome one in this room.

He cleared his throat ready to speak, conscious he was
choosing his words with the inevitability of trouble, as if he
were trying to tiptoe over hot coals. 'It isn't that bad, you
know.'

She spun her chair around. 'What isn't?'

'Parenthood.' He tried again. 'Being a mother,' he said. 'It
isn't that bad.'

She regarded him, tossing her hair over her shoulder, her
back ramrod straight now, ready to do battle. 'Motherhood,'
she said slowly. 'So you know about that, do you?'

Korpanski gave a lop-sided grin and braced his shoulders.

'Not exactly,' he said, carefully stepping around his prickly colleague. 'But I do know about fatherhood.'

And then the squall was over, the anger dissipated, replaced now by curiosity. 'Were you there when your two were born?' she asked.

'Not for Ricky,' he said frankly. 'I couldn't face it, truth be known, but when Jossie was expected Fran made such a fuss about me being there that . . .' He looked into the distance, which was not very far as their only window faced a brick wall no more than three feet away. 'To be honest, Jo,' he said, grinning now, 'I'm glad I *did* go. It was fantastic. Magical.' He couldn't prevent his smile from broadening. 'I think it's made me closer to Jossie, actually being there at the very moment of her birth.'

Joanna frowned. 'Did it matter her being a girl?'

Korpanski gave a slightly embarrassed laugh. 'No, why should it? They always say fathers are closer to their daughters.'

'So why do men make such a fuss about having sons?'

'Do they?'

She nodded and leaned back in her chair, relaxing now in the presence of her sergeant. 'You've only to look at Henry the eighth,' she teased.

'Oh, that was different,' Korpanski said bluntly. 'He needed someone to look after Merry England after he'd gone.' He knew she was pulling his leg, and was relieved to see his old DI back to her usual self.

'So why is it important to . . .' She didn't say Matthew but she knew that Korpanski would know exactly whom she meant.

And Detective Sergeant Mike Korpanski knew he had to come up with some sort of an answer. 'Maybe it's because they think they can do all the boy things together: footie, cycling, activity stuff. You know. Though when I say "boy things", they could do all that with a daughter too, of course. Not all girls like dolls.' He smiled at her, hoping to lighten the tone.

Jo nodded, then: 'So,' she followed up briskly, 'what have we on today's menu?'

'Rush rang first thing,' he said. 'He's been contacted by the French police.'

'Oh?'

'They're looking into two missing girls from Paris who last contacted their families in July – sent a postcard from Rudyard Lake. They say their bank account and mobile phones haven't been used since mid-July. And then we got a phone call this morning,' he said, 'from a French lady, mother of one of the girls. A Madame Bellange.'

'Nice accent, Mike.' She grinned.

'Piss off, Piercy,' he said gently, and they were back in the old familiar rut of working life again. 'She's come over on the Eurostar,' he said, 'to look for her daughter and her friend.'

'Why here?'

'Since that last postcard there's been absolutely no sign of them. They seem to have vanished, Jo.'

She sat up. 'What was the date of the postcard?'

'It was posted Friday, nineteenth of July. The girl – Annabelle – was hitchhiking with a friend, Dorothée.'

'And they came here? It's quite out of the way. Not the usual haunt for a couple of French girls. I'd have thought they'd have stayed in London.'

Korpanski simply shrugged. 'She said she'd be calling in and Rush seems to want us to help her as much as we can.'

Joanna's eyes clouded at the second mention of their new chief superintendent. 'How old are the girls?'

'Seventeen. They're due to go to college in a week or two.'

'OK,' Joanna said. 'Maybe we'll be able to help this Madame Bellange, but the probability is that the girls left this area after posting the card. Maybe they've run out of money or something. Or met some blokes and don't want their mothers to know. Or simply decided they don't want to go to college and the holiday's not over yet. After all, there's two of them. If they were here in July they've almost certainly moved on.'

'Let's hope so,' Korpanski said fervently. 'Don't want stuff like that on our patch.'

'Is there anything else?'

'Only the usual. Car thefts, illegal booze, drugs in school, fake fags. And there's a couple of undercover cops looking at Sergio Patterson.'

'Whatever for?'

Korpanski shrugged again. 'Who knows,' he said. 'Links with al-Qaeda.'

Joanna made a face. Sergio Patterson was one of those local petty criminals who seemed to have been around for ever. He'd been convicted of theft, fraud and false accounting. There were suspicions of money laundering and a fairly tacky internet site which promised the love of your life for three easy clicks of the mouse – oh, and a thousand pound membership fee.

But al-Qaeda? An emphatic *no*.

Then again, undercover cops were not going to reveal their sources.

Monday, 9 September, 10.30 a.m.
Stoke-on-Trent railway station.

Stoke-on-Trent appeared an old-fashioned sort of city to Cécile Bellange as she stepped on to the platform and looked around her. Overhead was a glass roof, through it blew a cool wind so it felt chilly in spite of the warm weather elsewhere. Her entire journey had been blessed with sunshine and she had looked out of the window at some very pretty countryside. Small fields, cows grazing, interesting-looking towns and villages. The people who were also on the train appeared to have been summoned from all four corners of the earth: Africans, Asians, Germans . . . She'd screwed up her eyes. Were there actually any English on the train – apart from the ticket collector?

But her fellow passengers seemed friendly and she kept herself to herself while watching them carefully. Annabelle had probably travelled on this train.

She smiled. Maybe England wasn't such a bad place after all. But as she stepped from the train she wasn't sure. It might have looked pretty and rural through the windows, but here, on this station, it appeared dull. Dingy, dirty and cold. However, all was not lost. As soon as she left the station she realized that Stoke had one major advantage – a hotel right opposite the railway station. She only had to cross the road to the North Stafford Hotel and she was there. And they were very obliging indeed, providing her with a perfectly satisfactory lunch and the use of a washroom.

Had the girls stayed here?

Added to all these advantages they also had a French waiter named Alfred who had had been very helpful, organizing a car for her complete with satnav which, with a bit of fiddling on Alfred's part, gave her directions in French. Madame Bellange felt even more optimistic. She would find the girls and bring them home – both of them. She would soon see her daughter, and scold her for not doing as she had promised and keeping in touch. Her expression changed to one of worry. Surely the girls *were* safe, they *were* simply being naughty? Annabelle was a pretty girl with an eye for the opposite sex, and it was well known that British men liked French girls. Oh, yes. That was probably it. They had met some boys who had distracted them. The worry faded into anger again as she contemplated this scenario. Perhaps they did not want to go to college. Was that it? Or was something, some*one*, keeping them away?

As she ate her lunch of lamb steaks in red wine sauce with sautéed potatoes she amused herself by picturing the girls' faces when she confronted them. They would be so surprised to see her. Shocked. Annabelle knew full well that her mother had never been to England, reluctant to leave her beloved France. Yes, this would really surprise them. All she needed to do was to find out where they were and what was keeping them away from home, preventing them from keeping in touch as they had promised. It was true that Annabelle resented the strict conditions she imposed on her but surely . . . Cécile stared out of the window. Even on a lovely day like today the railway station looked a little sordid and industrial, the figures bent and scurrying, reminding her of paintings she had seen by Mr Lowry. Maybe it was those very pictures, loaned for an exhibition to the Louvre, that had put her off visiting England before. She frowned. Of all the places in England that French tourists usually visited: London,

Stratford, Chester – why had the girls come here? The answer swam into her mind as she recalled Annabelle's bedroom wall and the mantras pinned up there: '*Fill the unforgiving minute . . . If you can bear to hear the words you've spoken twisted by knaves to make a trap for fools . . . If you can keep your head.*'

Of course. His most famous poem. The answer was in the postcard which was now in her handbag. Rudyard Lake, Rudyard Kipling. So was the clue to their silence wrapped up in Kipling?

She was sure Annabelle had *not* been angry with her, she was sure of that. Something must have happened. She stared bleakly at the wall. If the police couldn't find her daughter . . . What then?

She sat up straight and squared her shoulders. She would jump that fence when she reached it.

Monday, 9 September, 2.30 p.m.

Madame Bellange was driving north-east out of the city along a crowded A53 which bristled with the yellow speed cameras Alfred had warned her about. She found them both confusing and distracting, trying to translate miles to kilometres. It was bad enough driving on the wrong side of the road without all this. She had to concentrate very hard. The road was lined with a hotchpotch of houses, some old, some new, a very smart-looking Indian restaurant, garages and two schools, a high school and a primary. She smiled, taken back to the first time she had dropped Annabelle off at school when she had been four years old. She'd tilted her face up for a goodbye kiss and as Cécile had touched her cheek she had felt it wet with tears. My brave little girl. She sighed. She wanted her brave little girl back again.

She focused back on the road. And then something magical happened. The houses retreated; the city melted away behind her and she had a perfect view of a wide scoop of a valley, a stone farmhouse ahead. She sat forward in the car, looking around her, drinking in the beautiful vista.

So this was where Annabelle had been? Had her eyes opened

wide too when she had finally seen this lovely English countryside?

And then she saw it, a simple signpost to the left which read *Rudyard*.

Dorothée and Annabelle would have whooped with delight. She could almost hear them.

'Here. *Ici. Ici.*' And because they were such great friends they would have hugged each other. She was sure of that. But how had they got here? Had they hitchhiked as they had threatened? Or had they caught a bus like the one she had trundled behind for the last few miles? Who had brought them here? What kind of motorist had picked them up, sweaty and burdened with their enormous rucksacks, their jeans low slung? She forced herself not to shudder at the thought. They would have giggled as they climbed into his car. (She imagined it would have been a man rather than a woman who would have picked up two attractive young French girls provocatively dressed as usual and giggling.) Being also polite girls they would have thanked the driver whoever he or possibly she was. '*Merci. Merci.*' They would have sung out their gratitude in their excitement at almost arriving at their shrine. Her hands gripped the steering wheel. How she ached to see them again.

But she would not go to Rudyard first – she'd go straight on to Leek. Alfred had kindly given her the postcode of the police station so she drove straight there and parked next to a bicycle. She'd brought her French/English phrase book with her as she wasn't too confident that her English vocabulary was going to be up to this. And the English people, particularly out here in the country, had a reputation for speaking one language only. Their own.

From the hatch, once she had explained both who she was and why she was here, she was ushered into a small interview room and waited. A few minutes later a tall, slim woman with thick dark hair and fierce blue eyes who introduced herself as Detective Inspector Joanna Piercy was sitting opposite her. Her colleague, who had been introduced as Detective Sergeant Mike Korpanski, a tall, muscular man with dark eyes and black hair, sat by her side.

Joanna, for her part, saw a tiny woman, chicly dressed in navy trousers and a white sweater pushed up to reveal thin brown arms. On the table between them stood a large, white, expensive-looking leather handbag.

Inspector Piercy began. 'How may we help you?'

In answer, Cécile slid the postcard across the table. The words by now were so familiar that she could translate them perfectly into English. Then she leaned forward and challenged the angry blue eyes. 'But I don't understand. What is this letterboxing?'

It was Korpanski who answered. 'People hide things in a tin or a box and then other people find them, take a stamp and put the box back again. They collect them,' he finished lamely.

He wasn't surprised that Madame Bellange looked bemused.

Joanna slid a latex glove on and picked up the postcard, turning it over. Rudyard Lake. A place as familiar as her own back garden. She and Matthew had spent hours here, walking, even sailing, art exhibitions, lunches at the hotel and coffees and ice cream in the café. Of all the places she could think of it was the most innocent. The photo on the postcard was a nice view taken from the Dam End showing the entire length of the lake, the water calm, sails billowing. She studied it, used a magnifying glass to read the postmark and the writing on the back. She only knew schoolgirl French but could translate the gist of it.

'They were together,' Cécile managed. 'They were friends. Good friends. Dorothée and Annabelle. They decided to hike using the, how you say it? The thumb.'

'Hitchhike,' Korpanski put in. 'They didn't realize it was so dangerous?'

'Dangerous?' Madame Bellange queried, alarmed.

'Well, risky,' Korpanski corrected. 'We don't recommend it,' he said, frowning, 'particularly not for two girls.' He didn't say *two foreign girls*, or *two girls in a foreign country*. Both sounded dated and xenophobic as well as the even less forgivable misogynous. None of these were tolerated in 'Today's Modern Police Force'. How many lectures had he been to that had bleated this basic mantra? Too many.

Cécile turned anxious eyes on him. 'But two of them, surely, are safe?'

'It still isn't a good idea.' He stuck to his guns stolidly.

Joanna was watching the woman's face. She appeared calm, composed, more curious rather than frightened that anything sinister had happened to her daughter and her friend. 'And the girl who was with your daughter – Dorothée? Have her parents heard from her?'

It struck her that Cécile Bellange's eyes were guileless. It was as though she had never looked at anything bad in her life, that she could not suspect trouble or evil.

'Dorothée was not as . . .' she searched for the word, '*habituée* . . .'

'Regular,' Mike put in. Cécile Bellange nodded vigorously. '*Oui*,' she said. '*Oui*. Regular in her contact home. Her *maman* is a busy business lady.'

Joanna aimed raised eyebrows at her sergeant, who gave her a perfectly innocent and bland look back.

'Dorothée was not writing home often and I don't think her parents are as *concernés*.' She looked to Mike for help.

'Concerned,' he put in, and she could have kicked herself for not realizing.

'At her not writing home,' Madame Bellange continued. 'Her father has a new lady and is . . . umm . . . how shall I put it? He is often not quite well.'

Joanna sucked in a shallow breath of irritation. It was time to get down to business.

Madame Bellange placed several sheets of paper on the desk next to the expensive-looking white handbag.

'I have written here,' she said, 'Annabelle's personal details, bank account and mobile phone number, and here are some photographs of the girls.'

She looked hopefully at Joanna, who spoke awkwardly. 'I understand the French police have already been in touch with my chief superintendent asking him to look into the two girls' disappearance. And I think they've drawn a blank as to their phones and bank accounts. But we will, of course, recheck all the details.' She tried to give Madame Bellange a reassuring smile. 'You can be sure of that.'

Cécile Bellange didn't look reassured at all.

'We'll need your contact details too,' Joanna said, 'so we

can keep in touch with you. But you do understand, the girls may well have left this area and gone elsewhere. We may not be able to help you.'

Cécile Bellange simply nodded and bowed her head.

SIX

Martin and James had camped out the previous night in a field attached to a farm in Longsdon, three miles out of Leek. Local farmers welcomed the tourists with open arms – provided they kept their dogs under control, closed the gates behind them and didn't leave litter. So after a hearty breakfast at the Hungry Horse in Leek – which filled you to the brim with a fry-up and as much tea as you could down without bursting your bladder, and all for less than a fiver – they drove back out to Rudyard and located Mandalay.

It proved to be a surprisingly smart house, detached, large and white painted with a nice symmetrical frontage and plenty of parking along the drive. First impressions were good. They looked at each other and resisted the temptation to high-five. Their plan was to find out anything they could about the girls and then take a peek at the visitors' book to see if they could find an address, maybe a mobile number so they could track them down. What had seemed like a fun adventure to start with had become more determined now James was fully on board, though Martin hoped that, if they weren't at Mandalay or somewhere in the surrounding area, the search would stop and he could get back to Camilla and their wedding plans.

But James could be quite tenacious – once he'd got his teeth into something he was very unlikely to let go at least until he'd tasted blood. James couldn't have said what it was that drew him towards the girls, except that fun was something sadly lacking in his life at the moment. He naturally veered towards pessimism. He wasn't so much grieving the break-up of his romance but he was aware that his life had become dull and lacked that vital ingredient. He craved excitement. Besides, they wanted to be found, didn't they? And they were gorgeous if, he admitted to himself grudgingly, perhaps a little out of their league. Still, Martin had been all for it, and it was a challenge he couldn't turn down. It helped that he had something new to focus his energies on, rather than pining for his ex. It felt good.

James glanced across at Martin and grinned. They parked the car and approached the front door.

Barker opened it slowly, peering round it as though he hadn't just put up the *Vacancies* sign. He looked suspiciously at the two fit, young, healthy men. 'Yes?'

'Have you got a room?'

Barker's eyes flickered. 'Uumm,' he said. He did, but only the twin-bed room. And he didn't want these two young men there. What was the point in watching men? He preferred women. He felt his mouth twist. Preferably *young* women, but even older women were preferable to these two strong-looking males. Then again, Barker always felt he needed more money. One couldn't afford to turn away guests. The B&B trade was fickle and Mandalay was an expensive house to keep up. One wet, miserable summer's holiday in Staffordshire could have a knock-on effect for years. People didn't forget terrible holidays, and sitting in the Rudyard café, watching rain splash down on the water's surface, too cold to eat ice cream, counted as one of those.

But so far this year he was having a good season. Since May there had always been someone in the room for him and Supi-yaw-lat to keep an eye on. Most of the time they were young couples, though he tried to give them the double rooms. Families almost always plumped for the two family rooms – it worked out cheaper. But the nice thing about having two twin-bed rooms was that he could choose who to put in his *special* room. Oh, well.

Inwardly he sighed and spoke up in his reedy voice. 'I have a very nice twin-bed room as it happens,' he said, almost hoping the pair of climbers with their muscly legs and expensive-looking boots would decide to give him a miss. 'But it's eighty pounds a night.'

James made a face at his brother. Imperceptibly, Martin nodded. 'OK,' he said, resigned. 'We probably just need it for one night, but it might be two.'

Barker couldn't prevent his palms from rubbing together. 'Would you like to *see* the room?'

'Yeah. Suppose we'd better,' they answered in unison, their words tumbling out untidily as they stepped inside Mandalay.

They followed him up the stairs and, mirroring the cared-for exterior of the house, they were pleasantly surprised at the room, which was clean and nicely decorated with cream walls, a beige carpet, two beds with wine-coloured bedspreads and a nice view over the lake. The only discordant note was the . . . the brothers looked at each other, suppressing laughs. The truly dreadful picture. A tacky, odd-looking foreign woman trying to look seductive.

Barker followed their gaze. 'Lovely, isn't she?'

James cleared his throat noisily while his brother merely nodded and gulped.

'And the room,' Barker continued, 'is it all right?'

'Oh, perfectly.' Martin was also smothering a giggle.

'It's really nice, actually,' his brother put in kindly. 'Really nice.' He shot a warning glance at Martin, who was pushing open the door of the en suite. That, too, was a nice surprise – plain white, clean and smelling faintly of bleach, it had a power shower. It was a joy to behold, he was tempted to say, particularly after a day's hard climbing followed by a night under canvas. Inwardly, he was thinking that Mandalay represented value for money – providing the breakfast was good.

Barker looked pleased with the response. 'It's been refurbished recently,' he said. 'In fact, I decorated this room myself back in May.' He paused before adding, 'It took me almost three weeks.'

The brothers were both struggling to smother giggles now. 'You've done a nice job,' James praised, looking curiously at the picture again. He'd seen it somewhere before but couldn't remember where.

Seeing him focus on the print, Barker couldn't resist showing off his knowledge. 'It was a very popular picture in the sixties,' he said, giving her a fond glance. 'In fact, she's the most reproduced picture in the world. They call her the kitsch Mona Lisa. She's painted by a Russian guy called Tretchikoff.'

Martin's face was contorting with the effort of not laughing out loud. Pompous little fellow, he was thinking. And the picture was awful. Dreadful. That completely unrealistic stylized face, the blue-green tinge of the skin and the ridiculously exotic costume – it couldn't be a kimono, surely? It was repulsive. Sickly.

The way Barker was looking at her was practically lascivious. 'Chinese girl,' he added. 'That's what they call her, but I believe she's Burmese. Like the girl in "Mandalay" – Supi-yaw-lat.'

Something in the way he spoke made James's flesh crawl. 'The poem,' he said, suddenly understanding.

'That's right. Kipling. Clever man,' Barker said in his soft voice. 'That's why I chose the name.' He glanced, almost surreptitiously, as though asking permission from the picture and changed his voice to estuary English Mockney. *"'Er petticoat was yaller an' 'er little cap was green.'* He laughed. *"'I've a neater, sweeter maiden in a cleaner greener land! On the road to Mandalay."* He turned back to the brothers. 'One day,' he said, 'I'd like to go there.'

'Where?'

'Mandalay. Burma. Myanmar they call it now, but it doesn't sound quite the same, does it?'

It was difficult to find a response to this wish. 'I daresay it's a bit different these days from Kipling's time,' James said stiffly.

Barker bored into him with his sharp little gimlet eyes. 'Oh, I doubt it,' he said. 'I think I'll find it little changed.'

The brothers simply shrugged. They were bored with him now. James moved over to the window and gazed out across the lake. 'You've got a lovely view here,' he said.

'Ye-es,' Barker responded. 'I'm very lucky. There were some trees in the way, you know. They cut them down last year and I got my view back. We have a lot of visitors here and they all want to see the lake. It's a popular place of pilgrimage.'

'Pilgrimage?'

'Ye-es. Pilgrimage,' Barker said.

The brothers frowned, their faces suddenly announcing their consanguinity.

Barker waited for a response and when he got none moved
to leave but hesitated in the doorway. 'I prefer to be paid
upfront,' he said pointedly.

'Yeah. Of course. We'll just get our stuff out of the car.'

The brothers were both thinking the same thing. Shower,
change, the Rudyard Hotel, food and drink. Sleep and pursue
their hunt for the two girls.

'And what time will you be wanting breakfast?' It was
Barker's Parthian shot.

'Half eight?'

Barker nodded and left. When they were alone in the room
Martin couldn't resist mimicking him. '"The kitsch Mona
Lisa,"' he said in an Estuary accent, hand on hip, mincing
around the room. '"And isn't she . . ."' He stood in front of
the picture and searched for a word. '"*Er petticoat was
yaller an' 'er little cap was green*,"' he mocked in a gothic
tone.

'Ssh,' his brother warned. 'He might hear you.'

But Barker hadn't needed to. He had seen the look in the
boys' eyes as they had first of all regarded him and then
her. Why oh why did he always feel the need for people to
appreciate *her*? What did it matter? He descended the stairs,
shoulders slumped. Men like them, the hearty sort, always
despised him. It had started in school – possibly even before
that. He had a vision of his mother keeping the hood up on
his pram, omitting to enrol him in nursery, to shield him
for as long as possible from the taunts of other children,
knowing that in the end he would be an object of derision.
Always the odd one out. Barker reached the bottom of the
stairs and glanced up. He could hear their door opening.
They would be tumbling down the stairs at any minute in
their galumphing great boots, banging doors and making the
entire house shake.

Why hadn't they camped for a second night? He'd seen
their equipment in the back of their car. The weather was still
fine. They weren't being rained off. So why had they come
here?

He went into the kitchen, determined not to worry too

much, and shut the door firmly behind him. People still made
fun of him, recognized within minutes that there was something different about him, that he was the odd one out, a
misfit. Perhaps it was his mother's fault. Perhaps she *shouldn't*
have shielded him with her constant presence. She'd been
so overprotective, and it had only served to draw attention
to his inadequacies, his short legs and large head, his pale-
fish skin and podgy middle, even as a child. The other kids
had pointed the finger at the little boy who peeped from
behind his mother's skirts. Sometimes he wished he could
stick pins in a wax effigy of her. Why, knowing he would
be a misfit from birth, had she given him that awful name?
That label.

It wasn't even as if he could substitute his middle name. In
this area that would have caused even more leg-pulling.

And yet he knew he had Dora to thank for all this, for the
rebranding of Mandalay and the tourists that it drew in. Yes,
thanks to her he, Horace Gladstone Barker, was a rich man.

He busied himself with cleaning the kitchen, emptying the
dishwasher and checking that he had the ingredients for
the following morning's hearty full English, and listening out
for the two men who had just booked into Mandalay.

Ten minutes later they knocked on the door and held out
four twenty-pound notes before returning to their room.

He heard the sound of water running, felt the shake of their
heavy footsteps overhead, heard their boots clattering downstairs. The door slammed and Barker was alone again.

The Rudyard Hotel was quiet that evening and the barmaid
was different – a ginger-haired girl called Cheryl who'd looked
at them blankly when they'd mentioned two French girls,
friends of theirs, who'd been on holiday here a couple of
months ago. Her only, unhelpful response had been a grudging,
'We get a lot of visitors round here. It's a popular spot, you
know.' As with Sarah Gratton, they'd had to be content with
that.

So they ate their meal wondering whether the overnight stay
at Mandalay had been a waste of time. The girls had gone.
The question was had they left a forwarding address?

Martin, as usual, was upbeat. Not so, as usual, his brother. Walking back up the hill to the guest house they reflected that so far their quest had not exactly been successful. Tomorrow they'd pump Barker for information.

But the room was comfortable, even if they did feel watched by the strange eyes of the girl in the picture. They tried to turn her around, but she was screwed to the wall. In the end Martin draped a pair of trousers over her face.

They waited until Barker was serving their breakfast before broaching the subject of the girls. 'Do you remember two French girls staying here?' James asked idly. 'A little while ago?'

Barker took a step back. 'What were their names?' Buy time. Tread carefully. He eyed them suspiciously.

'Annabelle and Dorothée,' James said casually. 'They're friends of ours. We promised to catch up with them.'

Barker knew his voice would squeak. 'What makes you think they stayed here?' He felt an instinct to conceal the truth.

'They emailed us a little while ago.' James had made it up on the spur of the moment. A brainwave to flush out the truth. 'They were hitchhiking and suggested we meet them here. They said they'd stayed here before and could recommend it.'

Barker made one desperate attempt at getting his voice under control. 'When exactly was that?' He felt sick. He'd known these two were trouble.

'At least a month ago. Maybe longer.' The two brothers exchanged glances.

'Well, they're not here now.' His mother, Dora, had taught him this mantra. 'Attack,' she had said in her deep voice, both mother and father to him, 'is the very best form of defence.' It had been advice that Barker, the child, had taken on board, only for it to result in a succession of bruised ribs and bloody noses. 'And in fact, I don't know what you're talking about. I don't know any French girls.'

Martin spoke up. 'But they did stay here. The barmaid at the hotel told us.'

'She could be wrong,' Barker said quickly.

James's voice was calm as he continued as though Barker had not spoken. 'Do you know where they went after here?'

Barker shook his head and managed to face them. 'I don't know what you're talking about. You're mistaken. I'm sure I haven't—'

'Let's look in the visitors' book,' Martin suggested. It was a line they had already practised.

Barker was tempted to protest that he didn't keep a visitors' book but had a feeling that the brothers would have noticed it on the table that stood in his hall.

He stomped out of the breakfast room, the brothers so close behind him they practically nipped his heels.

They flicked back the pages and soon found what they wanted.

Annabelle et Dorothée, 18 Juillet, 2014. Merci. C'est Magnifique. Nous aimons le lac et son lien avec Rudyard Kipling, le plus grand de tous les poètes.

And . . . the jackpot. A mobile phone number.

James eyed Barker. 'So where did they go next?' he enquired innocently.

Barker felt faint. He could taste bile rising up in his mouth and hear a rushing in his head. Signs of panic, Dora used to call them.

'I don't know,' he managed to squawk, his throat as dry as the Gobi desert. In desperation, he called on his mother's advice. *Attack! Attack, Horace.* 'How should I know?' he almost shouted. 'People don't tell me where they're going next. I have lots of people here. Coming and going all the time. Are you going to tell me where *you're* going next?' Then he realized he was shouting.

James and Martin looked at each other. This seemed a bit of an overreaction to an innocent enquiry about the where-abouts of two supposed friends of theirs.

'Maybe,' Barker continued in the same voice, 'they didn't *know* where they were going next. They were hitchhiking, you know. They would have to arrive where they were taken, wouldn't they?' It seemed a wizard of an idea to him.

But not to his two adventurers. The brothers simply exchanged more puzzled looks. The silence dropped between them like a curtain of iron mesh.

It was James who finally broke into the awkwardness. 'I expect you're right,' he said. 'They would have to go where they were taken. Let's finish our breakfast.'

SEVEN

Joanna looked at Mike. He appeared to be bending over his work a little deeper, concentrating harder, as though wanting to shut her out. She sighed. This is how life is. One little hiccup, one trauma, a decision and the ripples spread far and keep on spreading. You can never gather them back into your arms. Somehow the small confidence about parenthood had distanced him. He was a devoted father. And husband, too. Although he would never have admitted it his fiery wife, Fran – a petite, attractive and energetic nurse – was his perfect partner. She eyed his dark hair, cut a little shorter these days, almost army regulation, the square shoulders and thick neck, the bulky arms in his Polo shirt, and wondered how to break the silence. With DS Korpanski there was really only one way – head on.

She caved in. 'OK, Mike,' she said, 'forget the tetchy, awkward subject of parenthood. It's my business anyway – not yours. Let's do what we're paid for. Work. Two French girls who seem to have vanished. Last known location the lovely Rudyard Lake.'

He fixed his dark eyes on hers, waiting for her next comment.

'They're in their late teens,' she said. 'Seventeen years old. Very attractive, possibly a bit mischievous.' She frowned. 'There isn't anything really worrying about their disappearance at the moment,' she caught his eye and added, 'is there?' She stopped. Of course there was. When do you ever see a teenage girl without a mobile phone glued to her ear? And how would they live without money?

Korpanski blew out his lips. 'We-ell,' he began in his slow way. 'We'd better hold fire at that, Jo. We'll need to recheck bank details from over here, mobile phone records, et cetera. But I agree with you. Let's start nice and slow. A couple of girls none too anxious to go home after a holiday, trying to avoid parental interference. It sounds as though both come from broken homes and it's only Madame Bellange who's actually chasing this up. Maybe we should talk to the other girl's mum. Just to check – you know?'

'In French?'

Korpanski simply grinned at her and she had her ally back. A friend, a colleague, someone who would make no demands on her. 'In French,' he said. 'I do have an A-level, Jo.'

She smiled back at him, feeling happy. 'You take Dorothée and I'll take Annabelle.'

'OK. That's fine.' Then, turning around, he added, 'but if this doesn't come to a swift conclusion you'd be much better using DC Alan King. He's positively fluent.'

'I'll keep my fingers crossed we don't need to,' she said.

Tuesday, 10 September, 8.30 a.m.

Barker had a problem: two hulking great big rucksacks. He sat at the kitchen table and pondered. What on earth was he going to do with them? He hadn't bothered up until now because he hadn't thought he needed to. No one was looking for them. But now these two men had turned up asking questions. Barker wasn't a person to panic; rather, he worked his problems out slowly and carefully. He'd thought he had plenty of time. He'd deal with it later. Always later – if at all. Barker was a procrastinator and also a person who shied away from unpleasantness, tried to pretend it wasn't there. Convinced himself that if he only looked the other way any nasty things would simply melt away. His mother had lectured him more than once on this. 'Face up to your problems, Horace,' she'd said sharply. 'Running away from them only makes them bigger, you know.'

But now . . . he gave an anxious glance at the kitchen door, which was very slightly ajar. He could hear the brothers at the breakfast table, the sounds almost pricking his senses: the dry rattle of cereal being poured into a round bowl, the soft sound of the milk splashing over it. Coffee. He could smell it from here. Poured and drunk. He shifted in his seat. He'd better ask them if they wanted a full English. He already knew they would. Two hearty climbers? Of course they would. He stood up, and felt a little shaky. He couldn't ignore them. They were there, an undeniable physical presence. He was apprehensive and nervous.

Somewhere in the depths of his character Barker was a superstitious man, and this had the tinge of terror around it. At the back of his mind sat a prescience of impending doom. Something hung over him, just out of sight, something that even Supi-yaw-lat couldn't put right. Not even her soft (imagined) fingers could smooth away this worry, this black crow, wings a-flapping, warning him. He had often wondered why black is the colour of evil when it is simply an absence of colour. Is colour good, then? All colour? Muddy green and khaki? Shit brown and blood red? He scooped in a deep breath. He had to acknowledge that this was not a big problem. It was *huge*. And the items that currently stood in the corner of his kitchen wouldn't simply go away. They wouldn't vanish or self-destruct however much he ignored them. He was going to have to do something with them. And for once he couldn't think what. Barker rubbed his hands through hair so thin so you could not only see his scalp but a couple of throbbing veins lying like worms over his skull. He was worried. *More* than worried.

He stood up and went into the dining room.

The two brothers were shovelling cereal into their mouths as though they hadn't eaten for a month. Barker almost shuddered. It was OK for people to enjoy food but something about these two men's heartiness troubled him. They had too much energy, he thought.

He almost extruded out a kind, conciliatory voice. 'Good morning. I hope you slept well?'

The brothers looked at each other and smirked. Barker knew they had been talking about him last night. He'd seen them through Supi-yaw-lat's eye. They had been laughing at him. Mocking him. Mimicking his accent, stealing his phrases. Even doing a ridiculous walk. He'd felt affronted. He didn't walk like that.

The taller one responded casually, 'Very. Is it OK if we stay another night?'

Barker felt his face stiffen. No, it bloody well wasn't OK

if they stayed another night. He didn't want them to. He felt
like shouting, no, I want you to go away and never come back.
I don't like you. I feel you are my nemesis. I don't want you
here. You're worrying me.

What he actually said was, 'Of course,' in a voice deliberately soft as velvet. 'Now, then. Cooked breakfast? Two full
Englishes?'

They nodded.

'And have you enough coffee?'

The brothers exchanged glances and Barker remembered
last night. *Have you enough coffee?* And, *The shower is new.
I put it in myself.* Hand on silly hip.

He returned to the kitchen to grill the sausage and bacon
and fry the bread, eggs, tomatoes and mushrooms. When he
said full English he meant exactly that. He took pride in this.
A bed and breakfast, he sometimes reflected, must take pride
in both – the bed, comfortable and clean, and the breakfast
well-cooked, made with local ingredients and well presented.
Barker loved cookery programmes – and the one where two
people who have a bed-and-breakfast business swap places
and pull each other's establishments to bits. He would love to
take part in that programme.

As he cooked, he dreamed. But as he put the bacon, sausage
and other items on the plates his unease grew. How he wished
he could wave a magic wand, say abracadabra and make those
two objects vanish in a puff of smoke, as well as the men who
were going to tuck in to his *poisoned* breakfast. He made a
face. Poisoned? I wish, he thought and stomped through, giving
one brief glance behind him.

He put the plates in front of them without a word, gave a
vague smile when they acknowledged their appreciation of his
cooking and tucked in, and returned to the kitchen.

The question was now obsessing him. How was he going to
get rid of them? Get rid of the evidence? He felt a creeping
uneasiness.

He'd procrastinated for too long, and for some reason hadn't
anticipated that people might come to Mandalay searching for
the girls. They were far too huge to simply hide, and they'd
been far too big for the girls, who had hefted them so easily

on to their slim shoulders. He'd thought that at the time. He should have got rid of them weeks ago, he now realized. Not waited. Leaving them here looked even more suspicious. And now their friends had come to look them. Like hunters, guns levelled, they were tracking the girls' movements, following their footprints, searching for markers, indicators, as to where they were now.

He felt sweaty when he thought about the two men two doors and a short corridor away, still eating their breakfast but probably plotting their next step to find their friends. Perhaps they were still whispering about him. Barker twitched. When were they going to leave? OK, tonight was just one more night. But what if they asked to stay yet another night? What if . . .? What if they never went? He looked up.

James was standing in the doorway, plates in hand. He grinned. 'Thought we'd give you a hand as you're on your own.'

Barker paled and felt himself go all dizzy. Automatically, he stretched out his hand and took the plates.

'Thank you,' he managed and, as he'd known he would, James spotted the rucksacks. How could he have missed them? They stood as obvious as Stonehenge.

'I'm minding them for a couple who've gone into Stoke for the day,' he explained, realizing it didn't sound credible, even to him.

'Nice,' James said, and returned to the dining room.

Barker waited until he'd heard them clomping back upstairs then tore off a piece of kitchen roll, held it under the tap and sat at his table, holding the compress to his forehead.

He wanted them to go. Now. *Right now*. He regretted not lying and telling them he was fully booked for the foreseeable future. For ever, actually. He had bad vibes about them. There was something about the way the taller of the two men had studied him, as though he was looking right through him, that made Barker shiver. Go, he wanted to shout. Go right now.

He looked again at the rucksacks. One was khaki, the other dark blue. They were large, with metal frames. Heavy. He

knew that because he'd had to lug them down the stairs. Get
them out of the way. Remove them. Otherwise he could never
have let the room again. It would have been a waste. So he'd
packed them up and put them somewhere out of sight. For a
month they had stayed in his cellar, at the bottom of the steps.
Recently he'd felt compelled to bring them up the steps, but
he'd never opened them.

Was there anything inside which would incriminate *him*?
he wondered. Gingerly he undid the dark blue buckle on the
closest one. Barker was not a big man. That had been part of
the reason why he had been bullied and teased at school. Both
his size and something about his timid character had alienated
his peer group from him. That plus the domineering mother
who had been in such evidence around the small boy. He lifted
the top, and an evocative scent wafted out. He closed his eyes,
breathed it in and remembered. Supi-yaw-lat had seen much
that night. Giggling girls with tanned skin, tiny white marks
where small bikinis had been. He breathed in perfume, soap
and deodorant. And an underlying scent of woman. Unmistakably
woman. He looked down to a pair of jeans. Neatly folded.
When they had gone out for that last day and he had heard
them laughing and talking all the way down the drive, he had
entered their room and lifted one corner of the jeans up. It
had been hot enough for shorts that day. Underneath the jeans,
in a little more of a higgledy piggledy pile, had lain some
underwear. Underwear. He had smiled and involuntarily his
fingers had stroked the soft material. It was nice underwear.
He'd heard French girls wore nice underwear but it had been
his first chance to find out if it was true. The bra was purple
and soft with spiky lace, and there'd been matching panties.
Barker dug his hands in now and felt something else silky. A
nightdress?

He dug in a little more, careful not to disturb the neat
packing, and pulled out a packet of contraceptive pills. He
knew exactly what they were. All the days of the week. Out
of this packet, the last one taken was Friday. Saturday and
Sunday still waited. Barker touched them. Should he destroy
the evidence which told a story so clearly? Better not. He
recalled seeing the packet of pills. They had lain at the side

of a toothbrush in the bathroom on the bedside cabinet. People staying in B&Bs leave plenty of clues as to their characters. He had seen these and known the girls were available. He'd smiled at them at the breakfast table knowing that he knew intimate facts about his two guests. He knew things about *all* the people who stayed here in the rooms people thought of, temporarily, as their own private places. But they weren't. Not really – even temporarily. They were his. He would reclaim them when they had gone. And somebody else would come.

He recalled Annabelle carrying the navy rucksack the first time he had seen her. And her silky hair. It had been the first thing he'd noticed about her. Her long, straight, shining silky hair. The colour wasn't great. Not black like his lady, but brown. In fact, a sort of disappointing mousey brown. But it had been the texture which had drawn him.

'Ye-es,' he'd said.

'*Avez-vous.*' She had laughed, showing a tiny gap between her incisors. 'Sorry, do you have a room?' Her accent had been unmistakably French, the 'r' bubbling from the back of her mouth, somewhere near the tonsils. 'For we – two,' she had added hopefully. 'Not *trop* . . . not too expensive,' she had corrected quickly.

He had warmed to the girl . . .

He heard a noise. One of the brothers – he hadn't quite distinguished between them, the taller one – was downstairs again poring over the visitors' book, now copying something down from it. Barker moved into the hallway and cleared his throat – a dry scrape of a noise that sounded guilty.

The guy was grinning at him, his finger on a page in July. 'I'm going to try this mobile number. I didn't write it down before.'

Barker swallowed. He had to get rid of the rucksacks.

Perhaps he could . . . drop them into someone's wheelie bin. But all the wheelie bins he knew were always full well before bin day. And if they happened to notice him with two large rucksacks them they might well call the police in. Besides which, only one at a time would fit into a bin. That meant *two* wheelie bins.

He could . . . burn them. People had bonfires, didn't they? All that would be left would be the metal frame. Yes, this sounded a good idea. He liked this one best. Then his spirits dampened. Someone might see the fire. And the police could gather much evidence from charred remains.

Take them down the dump? Two weeks ago he had struggled with a stained mattress. One of the men who ran the recycling centre had come up to him, taken down his car number plate and informed him that the recycling centre was being taken over by a private contractor and that in future the rubbish would be monitored. Not such a good idea, then.

It was tricky and a challenge. But blindly, all Barker really knew was that had to get rid of the evidence. If he didn't it would incriminate him. Big time. But maybe he could divert suspicion. Barker had an idea.

Joanna and Mike had spent three hours checking up on the girls' details, staring into computer screens and making a couple of phone calls. Mike had stumbled through a terse call in 'Franglais' first of all to Madame Caron, who had told him that her daughter had not been in touch but that she was not worried unduly. 'She's a big girl,' she had said. 'She does not have to be talking to her *maman* every day.'

Korpanski had pushed. 'When did you last talk to her?'

There was a pause before Renée had responded. 'Sometime in July, as far as I remember. I am not worried, *monsieur*. Dorothée will turn up just like you say in the UK . . . a bad penny. *Mais oui?*'

There was nothing Korpanski would have liked better than to respond with an equal surety and affirmative sentiment, but the truth was that as he watched Joanna come up with an equally negative response, he felt his pulse quicken. There *was* something in this. These girls really were missing. But from where?

By three o'clock they'd updated each other.

'Nothing,' Joanna said. 'No mobile phone used since mid-July, no signal since then. No money drawn out of Annabelle's account. Nothing.'

'Same here,' Korpanski agreed. 'Nothing gone from Dorothée's either.'

'So we have to put out two missing person's reports and do a bit more digging.' Joanna looked out of the window. 'Hey,' she said. 'It looks a lovely day. Fancy a trip to Staffordshire's seaside?'

'I take it you mean Rudyard.'

'Yeah. I'll drive. And I'll even buy you an ice cream if you're a good boy.'

Korpanski started laughing and they left the station in high spirits.

This, after all, was the job they were paid to do.

EIGHT

I t being a week day and duller and cooler than the weekend there were few boats on the lake, just a couple of sturdy men in Canadian canoes making good headway. It was much quieter than before but the ice-cream stall was still open, the eager-faced boy patently hoping to sell a large 'ninety-nine' to the burly sergeant and his companion.

Korpanski eyed the lake. 'You know what, Jo, we don't know they vanished from here.'

She gave him a sharp look. 'This is the last place we know they were.'

Korpanski shrugged. 'OK. So where do we start?'

'It's obvious.' Joanna grinned at him.

The hotel was still open all day so they simply walked in and took a look around. Rudyard Hotel was a sturdy Victorian building which had recently had a facelift and was very much open for business.

As they walked in, they caught the eye of one of the staff members and Joanna spotted a name tag: Sarah Gratton. They walked straight up to her.

Joanna flashed her ID card and Sarah gave a watery smile in response. *Right.*

'So what can I do for you?' she asked silkily, a note of sarcasm leaching any politeness or pleasantness out of the phrase. *Not those French girls again?*

Joanna flipped the photographs on to the bar. 'Have you seen these girls?'

Sarah frowned and looked up. 'You're the second lot of people in the last couple of days to ask about these two.' She looked up. 'French, aren't they?'

'That's right.'

'So what is it about them?'

'We're just trying to find them.'

Behind her Korpanski put in, 'So who were the first, love?'

The barmaid's gaze softened as she met Korpanski's dark eyes. As many women did, she immediately morphed into a coquette. 'Couple of fit-looking climbers,' she said, flashing a smile at him.

'Know their names, love?'

Inwardly Joanna gave a groan. Oh, let Korpanski get on with it. She gave a tut of irritation – which neither her sergeant nor the flirting barmaid took the slightest notice of.

'I don't think I ever heard their names,' Sarah said, smiling more broadly. 'I'll try and think about that one, see if I can remember,' she purred.

When would they learn? Joanna fumed. Korpanski was a married man – not up for sale. He was devoted to Fran, Ricky and Jocelyn. But he was adept at using his obvious charms to get what he wanted – particularly out of witnesses. *Female* witnesses. Men tended to perceive his powerful frame as a threat. Inwardly, Joanna smiled. Quite right, too.

But as he was doing so well she should probably let him continue.

'When were they asking, love?'

'A couple of days ago.' The eye contact between the two of them was cringeworthy. Sweet and sickly as a river of treacle.

She intervened. '*What* did they ask?'

Reluctantly Sarah Gratton tore her eyes away from Korpanski and focused instead on the inspector. 'Said they were friends of theirs and asked if I'd seen them.'

'And had you?'

Sarah Gratton shook her head. 'No,' she said, still frowning. 'At least, if I did I don't remember.'

Korpanski pursued the point. 'Ever?'

'I seem to remember a couple of French girls coming in here once or twice back in the summer, but that was a couple of months ago.'

'When?'

'July, I think.' Her eyes swivelled towards the corner of the lounge bar. 'They'd order their food and sit over there.'

Joanna pressed the point. 'Were they *these* girls?'

'Look, I really don't know. I couldn't be sure.' She met the inspector's fierce gaze. 'They might have been,' she capitulated.

'And did you ever see the pair of climbers with them?'

Sarah shook her head. 'No. I don't think I'd ever seen the climbers before.' She returned her gaze to Korpanski. 'And I would have remembered such a fine pair of guys.' Her grin was teasing and challenging and Joanna smiled, suddenly seeing the funny side of things because Detective Sergeant Mike Korpanski, happily married father of two, was blushing.

'Did you ever see *any* men with them?'

'No. They were always on their own. They kept themselves to themselves, simply ordered their food and drinks and sat on their own.' She shrugged. 'They were often reading from a book.' She frowned. 'Poetry, I think.' Again she appealed to Korpanski rather than to Joanna. 'But it gets ever so busy here in the summer. Kids running in and out, the boat people, trippers, sightseers. You know.' Again she shrugged, as though wishing she could wash her hands of this subject.

Joanna picked up on something. 'They weren't staying *here* then?'

The girl shook her head.

'Do you know where they *were* staying?'

'Yeah,' she said. 'I'm pretty sure they were staying at Barker's place.'

'Barker's place?'

'Mandalay. It's out on the road that leads up to Biddulph Moor. A sort of upmarket bed and breakfast.'

Joanna glanced at Mike. She was conscious of the fact that when they returned to the police station at some point Cécile Bellange would turn up again and ask for news of her daughter. And what could she tell her? Only what she already knew – that the two girls had been here.

Have you any news of my boy Jack?
Not this tide.
When d'you think he'll come back?
Not with this wind blowing and this tide.

It was the only answer she could give the woman: not this tide. She looked at the girl. Was this a dead end, as it appeared?

'Anything else you can think of that might help us find them? You didn't hear them say where they were heading next?'

The girl shook her head. 'No. Sorry.'

They used the well-turned phrase as Joanna handed over her card. 'Well, if you do remember something . . .'

Sarah made one last effort. 'Yes,' she said, smiling and looking straight at Mike, 'if I do think of anything, you can be sure I'll be right back in touch.'

You're wasting your time, love, Joanna wanted to say, but didn't. They left, both feeling that they'd missed something – something that Sarah had said that they should have pursued and hadn't.

It was the climbers. Just because Sarah hadn't seen the four together, it was still a lead they should have gone after. Two guys asking for the two girls. What did they know – or think?

'Mandalay,' she said.

Korpanski turned to look at her. 'So,' he said dubiously.

'So . . . *"By the old Moulmein Pagoda, lookin' lazy at the sea,"'* Joanna quoted, *"'There's a Burma girl a'settin', and I know she thinks o' me. Come you back, you British soldier; come you back to Mandalay!"'* She grinned at Mike. 'It's a Kipling poem, Mike.' She couldn't resist teasing him. 'Didn't you study Kipling at school?'

'No,' he said stolidly.

'Never heard of *The Jungle Book*?'

'That,' he said, 'was Disney.'

'Not originally. It was Rudyard Kipling. Who also wrote "Mandalay". Agreed?'

They took the back road out of Rudyard, taking the higher road rather than the road to the lake. It was a steep climb through a wooded narrow lane until they reached a driveway with a *Vacancies* sign dangling from a chain, rattling ever so slightly in the breeze. The gate stood open, inviting them along the rhododendron-lined drive. Mandalay was a large, Victorian house, well kept, with plenty of parking. Currently only two cars were there, a red Mazda sports car and a five-year-old Volvo, dark green and mud-spattered. As they pulled on to the drive the view opened up and they realized that the felling of

trees between Mandalay and the lake which had happened in
the late spring had opened out the view to its advantage. The
long lawn sloped downwards, and although the lake was far
below it had the effect of being an extension of the garden.
At the front of the house was a flat terrace with tables and
chairs. The place looked elegant and well cared for. And yet
. . . did it hide a secret? Had the two girls disappeared from
here?

'Nice,' Joanna said approvingly, then glanced at Mike, who
was also staring admiringly at the house. Joanna had always
had a soft spot for Rudyard with its lake and air of Victorians
at play. The lake itself had the atmosphere of a holiday destin-
ation and she had always shared the Kiplings' enthusiasm for
the place.

Korpanski was out of the car, looking down at the water,
which today in the stiff breeze sported white horses and almost
threatening-looking waves. Not a great day for canoeing,
he thought, watching the canoeists toss and tumble in the
spray. They were obviously enjoying themselves.

Mike gave a chuckle. 'We used to bring the kids here, to
Rudyard,' he said, 'for a treat when they were little. They just
loved the little train that goes up and down the valley. We used
to bring our bikes here as well. There's a good cycle track
down there that leads to a nature reserve.'

'Not so nice now they're teenagers?' Joanna ventured.

Korpanski looked at her sharply. He knew exactly what she
was searching for: a negative attitude to children. And he wasn't
going to give it to her.

'Equally nice,' he said firmly, stepping forwards, 'but
different.'

His words had set Joanna thinking. Would she and Matthew
bring their child here too to sit on the undersized train, eat
ice cream, sail a dinghy up and down the lake? Would they
bring picnics and walk to a grassy quiet spot to eat? Cycle
along the track? Would they? She couldn't picture it. Why
not?

She caught up with Mike. Good job he couldn't read her
thoughts.

Barker had heard the car crunch over the gravel. He'd seen

them through the window and, like Sarah Gratton had, recognized them instantly as police.

That was when he panicked. The evidence was here. He locked the door of the cellar behind them just as he heard the bell ring at the front door. He opened it with his landlord's smile.

'Ye-es?' Feign ignorance.

He looked at the big guy with black hair, half smiling, then at the woman at his side whom he instantly recognized as being the boss, even though she too was smiling at him. But it was a tight, sharply appraising smile. Suspicious, too.

'Detective Inspector Joanna Piercy,' she said brightly. 'Leek police. May we come in?'

He tried to look innocently enquiring, as though he was simply curious as to what all this was about. They stepped into the hall, noted the encaustic Victorian tiles polished till they gleamed, breathed in the universal scent of the bed and breakfast – the scent of the full English mixed with furniture polish.

Barker forced his eyes to open wide in enquiry. 'How can I help you?'

'We're trying to find the whereabouts of two French girls,' Joanna said, 'who haven't been in contact with their families since July.'

'That's a very long time to stay incognito,' Barker said steadily, in what he hoped was a sympathetic tone.

'We believe they stayed here.'

Barker tried to head them off at the pass. 'I don't remember two French girls.'

The big guy spoke. 'I expect you have a lot of people staying here.' He had a local accent. Leek born and bred at a guess. Barker narrowed his eyes.

'Do you keep a visitors' book?' It was the woman who was pursuing the point. Barker eyed her. Trouble, he thought. There lies the trouble.

'I do,' he said carefully, 'but of course not everyone bothers to sign it. Only the people who want to.' He waited, the smile pasted on his face. 'Those who wish to make a comment.'

'Yeah. Quite.' The big guy was grinning chummily at him but the woman was sticking to her purpose. Like a tube of bloody glue. 'May we take a look at it, please?'

Barker wasn't sure whether they should have a warrant to take a look at the visitors' book but he thought it would look more suspicious if he said no. He should have hidden that, too. He sighed. When would he learn? He harrumphed out of the room, returning with it a minute later.

Joanna flipped back through the pages. *Lovely place* came up a few times. *Delicious breakfast* a few more times. *Beautiful view. We so love being here. We'll be back. Rudyard is so beautiful. Tranquil. Great rooms. Great breakfast.*

And here it was.

Annabelle et Dorothée, 18 Juillet, 2014. Merci. C'est Magnifique. Nous aimons le lac et son lien avec Rudyard Kipling, le plus grand de tous les poètes.

Written the day before the date on the postcard. And after that – nothing. No more contact.

Joanna took a good look at the landlord. Bowed shoulders, nervous eyes, pale skin, clean fingernails – and Mandalay itself looked so well run. An above average bed and breakfast in a great location. And he'd had the savviness to exploit the Kipling connection with the name. She'd also noted a framed copy of 'If' in the front hall. Barker had a bit more about him than first appeared.

'These are the girls we're looking for,' she said, trying to make the connection. 'Do you remember them now, Mr . . .?'

'Barker.' He supplied his surname only. He wasn't going to allow the humour his first names usually evoked.

Korpanski spoke. 'Mr Barker, do you remember the girls? They were hitchhiking?'

'Not really,' he lied. 'I don't really remember them at all. I'm so busy in July, you see, what with it being the school holidays and always busy here.'

'But you don't get many foreign girls?'

'You'd be surprised.' He tried to inject a little innuendo into his voice.

Joanna interjected. 'Would they have pre-booked?'

'Some do,' he said firmly, 'but I wouldn't have the documentation. Not now. Not any more.'

'Do you have the passport numbers of foreign visitors?'

He drew in a deep breath. 'To be honest, Inspector,' he tried a smile on her, but soon realized it was a waste of time as her frown deepened, 'I don't always bother,' he said lamely.

Joanna frowned. 'If they were hitchhiking,' she said, 'how would they get to the main road from here? It's about four miles.'

'I don't know. I really don't know.' He knew he was sounding flustered. 'Walk, I guess. Sometimes other guests, if they see girls hitchhiking with those big rucksacks . . .'

Rucksacks. Why on earth had he mentioned rucksacks?

And the two police had picked up on it. Antennae were quivering.

'So you *do* remember them.'

He wished she wouldn't fix her eyes quite so unblinkingly on him. They seemed to be looking right through him. Skewering him to the wall.

He gave a little laugh that even to him sounded nervous. 'I was assuming,' he said, 'when you mentioned hitchhiking . . . they wouldn't have had suitcases, would they?'

Neither of them responded to this except by both continuing to fix their eyes on him. Perhaps it was a police trick.

Help.

Then they stopped looking at him and instead exchanged glances with each other, as though they could communicate without speaking. Both gave a little nod. What the hell did that mean?

He tried to convince them by repeating, 'I get so many comings and goings, you see.'

Joanna nodded. Could this guy have anything to do with the girls' disappearance? On the surface he seemed too . . . ineffectual.

Barker put his head on one side. 'I do apologize,' he said. 'I'm not being much help here, am I?'

Joanna heaved out a big sigh and felt a splash of sympathy for the guy. Gosh – they weren't going to close him down just for not taking the passport numbers of a couple of French girls.

'It's OK,' she said kindly. 'We can't expect you to remember everything and everybody who stays here. It *was* a little while ago – and in your busy season.'

Her response made Barker *want* to help. 'I suppose,' he said, conceding, 'that most people sign the visitors' book when they're leaving so that's probably when they left Rudyard and moved to another location.'

Without their rucksacks?

'OK,' Korpanski said kindly. 'OK, Mr Barker. You've been a great help. Thank you very much.'

'Do you think we might have a quick look at their room?' Joanna didn't even know why she'd asked it but it seemed to make Barker nervous.

A small bead of sweat squeezed out of a pore on his upper lip. 'Of course,' he said politely and led them upstairs. The stair carpet was pale beige and Joanna almost felt she should have removed her shoes, the place was so clean.

'You manage this place yourself?'

Barker turned. 'I do,' he said solemnly.

'You make a great job of it.'

For the first time she saw his smile, tentative and proud. 'Thank you,' he said simply. 'It seems to come naturally to me. Here . . .' He unlocked a door and pushed it open.

The room was neutral with only one note that jarred: a garish picture on the wall. Barker followed her gaze and misinterpreted her opinion. 'Lovely, isn't she? I like to think she's the girl from Kipling's poem, "Mandalay".'

'Yeah.' Behind her Korpanski's eyes had widened and the suspicion of a smirk was making his mouth wobble. She turned and glared at him. Whatever their opinion, the owner of Mandalay obviously loved this print. Still, there was nothing to be gleaned from here. The room was characterless. The French girls had well and truly gone, apart from the vaguest smell of perfume. She breathed it in. Or maybe it wafted in, riding on the breeze from the open window.

'Thank you, Mr Barker,' she said. 'That's all. Thank you for your cooperation.'

'My pleasure.'

He returned them to the front door, his relief so intense that when the detective held out her hand he practically kissed it instead of simply shaking it. But she hesitated on the doorstep. 'I don't suppose,' she said, 'as you don't seem to remember them well, you won't recall seeing them with a couple of male climbers, or if they mentioned where they were going next?'

The question gave Barker the worm of an idea, but he also had to be careful. 'No, and I have no idea. Probably somewhere on the tourist trail,' he said, wafting his hands around. 'Stratford? London. Edinburgh, maybe. Somewhere like that, I expect.'

She turned away from him then. He watched them go with initial relief. But it was soon followed by worry flooding back and a conviction that he and the detectives would be meeting up again sometime in the future.

NINE

I t was an unusual evening for them. There was a long film on and they lay slumped on the sofa together. But as they hadn't pre-recorded it they couldn't fast forward through the adverts. It was during one of these breaks that they started talking and the film seemed to fade into the background.

'What was it,' Joanna was asking, her head against Matthew's arm, 'that made you want me?'

'You really want to know?' Matthew said comfortably, his hand stroking her hair.

'Yeah.'

Moments like these were rare. Too rare. Matthew was a senior home office pathologist and his work load was awesome. He tried hard not to bring it home: studies, lecture preparation and papers, but it was a struggle. And Joanna? The life of a DI is irregular, unpredictable and never-ending, particularly when she had a new chief superintendent putting her under the microscope every second, waiting for her to make a slip. She could see it in his hard little eyes and mouth so thin it resembled a scar. Chief Superintendent Gabriel Rush had been in the post for almost four months and she had yet to see him smile. Added to his other unpleasant attributes – he had dry skin that looked flaky and lacking in vitamins or sunlight – she would have given anything, *anything* to have had Colclough back. But he had hopped it to a holiday home in Cyprus, so she couldn't even pick his brains or ask for advice. Arthur Colclough was not into Facebook or even emails.

'It was . . .' Matthew said, answering her question, leaning forward and taking a sip from a glass of very cold white Chablis. He thought for a minute, smiling to himself at the memory. 'I thought of you like a Minstrel,' he finally came up with.

'Uh?' she said, turning to look at him.

'Crisp, brittle shell and underneath such a piece of soft, sweet chocolate,' he said, planting a kiss on her cheek.

'Matthew.' She wanted to scold him but he continued.

'Oh, yes,' he said, laughing. 'Such a stroppy, defensive exterior and there you were, as vulnerable as a new-born lamb, puking up in the sink.' There was a silence before he asked, 'And what about you, Jo? What was it about me? Why did you agree to have dinner with me?'

She had three options here. She could tell him the truth. *Are you joking?* she wanted to say. Look in the mirror, Matthew Levin, take a good look at yourself, at that wide, generous mouth and tousled, tawny hair the colour of damp sand, at those merry green eyes that are so expressive, at your six foot lean and muscular frame.

Or she could have quipped, having puked up my breakfast, I was starving hungry and you offered to buy me lunch. Instead she opted for the half-truth. 'It was the fact that you were laughing at me. Everyone else was taking me so seriously, as though I was the bogey man – or woman. They were embarrassed at the fact that I was throwing up in the sink, standing back, awkward and not knowing what to do. And there you were, laughing at me. I warmed to you then, Matthew.'

She could have added that she had been impressed at his deft skill as a pathologist, at his meticulous examinations, the careful note-keeping, the simple yet profound explanations. Science and facts without drama. That and a certain modesty, as though the job he was doing anyone could do. Oh yes, the attraction between them had been hot and instant and, in spite of the fact that he had been married, their love had flourished. A forbidden hothouse fruit. Sweet as honey.

'Mmm,' he said comfortably, turning the sound back up. The film had restarted but neither was concentrating quite as hard as they had been. By the time it had ended they were both half asleep, their bodies tangled together.

The nights were drawing in towards autumn but the weather was still warm. No need to light the log burner yet.

By 8.30 p.m. the lights were being turned on in Mandalay. The brothers were changing into clean clothes having showered.

They were getting ready to head back down the road and eat
again at the Rudyard Hotel. They had read the board outside
earlier on in the day. It had boasted home-cooked steak and
kidney pie and they were already salivating after another day
spent canoeing and climbing. The full English seemed weeks
ago now – not twelve hours.

Martin was combing his hair, using the wall mirror next to
the Chinese girl while his brother brushed his teeth. Both were
dressed in rugby shirts and cargo pants.

Martin stared hard at the girl's left eye. It was as though she
was watching him. In front of his own eyes she appeared to blink.
And then all was black. 'James,' he said softly, 'come here.'

Barker drew back. His eye had met another. He'd known these
two were a dreadful mistake.

James crossed the room. 'Look at this.' As Barker shrank,
another eye took the place of the first one. Someone was
staring at *him*.

He froze. He dare not blink but forced his eyes to stay open.
Then he took two, three steps backwards and slid to the side,
trying to keep his breaths shallow and noiseless. The box room
was dark, deliberately so. Windowless. But he knew. He just
knew that one of them had his eye pressed to the hole. And
that he had been seen.

He swallowed and gulped. Instead of he and Supi-yaw-lat
looking together into the room she was now regarding him with
these strangers, looking backwards into herself. Why had he
risked discovery by spying on them? They weren't females. They
weren't even interesting. Why hadn't he kept away? Because
he'd needed to know how suspicious they were about the rucksacks, and if they'd recognized them as belonging to their French
friends. Oh, why hadn't he got rid of them before now?

In the next room, Martin put his finger to his lips, jogged his
brother's arm and, like Barker, they too moved to the side.

He's been spying, James mouthed, touching his eye with
his index finger and pointing to the picture to illustrate his
meaning. *Watching whoever was in the room*. Out loud he
said, 'Time to go to the pub.'

In the car they were free to speak. 'I bet those French girls were in that room,' Martin said. 'It's a twin-bed as opposed to a double. He'd put two of the same sex in there, wouldn't he? I bet whenever a couple of attractive women stay he keeps his eye on them.'

The brothers looked at each other, not quite sure either what this meant, whether there was any significance to it or whether they should do anything about it.

Barker had crept out of the room and on to the landing where he stood at the window and watched their car turn around and head down the drive. Tomorrow, if they wanted to stay another night he would tell them, *No. No. You can't.* He practised saying it in a forceful, angry voice. *No. No. You can't. Definitely not. No possibility at all. It's quite impossible. The room needs decorating.*

It was the best he could come up with. By tomorrow he would be free.

The pub was quiet. A couple of locals sat at a table playing dominoes, and there was a family with rowdy children – two boys who appeared incapable of sitting still, even to eat their sausage and chips – who left a trail of tomato sauce everywhere they went. And in the corner sat an ancient-looking man who drank with his dog sitting obediently at his feet. It was a Collie cross, sharp, observant and warily watching the two boys as though he feared they would step on his tail.

In the corner sat a slim woman, somewhere between forty and fifty, at a guess, with neat clothes and a self-possessed air. She gave the brothers a nod as they entered and caught their eye as they walked straight up to the bar. Conscious of her still watching them, they ordered their food and a couple of beers. Sarah Gratton served them, jerking her head in the direction of the woman. 'She one of your French friends too?'

'What?' James's head spun round.

'Well, she's French and she's been asking about those girls as well. Thought you might know her,' she added maliciously.

They turned slowly to observe her. Something in the quiet

manner of the woman, something self-possessed, should have warned them. It should have told them that to her they could not pretend. She would know the truth. And that they were in a tricky and potentially dangerous position.

They skirted past her and sat in the opposite corner, trying not to meet her gaze. But sweet little Sarah did it for them. 'Cécile,' she called out, her voice sugary, 'those are the guys who were asking about your daughter and her friend.'

The brothers looked at each other. Oh, shit.

The woman looked momentarily startled. Then she stood up, petite and slim in navy trousers and a pale blue sweater. She gave a tentative smile. ''Allo,' she said. 'Do you mind if I join you for a moment?'

Unmistakably French. What could they say? They gestured towards the empty chair. '*Merci*,' she said with a bright smile. But underneath they could see she was suffering. Her eyes beseeched them. 'I—' She appeared to have lost the power of speech. She glanced across at the barmaid, who was watching the scenario with a triumphant expression. She'd got her own back on the boys.

The woman tried again. 'My name is Cécile Bellange,' she said. 'My daughter is Annabelle Bellange.' She watched their faces for some response but both James and Martin looked impassive. Politely questioning. 'I – I believe you met my daughter and her friend, Dorothée?' Her face was schooled into brightness.

The brothers looked at each other. 'Not exactly,' they said together.

Madame Bellange shrugged. 'And what does that mean, *not exactly*?' Again, the two brothers looked at each other, unsure how to proceed.

Cécile Bellange stretched out one small hand and fluttered her fingers. 'Do you know where they are now?'

'No.' In chorus. This time there was no need for them to confer. The denial burst out of them. And Madame Bellange seemed to shrink, her eyes dulled with disappointment. She was silent for a moment, and then something of the fight returned in her. 'I have not heard from my daughter since the middle of July. Tell me what you know, please.'

The brothers looked at each other. Then James reached into his pocket and drew out the photograph. Cécile Bellange peered at it.

Then she turned it over and read the back. 'They . . .'

'The picture was taken at the Roaches,' James said helpfully. 'We found it on Sunday when we were climbing. It was in a plastic Tupperware box, half hidden so people like us would find it.'

'I do not understand,' Cécile Bellange said, her brow wrinkled. 'People like you? What does that mean? Why would they leave a photograph half hidden in a plastic box?'

'It's known as letterboxing,' James explained patiently. 'It's a sort of hobby. You collect stamps – and stuff. Then you stick them on a card,' he finished lamely as Cécile Bellange continued to look bemused.

James looked helplessly at his brother. 'Part of it is that you leave the stuff behind for others to find. Some people put bits in – photos and stuff – but we didn't.'

'So anyone else could have followed the girls to Rudyard?'

'In theory, yes,' James said, seeing a chink of light that might let them off the hook. 'Anyone else who found the letterbox before us will have seen the photo and might well have followed the girls to Rudyard.'

'But not many people would have found the letterbox,' James said, feeling even more stupid for exposing this fact. 'The habit or game or whatever you want to call it is less popular here than on Dartmoor where it all began.'

They could see from Madame Bellange's expression that she didn't really understand the concept at all.

'And you say Annabelle is – does this?'

The brothers nodded.

'Then where is she? Does this letterbox lead to her?'

'Well, it led to where she was staying at the time.'

'But you don't know where they are now?'

The brothers exchanged glances. 'No.'

'And you took the photograph away. Why?'

James spoke for both of them. 'We took the photograph because we hoped to find them and didn't want any other guys to get hold of it.' He grinned tentatively.

'They're very attractive,' Martin added. He felt this evening was not going at all well. 'We hoped to find them and maybe go for a drink.'

Madame Bellange continued to look bemused and the brothers shrugged. They'd done their best.

'And you say it was on a climb . . . somewhere?'

'Out on the moors. We found it at a famous climb site called the Roaches.'

'You will take me there?'

The brothers glanced at each other, both thinking the same thought. *Not in those clothes.*

James answered for both of them. 'If you want. In the morning, if you like.'

'*Merci,*' she said before dropping her bombshell. 'But first you will come with me to tell all this to the police,' she said. 'You still have your card with the stamps on it?'

Now they both felt very twitchy. 'Yes.' They spoke as one.

'Then you will bring it.' And she left.

They groaned. If these girls really were missing, as Annabelle's mother had suggested, what had happened to them? Even to them their story sounded lame – the chance finding of the letterbox, the apparently seductive invitation to join the two French girls at the lake and their pursuit six weeks after the photo had been left. Could they really have thought the girls would still be here?

No, but they had thought they might find another clue – possibly a further location or contact details. Something which would lead them nearer to the girls' tempting invitation. But now they realized how fishy the whole thing sounded – even to them. Imagine what a team of twitchy-nosed detectives would think.

And then there was the peeping Tom landlord. What was that all about? There was something unsavoury about Barker but they couldn't really imagine him doing away with the girls because they'd seen him watching them. If they had, they'd have just left and booked into somewhere else, surely? Somewhere other than Mandalay. But then James remembered the rucksacks standing in the kitchen, and Barker's apparent confusion when he had rounded the door. The Chinese girl's eye so carefully and precisely cut away to provide a peephole. What did the law call it? Pre-meditation. They looked at each other, troubled that they were booked in there tonight.

Oh, hell. They just wanted to leave.

They ate their steak and kidney pie with chips and mushy peas – home-made and cooked to perfection. But, in spite of their initial hunger, they didn't enjoy it half as much as they'd expected before meeting Cécile Bellange, even though the big fat chips were probably the best chips they'd ever eaten in their lives.

They sat with their heads together exchanging low words. They were going to have to get their story straight for the police.

TEN

Charlotte Bingley was planning a trip. She'd bought the book on the Roaches' climbs and planned every single day for four whole days – a different climb or walk each day, whatever the weather. She would go in early October when the weather should still be good, when children would be back at school and before half-term. Over the internet she booked into Mandalay, liking the exotic sound of the name and the pretty picture of the lake which accompanied the website.

Charlotte liked to climb alone so she had no one else to consult. There was another reason why this particular time suited her. Two years ago she and her long-term boyfriend, Stan Morton, had split up and she'd found the break liberating. Shocking, her mother had said, vinegar in her voice. She had been hoping for a wonderful white wedding and a couple of cute grandchildren that she could boast about to her friends. Charlotte had sighed and known that her mother was disappointed in her. *Very* disappointed.

'You're crazy,' her best friend Shona had said, 'letting him go. Stan's gorgeous, he's rich, he has a good job (an IT consultant in central London) and he loves you. He's fabulous.'

But Charlotte had taken absolutely no notice.

And so Shona had set her snares, which had relieved Charlotte of the dual burden of guilt and the accusatory presence, complete with hangdog expression, of her ex, who for the first couple of months after the split had seemed to be wherever she was socially. But eventually it had also relieved her of her best friend too. Shona's allegiance had changed. Her admiration for her friend's boyfriend had translated into a relationship with the result that, as her relationship with Stan had blossomed and bloomed, her shared confidences with

Charlotte had dried up. And now they were to be married. Shona and Stan had planned humongous nuptials in Italy in a big, fairy-tale, footballers'-wives-style wedding. Her mother had seen the invitation propped up on her mantelpiece in the tiny flat in Maida Vale and had read every word out aloud, including the nauseating and clichéd quote, *La amora tutto intorno – Love is all around.*

"The marriage will take place of Shona and Stan at the Villa Principessa, Napoli, Saturday fifth of October at three p.m."' She had read the words, using them as a cat-o'-nine-tails to whip her daughter with. Charlotte, to her mother's intense irritation, had simply smiled and said she was happy for them.

'Happy for them,' her mother had snorted.

But Charlotte really was. Shona and Stan had found each other and she had found herself. Her mother appeared to be the only one who had not moved on. When the wedding invitation had arrived, with its puke-provoking strapline, Charlotte Bingley had thought, *Not for me is la amora tutto intorno,* and had politely declined, saying she had a long-booked holiday. No one there would believe her, of course. Just about everyone at the wedding would form their own explanation for her absence.

She could just imagine it – all her old university friends: from *heartbroken* to *embarrassed* to *green-eyed jealous* and so on and so on. What she wouldn't have been able to stand would not have been the adoring glances between bride and groom, the *oh look how happy they are* moving on to plans for *one of each within two years I wouldn't be surprised,* which would have had her mother grinding her teeth in frustration. No – that was as it should be. It would have been the misguided pity aimed in her direction as they wrongly judged her, turning away from her to mutter, *she's made a terrible mistake,* and *I bet she's regretting it now.*

And however much she might protest that she was happy that Stan and Shona had found each other, no one would believe her. *She doth protest too much,* would be next.

They were all wrong. She and Stan would never have made

each other happy. She was, as she was finding out, far too independent and happy in her own company.

Charlotte was a tall, muscular thirty-eight-year-old. When her mother had advised her to remember the 'time clock' she had blown out an exasperated raspberry. She didn't give a monkey's tits about her time clock. In fact, if someone looked into a crystal ball and pronounced, 'You will end your days alone, childless and a spinster', she would have felt some relief. Thank goodness for that. Something I *don't* have to worry about.

She was a doctor who had passed all her exams a little late in life, having initially embarked on the same career as Stan – IT. Her abandoning such a well-paid career had been the thin end of the wedge between them. But she hadn't really decided which speciality she wanted to pursue (which would inevitably mean yet more exams). At times she fancied herself a GP but at others the idea of working in paediatrics as a saviour of children appealed more. And at other times she wondered about gynaecology and/or obstetrics.

The choice was vast. Too vast. One wouldn't have believed the human body could throw up so many different specialities. And then there was the adventure world of Médecins Sans Frontières, working in war-torn countries: emergency field work in areas his by crises – tsunamis, earthquakes, hurricanes, nuclear explosions, Ebola outbreaks and war. Or doing less exciting voluntary work, treating tropical diseases in village health centres. That attracted her too, so for the moment she fiddled around in A&E departments up and down the country while she made up her mind. She relished the idea of this holiday, travelling incognito, without her mobile phone, just wandering where the fancy took her. She would walk, climb and explore and spend her evenings reading. Bliss. She booked a room in Mandalay for early October for four nights.

Wednesday, 11 September, 8.30 a.m.

As though he had been lying in wait for her, Chief Superintendent Gabriel Rush found her at the very moment that she was walking into the station in full regalia: cycling shorts, garish cycling top (to make sure vehicle drivers *saw* her), helmet, SPDs. The lot. His pale eyes took in her fancy-dress costume and his scarred mouth looked even more disapproving as he greeted her coldly. 'Good morning, Piercy.'

'Morning, sir.' She removed her cycling helmet – a present from Matthew following a cycling accident when she had broken her wrist. And although a cycling helmet would be no protection against a broken wrist, she always wore it now. He tended to remind her if she 'forgot'.

'These French girls,' Rush said. 'Have you found anything out?'

She felt at a real disadvantage facing the CS in a pair of Lycra cycling shorts and the vividly coloured top – great to alert careless drivers to your presence but not exactly *de rigueur* for a DI. 'Nothing positive, sir,' she said, trying to sound dignified and in control and knowing she was managing neither. 'Only negatives. No bank transactions, no mobile phone usage. They haven't been on their email accounts since mid-July. Nothing's been picked up. The last record we have of them is on Friday the nineteenth of July, the day the card was posted.'

'Ah, the postcard,' he said, as though he understood the significance.

'We've tracked them back to a guest house in Rudyard at that time but they haven't been seen or heard of since that week.' *Oh, for goodness' sake, can we talk about this when I'm dressed?*

'The postcard,' he repeated. 'It was posted where?'

He was doing this deliberately. 'At the post box at the end of the road where the guest house is, sir.'

'So what next, Piercy?'

'We've spoken to some local people who remember the girls but no one seems to know where they were headed next, sir. It could be anywhere. They were hitchhiking. There's a possibility the girls were picked up by a driver and . . .' She didn't need to complete the sentence.

'So do you have a line of enquiry?'

'Two young men have been asking about them but we don't know their connection with the girls.'

Rush waited, his face impassive.

She tried again. 'Madame Bellange is coming in at nine o'clock this morning to see me, sir.' *And now can I bloody well get changed?*

'Then you'd better get changed, hadn't you?'

Had she been glaring at him? She smothered a smile.

Heaven help me if Chief Superintendent Gabriel Rush can read my mind.

She changed into a more suitable short black skirt, wedge-heeled shoes and a blue shirt, then went into her office where Korpanski was already working hard, checking into the PNC for any sightings of the two girls. He'd done two missing person's posts yesterday but so far nothing had come up.

He aimed a look of sympathy in her direction. 'Get copped by Rush, did you?'

She dropped into her seat. 'I swear he was waiting for me, Mike – lying in wait like a bloody predatory animal.'

Korpanski simply chuckled.

She glanced at his computer screen. 'No line on the girls then, yet?'

'No,' he said, then swivelled his chair around to speak to her. 'We're going to have to escalate the enquiry. Widen our search.'

She nodded.

Wednesday, 11 September, 9 a.m.

Nothing was said as Barker served the brothers their full English, but there was a general air of embarrassment and the Stuart brothers didn't even ask if they could possibly stay another night. Neither did they mention their impending trip to the Leek police station with the mother of Annabelle Bellange. Feeling slightly sick, they didn't even finish their breakfast.

They paid their bill with a debit card, loaded up their rucksacks and left.

Barker watched them go, his feelings a mixture of anxiety at what they would do next and relief. Then he went into his study and thought.

Barker with was good with technology. Self-taught and with a natural bent towards IT: mobile phones, email, the lot. He was very proud of the website he'd constructed for Mandalay and he'd had an idea. A very clever idea.

What if, he thought, he charged up one of the girls' mobile phones which had been left in their rucksacks, switched off (he'd checked), and sent a text on it, telling mum they were heading for somewhere far away from here? Then he could switch it off so no one would have time to track it and no one would be any the wiser. At least, that was what he hoped.

Good idea or what, Barker? He almost patted himself on the back but could only manage his shoulder. He answered the question himself. A very good idea, Barker. He would just need to practice what he was saying. Do a little translation. Choose a city. London. Eventually, he settled on the message:

Hello, Mum, sorry we haven't been in touch. We're in London and we're staying here for a bit. Just to let you know we're both well. See you soon.

He had a French dictionary, but the online translator tool was much easier and quicker. *Bonjour, maman, désolé, nous n'avons pas été en contact. Nous sommes à Londres, nous allons rester un peu ici. Nous voulions simplement vous dire que nous allions, toutes les deux, bien. A bientôt.*

Barker smiled, feeling pleased with himself. He found *Maman* in the phone's contacts and sent the text.

At the station, Cécile Bellange was not only on time for her ten o'clock appointment but she had in tow two ruggedly handsome men who looked decidedly sheepish. Joanna looked at Mike, her shoulders raised in question. Were these the guys who had been asking about the girls? Did they know Madame Bellange? Why were they here?

She glanced at Mike who gave his *all-will-be-revealed* shrug. But unfortunately, the garbled story that came out didn't help her much.

Letterboxing. A photograph. Interpreted as an invitation. Rudyard. Poems.

They'd not actually met the girls. It all came out in a

complete jumble, and it didn't help that the brothers had developed the habit of finishing off each other's sentences.

There was only one thing to do. 'Start at the beginning,' she said, and tried to let them speak without interruption, only asking questions if she felt she needed further clarification.

'So what took you to the Roaches and that particular climb?'

'Pure chance,' James said. 'We'd done some of the climbs before and that seemed a challenging one, so we went ahead with it.'

'And the letterboxing?'

'That's a sort of sideline.' They glanced at each other, both obviously wishing they'd left the Roaches well alone. Who would want to get embroiled in this?

'Describe to me exactly where it was.' Joanna glanced at Korpanski and he could read the tacit question in the lift of her eyebrows. *How's your climbing skills, Detective Sergeant?*

He grinned back at her. *Easily as good as yours, Inspector.*

She looked from one to the other and when she caught Korpanski's eye she could see that he was as bemused as she was.

What the hell was going on?

Gradually she began to tease out the story. Last weekend these two young men had been climbing in the Roaches. On reaching the top of the climb known as the Valkyrie near the Winking Man's head they had found, partly hidden, a Tupperware box placed there by someone calling himself the King of the Roaches. This was an oblique referral to someone whose story was so amazing it had practically passed into folklore. It was the story of Doug Moller, King of the Roaches, his wife, Annie, and Rock Hall Cottage. Rock Hall Cottage was part cave, part home to this eccentric pair. They had lived in this remote position for years until it had become untenable. Tragically, Annie had died of burns a few years later. Doug was still around and their son, Prince of the Roaches, carried on the tradition. His ink stamp was considered a rare prize as he was adept at hiding his letterboxes. These days Rock Hall Cottage had been turned into a retreat or shelter for climbers.

'Show me,' Joanna said, and the brothers unfolded a climbing map of the area. The Valkyrie was clearly marked.

'And the letterbox?'

The brothers showed Joanna their notebook and the collected stamps from other letterboxes. They had stamps from all over the country – Dartmoor, Exmoor, Devon and Cornwall, the top of Brown Willie and the peak of Snowdon, Ben Nevis and Scafell Pike. Looking at them made Joanna wish that she and Matthew had more time for this sort of pursuit. It looked fun.

'And in the box was this photo,' James said.

Joanna slipped on a latex glove. 'Do you mind?'

It was a colour photo of two laughing girls, both extremely attractive with fine skin and teeth and long, straight silky hair. They were wearing short shorts with their bottoms to the camera, turning to laugh teasingly into the lens.

Scrawled on the back was the invitation. *We are two French girls on a voyage of discovery. Come and find us. We will give you a welcome at the poet's lake, love Annabelle Bellange and Dorothée Caron XXX*

There was no date.

'Was there anything else?'

'No.' James answered for both of them.

Joanna dropped the photograph into an evidence bag then removed her gloves. 'So,' she asked innocently, 'you didn't meet up with them?'

The brothers shook their heads violently and vehemently. 'No,' they protested. 'We never did.' They looked even more awkward. They were concealing something.

Joanna shot a glance at Madame Bellange. Her face was impassive, her black eyes bright and inquisitive as a bird's, her thin face almost quivering with attention. She turned her gaze on one brother and then the other, sharp as a drill. She looked dubious. And looking at her, Joanna wondered whether *she* believed their story.

Joanna was still bemused. 'So what exactly did happen? What did you do next?'

'Well, we found out through the barmaid at the Rudyard Hotel that the girls had stayed at Mandalay.' Martin had taken up the reins and was speaking animatedly. 'So we went there and searched through the visitors' book.'

'But the girls would have moved on.'

Again James seemed to take charge. No longer sheep-faced,

he spoke clearly. 'We thought we might catch up with them somewhere else, maybe through their mobile numbers. They left one in the visitors' book at Mandalay, but it went straight to answerphone when I tried to call it. They looked fun,' he said defensively.

'And attractive,' his brother put in with more honesty.

Joanna didn't even ask whether the brothers were in current relationships. The question *she* needed to ask herself was how much of this was true? Had they really never met Annabelle and Dorothée? Had they just followed a whim? Searched for two girls who appeared to have vanished? Just like she was now doing? Or . . .

The two brothers exchanged nervous glances which were not lost on either Joanna or Mike. She knew they were hiding something.

'Can I ask you something?' she tried innocently. 'Surely when you discover a letterbox the idea is to collect the stamp; some people leave stuff – a picture or a little souvenir – and then you leave everything as it was?'

'Ye-es. At least, theoretically.'

'So why did you remove the photograph?'

They had their answer sorted – just as they had explained to Cécile Bellange. 'We didn't want the competition.'

'But *anyone* prior to your removing the picture could have pursued the girls to Rudyard Lake and found them.' She gave Korpanski a swift glance and knew he was already compiling a list of things to do. Top of the list was to visit the letterbox site. Then return to Mandalay and ask Mr Barker again whether anyone had been searching for the girls, including these boys. Start asking questions and then ask some more.

'Is there any chance,' she said to the brothers, 'that you can take me to the site of the letterbox?'

ELEVEN

Timmis and McBrine, Moorland patrol, were waiting for them at the bottom of the climb. This wild and rugged area was their patch. They loved the challenge of the terrain which could be unforgiving in winter and almost always felt hostile to intruders, even in the height of summer. Visitors quickly grew aware of the isolation of the area, the miles and miles of nothing except buzzards and kestrels, rabbits and the odd domesticated animal, cows and a few sheep. Otherwise, apart from the more adventurous hikers, bikers and climbers there was an absence of people. The natives were used to isolation and felt crowded in when they went to Leek for market day or to fill their freezers with provisions. Out here one could take nothing for granted – not even a reliable supply of food. There had been snows in June and September, quite apart from the normal extended span of winter. The natives kept themselves to themselves. Visitors came at their own risk.

Either Josh Timmis or Saul McBrine would be happy to scale the heights of the Roaches. They could run crab-like up its rocky surface or wander along the easier paths. It was all the same to them. Joanna laced up her climbing boots, tucked her jeans in her socks and prepared herself. It was not a tough climb but it was strenuous and she didn't feel at her fittest. Since her marriage there'd been many demands on her which had cut down her cycling time. It didn't seem fair on her free Sundays to abandon Matthew and join her buddies in the Leek Women's Cycling Club, so reluctantly she simply stuck to her route to and from work. And when the clocks went back in October, it would be too dark to cycle the lonely and unlit country lanes which led from Waterfall Cottage to Leek police station. And then there was this business of Matthew wanting a family. He was a protective man and would not look kindly on her putting a child at risk by cycling. Heigh ho.

James and Martin were climbing reluctantly out of the car behind them. They were to act as their guides.

She looked up at the bony crags of the Roaches. And, as always, she questioned herself. What was she doing here? Chasing up a flimsy clue in the search for the two girls? What Mike had said earlier was right. If they were missing rather than just gone AWOL because they didn't want to attend their college courses, the likelihood was that something had happened away from this area. The probability was that they had returned to the main road, stuck their thumbs out and been picked up by someone whose intentions were less than honourable. They would have to widen their search. As she scrabbled behind Josh Timmis, who was well kitted out in climbing gear, she followed him into handholds and footholds, remembering the mantra to keep close bodily contact with the rock face and to use, monkey-like, hands and feet to secure her safety. At the back of her mind was the embarrassment of explaining this to CS Gabriel Rush: *Well, sir, I thought I might find a clue to the girls' whereabouts up there on the crags.*

Ha. She scolded herself. She would achieve nothing by this except a bit of extra exercise. Then, hands and feet secure, she looked around her. Gaining height had afforded an even wider, more panoramic view of the hills and valleys of the moors. Surely, on such a blue-sky day, this was better than sitting in her office and staring at a brick wall? Then the wind whipped around the corner and she was not quite so sure.

They had left Saul McBrine in the car and Korpanski was back at the station with Cécile Bellange. There was no way she could have climbed up here, particularly in her elegant Parisian clothes. Martin and James were well ahead now, climbing quickly and confidently in their natural environment, glancing back every now and again like true group leaders to make sure she was keeping up. Josh Timmis was next in line, his boots occasionally catching some shale and sending it spilling down below. You had to think here. One slip and you would tumble – admittedly not to your death – but to some very nasty grazes which could be quite painful. Joanna had done this years ago with another boyfriend who had been a keen climbing partner, and she had always thought he had taken malicious delight in applying some stinging antiseptic to her injuries.

The trouble was she was a cop. And cops tend to look for trouble. It's not that they are pessimistic, more that they have met the worst scenarios too many times. And so, nibbling away, like a mouse on cheese, at the back of her mind, in a hole no bigger than a mouse hole was something. Some feeling . . .

Perhaps it was Madame Bellange's manner – quietly dignified, dumbly pleading. That desperate appeal that pricked at her conscience.

Added to that . . . She glanced ahead of her at the brothers, moving crab-like up the surface of the rock, agile as athletes. She wasn't sure whether she trusted them. During the drive out she'd kept an eye on them as they led the way and was sure they were having a fairly heated argument about something. A disagreement. She'd seen the heads turning towards each other, mouths open, hard stares, and felt the anger that passed between them. She would love to know what it had been about, though she could well guess: which version of events they should stick to.

A piece of loose shale loosened by Martin's boot stopped her mind from wandering and forced her to focus on the climb. The brothers were far enough ahead to make a whispered exchange. She strained her ears, quietened her breathing and listened.

James was talking to his brother. 'We should have never . . .'

She heard three more words. 'Come back.' And then: 'Rucksacks.' Spoken with intent, it floated down from the ridge. Then, as though they knew she was listening in, as one they turned around, saw her and clamped their mouths shut.

But when out of earshot they continued speaking, their words wafted away on the wind before they reached Joanna Piercy's ears.

When they reached the top all four of them were panting. Even a short climb was strenuous. But despite considering the uncomfortable circumstances which had brought them to this point of time and place they grinned at each other, triumphant. They'd done it. They were on top of the world.

Joanna was the first to speak. 'Show me exactly where you found the letterbox.'

They indicated a small cairn twenty, perhaps thirty yards away, which did not look like a random fall of stones but as though it had been placed there carefully. Man made. Quiet yet inviting the attention of the observant.

'Let's take a look, shall we?' Joanna slipped on a pair of gloves and picked up a plastic Tupperware box, the size of a sandwich box. Carefully she lifted the lid. Inside was an ink stamp, some postcards of local views, a couple of business cards. She took out a large evidence bag and slipped the entire contents, sandwich box and all, inside. The brothers looked appalled. 'You can't do that,' they said simultaneously. 'You can't take it away. It's not fair . . .' The words died inside them as they recalled the stricken face of Madame Cécile Bellange.

PC Josh Timmis looked sympathetic. Maybe he too was a secret letterboxer. 'We'll bring it back,' he said kindly, 'when we've taken a good look at it.' And then, as the brothers looked dubious, he added, 'I promise. I'll bring it back myself.'

The brothers looked mollified.

'But we have to take it,' Timmis continued, 'just in case . . .' He risked a look at Joanna and explained further. 'Just in case there's something inside that gives us a clue where the girls are.' He put a kindly hand on James's shoulder who was, he judged, the more upset of the two and seemed to need further assurance. 'I'll put it back, I promise. OK?'

James was looking at his brother. 'That isn't the one,' he said.

Joanna looked around. 'No? How many of these things are there hidden?'

James answered for both of them. 'We don't know,' he said. 'But that isn't the one we found. It's in the right place but it's not the one we took the girls' photo from.'

Joanna looked around her again, puzzled. Where had it gone? Had it been moved deliberately and replaced with a different box? But as she studied her surroundings she was struck by another thought: Annabelle and Dorothée must have been fairly tough to have made it up here. They were girls

who could look after themselves, she argued. And there had
been the two of them to look out for one another.

And then, in this most incongruous of places, her mobile
phone went off, the jaunty ringtone, *Paradise Island*, set to
remind herself of her honeymoon in Sri Lanka sounding
strange, exotic and thoroughly out of place in this most English
of landscapes. The number began 01538. It was the station.

'Drama off,' Korpanski said, jaunty as ever. 'Tour duty over.
Come down off the mountain.'

Joanna smiled. 'Go on.'

'Mrs Caron has had a message from her daughter today to
say they'd decided to visit London.'

'And that's it?'

'That is it, Inspector,' Korpanski said, sounding even more
jaunty. 'Time to come home and get back to some real work.'

'OK,' she said. 'I'm on my way down.' She ended the call
and looked at the brothers. 'Drama over,' she said. 'Dorothée's
mother has heard from her. The girls are in London.'

'Right.' They looked at each other, as if not sure whether
to believe her. Then they turned around and led the way down.

The descent was easier and the exhilaration was wearing
off quickly. At the car Joanna returned to business. 'What are
your plans now?' she asked the brothers, more for politeness
than any real curiosity.

'Back to work,' James said.

'In Birmingham,' his brother finished.

James worked in financial planning while his brother was
'in the car industry'. He didn't enlarge and she didn't ask.

'If you wouldn't mind leaving your contact details back
at the station, that'd be helpful,' Joanna said, knowing the
invitation would rattle the two men.

The look they exchanged between them was a simple, shrug-
ging, *What for?* The drama was over, wasn't it?

Well, let them be rattled just a little longer.

Back at the station Joanna spoke to Cécile Bellange. 'So what
are your plans now?' she asked pleasantly. 'Do you intend
meeting up with the girls in London, madame?'

'*Mais non*,' she responded heartily. 'I cannot find them in such a big city. I shall return home. Back to Paris and my work and to wait for them to arrive back home. Then I shall give them a *réprimande*.' She smiled. '*Merci beaucoup*, Inspector. *Merci pour votre aide . . .*'

Joanna cut in. 'Have you actually spoken to Annabelle yourself?' She felt she was being a wet blanket. A pessimist. A Cassandra. A detective.

Cécile Bellange must have thought so too. Her response was irritable. '*Mais non*,' she said. 'It seems obvious to me that only Dorothée still has her phone. Annabelle's number is not working.'

'OK. And did Dorothée's mother ring her daughter back?'

'I don't know that.' She sounded irritated and defensive. 'Renée Caron rang me half an hour ago to tell me. I only know that the girl has sent a message and that they are both safe.'

Joanna was thoughtful. 'So,' she said slowly, 'Madame Caron did not actually *speak* to her daughter?'

Cécile Bellange was angry. '*Non*,' she said, even more crossly this time. 'I already told you. Dorothée sent a text to her *maman*.'

'OK,' Joanna said slowly. She would have preferred it if Mrs Caron had actually spoken to her daughter herself. Why all this silence until now, when the police were involved? But Madame Bellange seemed adamant that the girls were safe – and maybe they were. There was no point trying to keep the investigation alive if the girls' families were convinced they were found.

And Cécile Bellange clearly was. Her demeanour had changed. She was brisk and anxious to be gone. '*Merci. Merci.* Thank you and goodbye, Inspector,' she said firmly and quickly. She shook hands and was gone.

Joanna hoped the goodbye wasn't simply an *au revoir*.

TWELVE

S o Joanna filled Rush in with the result of the case. She completed her reports, emphasizing the fact that Cécile Bellange was content the girls were safe in London.

She couldn't pretend to be a hundred per cent happy at the result. With her suspicious DI's mind, like doubting Thomas, she wouldn't be absolutely certain until someone who knew them had actually seen the two girls. But still, she could settle back in relief at the fact that the errant French girls appeared to be safe and not dead on her patch.

And there were distinct advantages to this state. When there is a major case in progress, policemen, whether DIs or DCs, are not allowed to have private lives. Weddings, funerals, let alone holidays and any other commitments, have to be placed in a bin and the lid screwed down tightly. With this new situation, Joanna felt released. Her weekends and evenings could be freed up. There was no other major case on at the minute. Simply a couple of routine investigations which would tie her and Korpanski and most of their team to their desks for the next few weeks. Achingly boring, collecting statistics and proving, in time for the party conferences, that the current party in power was the one who could be trusted to achieve better law and order.

Wednesday, 18 September, 7.30 p.m.

It had been Eloise's idea to meet up at a pub not far from Keele, the university where she was studying medicine. 'The Mainwaring Arms, eight o'clock,' she had stipulated in her icicle-sharp little voice. From across the width of their sitting room Joanna had heard the words even though Eloise had been speaking to her father. Matthew had half turned towards her, his eyebrows voicing the question and she had nodded and smiled. Time for détente. She was weary with the hostilities that existed between herself and her step-daughter. If there was to be an absence of affection between them – and she suspected this was the status quo – then a truce, or at least a civilized tolerance, had to be the order of the day. She simply didn't have the energy for any more belligerence between them.

And so she had dressed up tonight as an indication of her new attitude. A couple of weeks ago she had treated herself to a very expensive new dress and some smart black court shoes and tonight, instead of dressing down in her usual skinny jeans and top with boots, she had decided, for once, to dress like a lady, which Matthew loved. Like many men he loved to see his wife in a skirt, legs on display. And more than once he had commented that with all the cycling she did which had toned her legs, it was an awful shame to see them encased in denim. So she was dressed not only to indulge her love of clothes but also to please her husband, and hopefully not displease her stepdaughter. As she slipped it over her head she had to admit that her new dress was unusual, with a panel of silky material in a rainbow effect down the front with plain black sides and the clever stitched effect of a black bolero over it. The shoes were skyscrapers, rather appropriately designed by Paris Hilton, black patent with a silk bow on the front. She wriggled her toes. And she could walk in them – well, just about. Unlike the TV detectives she wasn't sure she'd manage to run in them, though. One false step, she thought, as she almost tripped down the stairs, and you'd twist your ankle.

On the drive over she was quiet, pondering on the signifi-cance of this mid-week assignation. This was unusual for Eloise. Usually she came to Waterfall Cottage, liking the village and the walks nearby through the moorlands. She tended to come over at the weekends or more truthfully *for* weekends rather than in the week. For her to suggest they come over to this end of town on a Wednesday evening was different.

Joanna was also thinking about the two French girls playing hooky and not letting their mothers know where they were or where they were heading. She smiled. She sure as hell wouldn't like to be them when they faced their mothers again, although Dorothée's mother appeared a bit more easy-going than Cécile Bellange, who struck her as a rather intense woman. Come to that, Joanna wouldn't mind giving them a bloody ticking off too for wasting police time, although she had to admit she hadn't spent a lot of time investigating the girls' disappearance, and the climb at the Roaches had been an exhilarating bonus. She hadn't done too badly. Maybe she and Matthew would even get into letterboxing themselves.

Her smile broadened as she recalled where the embryonic case had taken them. Following a pair of fit legs up a rock face hadn't seemed like hard work – nor the ice creams she had shared with Korpanski on the lake side. Then there had been the creepy proprietor of the bed and breakfast and the brothers who had unsuccessfully made chase. She gave a little chuckle. She couldn't go around arresting people simply on account of their being creepy.

Matthew looked across, his eyes warm. 'What are you giggling about?'

She told him a summarized version, and he, too, found it amusing and said maybe they'd better stay at home instead of risking a weekend at a creepy bed and breakfast.

'What made him so creepy?'

That was always difficult to put into words. She tried anyway. 'I don't know. He was a bit Uriah Heap with funny eyes, sweating and looking guilty when he shouldn't have had anything to worry about. But it appears the girls simply left Mandalay and headed for London. Typical teenage girls,' she said.

'Thank goodness Eloise was always fixated on getting to medical school,' was his response.

They had reached Hanchurch roundabout, turning left then right at the traffic lights, over junction fifteen of the M6 and out on to the A53 towards Whitmore.

The Mainwaring Arms was a small pub popular with the locals and the hoi polloi of Newcastle-under-Lyme. It had recently opened a smart wine bar at its rear, which was where they were booked in.

Eloise was already sitting down when they arrived, a little late, as there had been a holdup on the 'D' road. Pale and thin, with very blonde hair and her mother's sharp, angular features, Matthew's daughter was a final year medical student; it wouldn't be long before she qualified. Another Dr Levin.

Tonight, unlike Joanna, she had not dressed up – her hair was hanging loose, a little rat-tailed. She looked tired and was toying with a glass of water. Water? Or gin? She looked distracted as they approached and her father picked up on this. He touched Joanna's arm as they reached the table, his face taut with concern. Joanna's guess was that Eloise Levin had been studying too hard for her finals, burning the candle at both ends, but working rather than partying. She would give the girl that. Like her father, Eloise was conscientious and took her studies very seriously. When she stood up to give her father a kiss, Joanna noted that she had lost weight, and this was emphasized by the patched jeans she was wearing and a baggy grey sweater that did nothing for her pale complexion. Eloise embraced her father and aimed a cursory nod in Joanna's direction – her customary greeting. If that.

'Hi, Dad.' She gave him a kiss.

Joanna dropped into one of the chairs opposite and watched Matthew kiss his daughter back, both cheeks, before holding her at arms' length then sitting down and teasing her about the patches on her jeans, which he knew were a fashion statement.

He tweaked her shoulder. 'Aren't we giving you enough of an allowance?'

Eloise gave a weak smile and didn't bother to respond to the tease, just opened the menu with the statement: 'I'm starving.'

'Obviously not, then,' Matthew said, still smiling and not abandoning his tease, even though it was patently boring his daughter, 'if you can't afford to eat *or* clothe yourself.'

Her response was . . . Joanna kept her eyes on the girl: nothing.

Eloise simply kept her eyes on the menu, averting her father's gaze. To Joanna it appeared rude. But then nothing his daughter said or didn't say could or ever had tipped

Matthew into ill humour. Though tinged with guilt for having left her mother, Matthew simply adored his daughter. As was Matthew's way, when he gave his love it was absolute – without dilution or compromise. His love for Joanna indicated that, so how could she complain when his daughter received the same degree of affection?

And the son he so badly wanted? Joanna watched him through lowered eyelashes. Yes. That son – or even second daughter – would receive no less.

Matthew continued to smile as he too picked up the menu and studied it.

They ordered their meal and a bottle of wine. Matthew kept glancing across at them both, from one to the other, from wife to daughter and back again. Joanna knew he wanted to comment on Eloise's appearance, ask if everything was all right, but there is nothing more annoying when you consider yourself an adult than a parent asking if you are *all right*. Matthew knew this and was wise enough to resist the temptation.

But halfway through the meal, having watched Eloise push her food round and round the plate, he couldn't help himself. 'I thought you were hungry,' he said sharply.

Joanna had hoped he hadn't realized what Eloise was up to, the fork hardly touching her mouth, the food uneaten, simply played with.

His daughter looked up, bones prominent in her face. 'Don't fuss, Dad.'

Matthew bit his lip, didn't look at Joanna but frowned into his plate, took a determined gulp of wine and was quietly thoughtful. Minutes later he looked up, bright again and hopeful. 'How would you feel, Eloise,' he asked enthusiastically, 'if you had a new brother?' He paused before adding, 'Or sister?'

After a brief startled, panicky look at Joanna, who gently shook her head, Eloise fumbled for words. 'We-ell,' she began. But Joanna had already read it. Anger, hostility. Rage, even. And the heat of that surprised and shocked her. She felt a brief pang, the tiniest sliver of pity, for this child, as yet not even conceived. Poor little thing, she thought. A mother who was distinctly unenthusiastic for the honour, a father who made a demand on its sex and a stepsister who positively hated the idea of its existence. What would Matthew do if he had another daughter instead of the longed-for son? And what if the son did not live up to his father's masculine expectations?

Joanna toyed with her own food. It was all very well for DS Mike Korpanski to tell her that she would love the child – if not from conception – the moment she held it in her arms. It was fine for him to reassure her that *all* mothers *always* did. It was natural. What if it wasn't for her? Was she then unnatural? Korpanski had assured her that she would nurture and care for it without a second thought. But what if . . .?

The evening remained subdued. Eloise hardly ate a thing. Matthew was fidgety, doing his best to avoid mentioning his concern for his daughter and Joanna, as always, felt outside the family circle, an uninvited and unwelcome intruder, someone who peeped in through the window but was left outside, feeling as cold as she had when she had stood on the top of the Roaches a week ago.

THIRTEEN

Matthew was quiet all the way home, which was not a good sign. Joanna kept glancing across at him. His face was set, his hands gripping the steering wheel unnecessarily hard. Her husband was generally a chatty, communicative man, particularly after spending time with Eloise. He would comment proudly on her progress at medical school, repeat remarks she'd made and chuckle at some of the funnier things she'd said. Generally he had plenty to say – except when he had something on his mind, like now. He appeared deep in thought and after a few attempts at conversation Joanna gave up. She didn't dare broach the subject of Eloise. Anything she said about the girl was often open to misinterpretation. So she too remained quiet.

It wasn't until they reached home and were having a good-night drink on the sofa that Matthew finally spoke. 'She's not eating properly, is she?' Before Joanna could find a suitable response he carried on: 'I don't know what to do, Jo.'

She put her arms around him. 'Matt,' she said, 'you and Eloise have always been close. You can talk.' Her suggestion almost stuck in her throat but she said it anyway. 'Perhaps,' she said tentatively, 'you might think about meeting up with her – on your own one night – and ask her then what the matter is because . . .' she ploughed on regardless, '. . . something must be wrong.'

She looked into his troubled face and felt a wash of pity. Matthew's guilt always made him feel he had let his beloved daughter down, somehow. She carried on: 'Eloise was never fat, you know. She's always been pretty slim but now – well – I agree. She is looking too thin,' she finished lamely.

Luckily for her, Matthew took her comment the right way. He gave her a hug. 'Thanks,' he said. His positive response encouraged her to say more.

'Maybe it's boyfriend trouble or the pressure of the exams coming up. You know how it is.'

He nuzzled her neck. 'Hmm,' he said, then moved away so he could stare into her face. 'Boyfriend trouble?'

She laughed and after a moment he joined her.

'Children,' he said. 'Nothing but trouble.'

She raised her eyebrows.

'Now, time for bed,' he said, smiling and setting his glass down.

Thursday, 3 October, 10 a.m.

Charlotte had arrived in Staffordshire that morning and the fine weather and sense of absolute freedom made her want to whoop for joy. Unfettered in her silver Skoda Yeti Adventure, she felt as free as the proverbial bird. She didn't even think about Shona and Stan tying the knot in *Italia*. She turned the radio up full. Andrew Gold's 'Never Let It Slip Away'. Oops! She just had. But to salve her conscience she had sent them a lovely card and lodged £200 in the appropriate John Lewis account. Now she could wash her hands of the past and focus on the future. Perhaps tacky pop songs said it all. Love is all around – indeed. They should be so lucky!

Joanna had plenty of other cases to occupy her mind and it was easy to forget about the two girls. The weather had remained dry. The level of the lake had dropped. From being a sparkling body of water reflecting summer sunshine it had changed to a sullen shallow basin with a sticky muddy edge. At weekends the train continued to thrill the children whatever the weather as September had melted into October. The screams of delight and the *toot toot* of the cheerful little engines were heard by Barker as he stood on the edge of the lawn that sloped gently in the direction of the lake, almost tipping him into it. He stood staring at the water's surface, which seemed to him teeming with life. It was full of day trippers, canoeists and inexpert sailors, quite apart from the people at the water's edge frolicking and shouting, dogs barking, the ice-cream vendor's tinkle tune playing, children screaming. He felt invaded. He shuddered, recalling another poem that had always haunted him: 'The Last Chantey' and the words, *Shall we gather up the sea?*

What if the lake dried up completely? As he stared at the waters and saw the clouds reflected, it was as though he could peer right down, down, down. To the bottom.

Barker scooped in a panicky deep breath. He still didn't know what to do with the rucksacks. It was a problem that still sat on his shoulders, a bird of gloom weighing him down. He had the wild idea of hurling himself down the lawn, straight into the mud and the water to lie on the bottom himself. He was frightened. Thank goodness the police had left him alone. He wasn't sure his nerves would have stood another visit. The big guy had been intimidating but, in spite of her attractive face, the woman had been even more so. The way she had fixed him with her cold blue stare had seemed to pierce his brain like a bolt of electricity and shatter it into a thousand brittle shards. He had been convinced she could read his mind. He stood, still on the lawn, motionless for minutes, his mind swimming through the waters, and then he heard a noise from inside the house and turned. Now he had a new guest. Charlotte, she had said her name was, and she was travelling alone. He had put her in the twin-bed room where he and Supi-yaw-lat could watch over her. Barker turned away from the lake back towards Mandalay. He must not neglect his new guest.

Upstairs, he pressed his eye to the hole in the wall. Charlotte had returned to her room and was now simply lying on the bed, her shoes thrown off. They lay as they had been thrown, drunkenly between the two beds. Her feet were bare, the small toe nails painted. She was still wearing her jeans and sweater. The window was open and she was reading from a Kindle. She looked peaceful and relaxed, as though she didn't have a care in the world. Barker watched and envied her.

She wasn't exactly a beautiful woman but she looked strong and yet feminine. Hard breasts, flat stomach, long legs. But it was her little jewelled toe nails that held his attention. Barker had felt a fascination with women's feet ever since he had read an account of foot binding in China. The idea of the tiny bones smashed – all for the weird desires of men – was quite disgusting. These feet were healthy and beautiful. There was a tiny tattoo of a rose on her ankle bone, and her toe nails were red as though blobs of blood had been dropped on them. Charlotte had the most beautiful feet he had ever seen in his life. Barker smiled. This would console him for his recent difficulty.

He wondered about Supi-yaw-lat's feet and decided that they would be small, undamaged and decorative.

Thursday, 3 October, 2 p.m.

It had taken them ages to find a place to hang their picture. Waterfall Cottage was not big and the slanting ceilings upstairs robbed them of hanging wall space, but the wall facing the front door had been available. When they had finally decided to hang it there Matthew had banged in a picture hook and then stood back to admire his handiwork. He turned around and grinned at her. 'It's a lovely day,' he said, 'I'm surprised you're not out on your bike.'

'I just fancied being at home for a change,' she said. 'And I'm owed so much overtime that the force don't want to pay me for I thought I may as well have an afternoon at home.'

Matthew raised his eyebrows but didn't say anything.

Friday, 4 October, 11 a.m.

Charlotte was tackling her first climb. It wasn't an arduous one – no need for ropes and crampons. Simply good handholds and footholds. And confidence.

Joanna and Mike were working in their office, not only cramped but with the depressing view towards a brick wall that made Joanna feel closed in. 'Mike,' she said tentatively.

He swivelled his chair around to face her.

'What if I don't like the child?'

He grinned at her, reminding her of a big grizzly bear. Big square shoulders, dark eyes, black hair and a wide grin. He was the sort of man who would crush you in a bear hug. ''Course you'll like it, Jo,' he said. 'It's like a feeling of warm honey – the minute you look at your own flesh and blood blended with Matthew's. It's magical. And,' he added, 'the love, it just happens. I keep telling you but believe me, Jo, it just does.'

But she didn't feel reassured by his confidence. She continued to frown into her computer screen, tense and anxious. Then the call came.

'Madame Piercy?' She recognized the voice at once.

'Madame Bellange,' she responded politely. 'I thought you had returned to Paris.'

'I have, madame detective. I am calling from Paris now.'

'Then what can I do for you?'

'We have heard nothing more,' she said, 'from either Annabelle or Dorothée.'

Joanna's heart sank. She gave Korpanski a quick, despairing look.

'But, madame, the girls were in London. You should speak to the Metropolitan Police now. There's nothing I can do from up here.'

'*Oui,*' she said. '*Je comprends cela, mais . . .*'

'I suggest you contact Scotland Yard . . .' Joanna repeated. She didn't envy the Met their job. She could just imagine how many missing teenagers were reported to Scotland Yard – it must be hundreds a week. And where would they start in such a huge, cosmopolitan city where it would be so easy to disappear if one wanted to? And yet. And *yet.*

She felt the familiar twitch in her toes. There was something here that she wasn't happy about. Something wasn't right and she knew what it was. A text? Anybody in possession of Dorothée's mobile phone could have pressed the keys and sent that text. And how anxious had they all been to believe it? Even Jo, in spite of her reservations. She had not tried to keep the investigation going. She and Mike and the mothers too. They had all believed what they had wanted to believe, Joanna because it would save her a major case, the mothers because they wanted their daughters to be alive and well.

More than ever, she wished Colclough was still around. It

was the sort of situation she would have talked over with him and together they would have decided what to do. As it was, having a superior who would question her every move, calculate how much a wrong move would cost the public, wait for her to make a mistake and then pounce, she felt as though she was dancing on thin ice. She would either fall over or crack the ice and fall under. Neither was an attractive idea.

'We've been thinking.' Madame Bellange's voice filled the silence and echoed Joanna's thoughts. 'Perhaps it was *not* Dorothée who sent the text message. We have heard nothing since and they do not answer. Why not?'

Joanna didn't have a response.

When Madame Bellange spoke again she sounded upset. 'Please, help us.'

Joanna shot an appealing look in Korpanski's direction. 'OK,' she said. 'I'll make a few more enquiries from around here. I'll be in touch.'

Mentally she allowed herself one week and a couple of desk side investigations. She took the distressed woman's contact details and hung up. Mike was watching her.

'Let's start with that text message,' she said. 'Run a check through. See where it came from.'

At the back of her mind was the little niggle. She could have done this before. But the fact that argued with was that the two mothers had accepted the text without question. So why shouldn't she have? Answer – because she was a cop.

Minutes later Korpanski straightened lowly. 'Well, well, well,' he said. 'Would you take a look at that?' And then the door opened.

FOURTEEN

What a sense of timing.

It would have to be Rush, wouldn't it? He would have to get involved at this particular point. Perhaps one of these days he might think of knocking before he barged into their office? Joanna winced at his heavy footfall. He stood looking over her shoulder.

'Piercy.'

'Sir?'

He peered past her at Korpanski's screen. 'You're still working on . . .?' His eyebrows arched to ask the question.

'The two French girls.'

Rush's mouth grew even more thin – if that was possible. Any thinner and he'd have no bloody mouth at all. 'But I understood that they'd decamped to London.'

She shook her head. 'It doesn't look like it, sir.' She knew, without him rubbing it in, that this was sloppy police work. She should have checked on the origin of the text. It was easy, and would only have taken minutes.

Rush's thick eyebrows moved together. 'But I thought,' he said, with ice in his voice, 'that you reported that you had had a phone call from one of the girl's mothers.' He scratched around in his memory, 'A Madame Cécile Bellange, who said that Dorothée had texted her mother to say they were heading for London.'

'Except the text didn't come from London, sir.' She resisted the temptation to hang her head like a naughty schoolgirl.

The eyebrows moved again. Korpanski had swung around in his chair, his bland expression and troubled eyes giving her tacit support. Which didn't blot out her sinking feeling.

'Explain yourself, Piercy.'

'Madame Bellange telephoned here about an hour ago, sir. She expressed doubt that the text had come from Dorothée.

They've had no contact since and have been unable to speak to either girl.'

She gave a deep sigh and continued.

'Although initially they were convinced that the text was from Dorothée, as time went on and they heard nothing more and Madame Caron failed to make further contact with her daughter, she and Madame Bellange began to wonder. And then they rang us. Again.'

Rush gave a tut of disapproval, rolling his eyes as if to say, *Women!* while Joanna risked a swift glare at Korpanski. Tacit support was all very fine but she would have liked a word or two of vocal support from her sergeant, preferably loud vocal support. She turned her attention back to the chief superintendent. He was standing still, hardly blinking, neither encouraging nor discouraging her from continuing. She took a risk and ploughed on.

'So we checked up on the phone details. According to GPS there was no signal from the phone in question from two p.m. on the twenty-first of July except for a very brief time on the eleventh of September, the time the text came through.' She paused. 'The signal came from Rudyard, which makes me wonder whether the girls ever left the area.'

She wished Rush would display at least some response but his face was impassive apart from a slight narrowing of his nostrils, which seemed to echo even more disapproval.

She put the least likely theory forward first. 'So the text purporting to be from Dorothée saying they were going to London was either a deliberate red herring from the girls themselves who had decided to play truant and mislead their mothers, or from someone else pretending to be them.' She wouldn't insult him by pointing out the implication behind this scenario.

Rush's eyes narrowed further but he still said nothing so she carried on, digging herself in right up to her neck. She gave the silent Korpanski a swift, meaningful look. She wouldn't have minded him speaking out – at least say *something*. Take joint responsibility but no, he was letting her ride this storm alone. She directed a scowl at him but his face remained impassive, his features schooled into blandness. Patently he was going to leave her to muddle her way through the maze of possible theories.

'Needless to say, Mandalay, the bed and breakfast the girls had been staying in, would be included in the area,' she added.

Rush's pale eyes widened now. 'And the other girl's phone?'

'There has been no signal from Annabelle's phone since Saturday, twentieth of July, sir.'

Rush's voice was silky smooth as he spoke the next sentence. 'Then I suggest the pair of you get back down to the bed and breakfast in Rudyard and start finding out what really *has* happened to the two girls.' His voice was heavy with sarcasm. His parting expression left a chill in the room even after he'd stalked out.

Joanna was tempted to stick her tongue out at his receding narrow back until she caught Korpanski's eye. His face was contorted with the effort of not laughing and after a minute she gave a chuckle. 'Shit,' she said. 'They couldn't have appointed anybody worse than him, could they? Sense of humour? Nil. He's . . .' She couldn't find the words and what made it worse was the fact that he had come into this job already disliking her. She knew that. What she didn't know was why. Where had that prejudice come from?

Then the reality of the situation hit her. She dropped her face into her hands. 'You realize this puts us right in the shithouse, Mike? We should have checked that one simple point.'

Korpanski crossed the room in two steps and rested his large hand on Joanna's shoulder. 'Not necessarily, Jo,' he said. 'We had good reason for believing the girls had left this area safe. The girls' mothers were initially convinced the text was from Dorothée. Even now we don't *know* that that isn't the case. And think of the hoo hah if we'd spent public money searching for two French girls who were living it up in London. But if this development *does* mean that something has happened to them on our patch and we *do* end up in the shit then it's up to us to dig ourselves out, isn't it? At least we have a good idea where to start.' He took two strides across the room. '*And* we already have a chief suspect.'

'In a *possible* disappearance, Mike,' Joanna said slowly. She was dubious. Cases which initially appeared simple and obvious usually proved to be anything but. Barker had appeared creepy – yes – but she couldn't quite see him as a murderer of two healthy girls. How would he have done it? Why? He didn't have a criminal record. There had been no complaints against him. He appeared to be a hardworking, capable man running a successful guest house.

She continued with her reasoning. They had nothing on him except the fact that girls had stayed there. And Mike was right. They still couldn't say for sure that the text wasn't from Dorothée, or that the girls had gone missing from Rudyard. But the one incontrovertible fact was that someone – be it the girls or not – had texted from this area in September before switching the phone off again. Someone had been on the end of that phone. Maybe Dorothée. Possibly Annabelle, or somebody else.

She sat drumming her fingers on her desk, knowing it would annoy Korpanski. Any minute now he was going to clear his throat and ask her to stop. Sharing an office can be more claustrophobic than sharing a marriage.

She looked across at him. He was watching her, his face very alert, his meaty thighs tensed, ready to spring. He was leaning forward. Ready for action. She smiled at him then, on instinct, she accessed her file on the Stuart brothers and found the mobile number of Martin Stuart. He picked up on the third ring.

'Yes?' He was shouting – probably speaking from outside or from a noisy workshop.

She shouted back. 'It's Detective Inspector Piercy here. Leek police.'

'Yes?' he repeated, sounding impatient.

'I could do with having a quick word with you.'

'What about?' Still shouting.

So was she. 'The French girls.'

'I wish we'd never got involved.' And now his voice had dropped and the background noise had filtered away. He must have found somewhere quiet. 'Have you found them yet?'

'No.'

'But I thought you said they'd rung their mums from London.'

'That appears not to have been reliable information. And it

was a text, not a conversation.' She was anxious not to give too much away.

'Oh?'

'Tell me,' she prompted slowly. 'Mandalay.'

'Yes?'

'Was there anything strange about Mr Barker?'

'How d'you mean?'

'Anything unusual?'

There was a long pause. Martin Stuart was patently thinking about it. 'Yeah,' he said finally. 'There was.'

Joanna waited.

'He was a peeping Tom.'

'Oh?'

'He used to spy on people. You remember the garish picture on the wall of the twin-bed room?'

'Yes.' Joanna smothered a smirk. Who could forget it? It was a picture with impact. 'Go on.'

'He'd cut one of the eyes out. I think he watched people through there.' Martin gave a snort of laughter. 'Not boys. I think he probably preferred girls. But then you never can tell.'

'I see.'

Martin badly wanted to mention the rucksacks he'd stumbled on in Barker's kitchen but the police would ask why they hadn't mentioned it earlier when it was patently obvious that they might have something to do with the two girls, and he desperately wanted to divert attention away from himself and his brother. He waited for the inspector's next words, knowing he and James had already tied themselves up in knots.

Martin shivered. Maybe they should have stuck to the truth from the start. It was too late now to backtrack, trying to find it. It would make them look suspicious and he knew that when the police had suspicions they often found the evidence to support them. He wasn't sure either he or James could remember exactly what story they had told. And he had a feeling that Inspector Piercy and her sidekick were pretty tenacious.

Put it this way, Martin, he thought. You're fucked either way.

Joanna thanked him and put the phone down. She'd just found Barker's possible motive.

Korpanski was on his feet now. He smirked when she gave him the content of the conversation. Joanna gave a private prayer up to whoever had sent her Detective Sergeant Michael Korpanski, half Polish, half Staffordshire. As loyal as a dog, as energetic as a puppy. She too stood up, slipped a jacket on and the pair of them headed off back to Rudyard.

The lake was peaceful and quiet today, weekends being its busy period this time of year.

'Let's stop for a coffee,' Joanna said. 'We're not in a rush.'

They walked to the small lakeside café, where the ice-cream boy served them. He grinned. 'Them French girls turned up yet?'

'Not in Europe they haven't.'

'Not gone home then? I heard they was in London.'

'You heard that?'

'Yeah. Someone told me.' The jungle drums of the Staffordshire Moorlands. The information made Joanna curious. 'Do you remember them, er . . .?' She didn't know his name.

'Will,' he supplied. 'Will Murdoch – at your service.' He had a pleasant manner. 'Not sure if I remember them. I don't think I remember serving two French girls. Maybe I did.' He changed the subject. 'Not much call for ice cream today,' he said, 'so I'm in here instead. It's a bit too chilly. Running our stocks down, we are. What about a nice hot chocolate instead?'

'Good idea.'

They sat down and waited. Mike leaned across. 'So what's the plan?'

'We'll go to Mandalay,' she said, determined and directed now, 'and take a look around. Check out that painting. If Martin's right we have enough to hold Barker. And I can't deny it gives him a motive. The girls might have discovered the peephole and threatened to report him to us. He might have panicked and . . .'

Korpanski was making a face.

'Have you got a better suggestion?'

'No – but it seems a weak motive for murder.'

'Think about it, Mike,' she said. 'Just think about it. That text,' she said, 'was designed to send Madame Bellange scurrying back to France, convinced the girls were safe, take the heat off the search and, if their parents were still convinced the girls were missing, divert attention to London. It isn't a weak motive at all but a very strong one.'

'How do you work that one out?'

'Mandalay is his life,' Joanna said. 'The fact that he was spying on his guests would have made for some tacky reading in the *Leek Post & Times*. He would have been branded a pervert. His business would go down the pan. No one would stay there. The scandal would close him down. So let's consider the options,' she said carefully. 'Option one, he nicked the phone *and* sent the text; option two, somebody else did; option three, it *was* the girls trying to send their mothers a message that they'd decamped to London when they were still here, though why they'd do that beats me.'

Korpanski nodded and she continued in her thoughts aloud.

'Option one is the most sinister, isn't it? Particularly now we know that Mr Barker has a motive.' She sat still, puzzling. 'But I'm still not sure I can see Barker killing them. He seems so ineffectual.'

'But we know, Jo, that quite a few murderers *are* ineffectual,' Korpanski offered gruffly.

'You mean they often aren't the big, strong, beefy boys . . .' Joanna couldn't resist a smirk in his direction. Korpanski had the build of a man who spent hours in the gym pumping iron, '. . . but inadequate wimps,' she finished.

He was right. She recalled some of the killers she and he had uncovered.

'Well, we'll bring him in for questioning at the very least.'

Korpanski nodded and slipped the car into gear.

As they took the road upwards towards Mandalay they couldn't miss the fact that the water level was still low and dropping. In fact, the level was the lowest Joanna ever remembered seeing. But then she'd been brought up in Stone, twenty miles to the south. She had arrived in Leek well after the drought of 'seventy-six. She turned to Mike. He was a local lad. 'Do you remember the water level being as low as that before?'

'In 'seventy-six,' he answered, almost without thinking. 'If it hadn't been for the mud, which I can tell you is quite treacherous, you could probably have walked right across it then.'

A few minutes later, 'Carver Doone,' Joanna said.

'Sorry?'

'*Lorna Doone*?' She looked at him. 'The villain of the piece, Carver Doone, sinks into the mud.'

'Nasty end,' Mike said, prosaic as ever. 'Well, as the water level fell and there was more of the mud quite a few dead cats and dogs turned up.'

'No humans?'

'No. No humans. Just old shoes, bits of fishing tackle, a few lead weights and animal skeletons. Even a cow's skull.'

'Nice thought.' And now they'd arrived.

FIFTEEN

They got the impression that Barker wasn't even surprised to see them. As they crunched across the gravel drive the front door opened and he stood there, peering round it, motionless, as though Nemesis herself was getting out of the car rather than DI Piercy and her sergeant. He showed no curiosity even when Joanna asked politely if they could come in, and that they had some questions they needed to ask him. Instead he looked defeated. Deflated as he backed into the house. Defeated and rather guilty.

Afterwards Joanna would puzzle and ponder that point. On the face of it, it looked bad. Barker had motive and, presumably, opportunity. Guilty of what? Two girls were apparently missing and they were linked to here. If they had been killed here there should be some evidence. And bodies.

They followed him into the sitting room, the bay window affording a wide view of the lake as a stunning backdrop. He was opposite the Boathouse which stretched right out into the lake. Barker perched on the edge of his armchair, his face practically twitching in anticipation.

'Mr Barker,' Joanna began. 'You *do* remember the two French girls who stayed here back in July?'

Barker nodded. He'd made a mistake. A silly mistake. And now he was going to pay for it. He waited for the axe to fall. He was pouring out clammy sweat. Looking at the faces of the two detectives, the blunt, strong features of the man and the determined face of the inspector he knew now that whatever he said they were not going to believe him. His mouth was dry. He needed to *think*. To work this out. But he couldn't. Panic was mushing his brain.

'The girls left,' he insisted stubbornly, desperation making his voice squeaky. 'They left here. I don't know where they went.' His story was perfectly credible, his gaze shy, his eyes moving around the room, flitting like a butterfly searching for

somewhere to land. He didn't find it. There was nowhere safe
for him.

His smile was begging them to believe him. He looked from
one to the other, wondering which one would be most likely to.

Joanna was finding that she wanted to believe him. But was
this clever manipulation on his part? Korpanski was standing,
as he always did, in the doorway, arms akimbo, legs apart,
blocking any idea of flight that Barker might have had.

'They left,' he said again in his voice soft as slippers. 'I
don't know why you've come back here when we heard they'd
gone to London.'

Joanna gave Mike a swift warning look. *Don't tell him.*

Barker continued looking from one to the other, questioning
with that bland, almost innocent smile.

She wanted to see the peephole for herself and dent his
confidence. 'Do you mind if we take a quick look around, Mr
Barker – perhaps in the room the girls slept in?'

'I've cleaned it many times since they've left. You won't
find anything there, Inspector.'

Oh yes I will, Mr Barker.

'Is it OK if we go in there?'

'Yes.' Barker so wanted them to believe he was innocent.
And leave him alone. For ever. 'Of course. I'll take you up
there myself.'

'Thank you.' They tramped up the stairs behind him.

Barker stood in the doorway while Joanna glanced casually
round the walls. Now that Martin had told them of the existence
of the peephole they couldn't think how they'd missed it before.
It was so obvious. How come no one but the brothers had picked
up on it? Perhaps it was the arrangement of the lights, situated
at the far end of the room, facing away from the picture, two
bedside lamps quite dim with dark red shades which must have
dimmed them even further, and the spotlights in the ceiling were
angled away from Miss Wong or whatever her name was.

She didn't want to make it too obvious so she signalled to
Mike to keep Barker occupied in the doorway while she examined it closer. She couldn't quite put her eye to it without
Barker seeing but she went up close and was tempted to put
her finger into the small hole.

Barker was watching her carefully.

'It's quite a painting,' she said – for something to say.

'It's a print,' he responded in his flat-fish voice.

She drew back. 'And the room next to this?'

'Just a sort of box room,' Barker said, twisting his hands together now. 'I keep old stuff there. Suitcases and things.'

How could he have been so foolish?

For some stupid reason he'd thought that putting the rucksacks in there would be a good idea. Amongst other luggage. Like hiding a branch in a forest or a needle in a workbox.

And now he could kick himself.

Joanna's antennae were up. She sensed a kill. 'Old stuff?' she asked innocently. 'Any chance we could take a look?'

'If I can find the key.' He stomped off.

Perhaps it was her imagination but looking around the bedroom Joanna thought she could pick up the scent of expensive French perfume. Chanel? Yves St Laurent? Though she could smell it she couldn't identify it. It was vague, insubstantial. Lingering. And impossible that the scent was anything but her imagination.

Too many people must have stayed here since for the girls' perfume to linger – if it even was their perfume. In fact, Joanna realized now, the room was currently occupied – by another woman, it appeared.

Barker was back with the key and looking very uncomfortable. He was mouth breathing – shallow, panicky adenoidal breaths that smelt of cups of tea.

Joanna watched him as he turned the key of the box room, switched on the light and stood back. At first she was only aware of the scent – the same, pleasant, underlying scent. Then she saw them, leaning against the wall. He should have put them in a better place.

Silly, silly me. And now he was in trouble.

The inspector was looking at him, waiting for an explanation.

'I needed the room.' It was all he could think of to say. 'They left them behind.' Even to him the explanation sounded limp and lame.

Detectives usually have a pair of latex gloves somewhere

on their person. Joanna fumbled in her pocket, pulled a pair out and slipped them on. She handled the rucksack closest to her and knew she hadn't been mistaken about the scent. She recalled someone from the pub.

'She 'ad a blue rucksack. Huge thing, it were.'

'Mr Barker,' she said very carefully, 'this isn't your rucksack, is it? Whose is it?'

He practically fainted with terror. He felt dizzy and unable to breathe. His mouth was too dry to talk. 'One of the girls,' he said hoarsely. 'Like I said, they left them behind.'

She nodded past it. 'And the other one?'

Barker's head nodded another affirmative.

Joanna's heart sank as she glanced at Korpanski. Now they had a fully blown case. The girls wouldn't have managed a day without their rucksacks, let alone weeks. She looked at Barker, who had all the appearance of a guilty man. This was damning evidence. And Rush would be breathing right down her neck all the way through it. Make a slip, one wrong move and . . . She could almost drag her finger along her neck. *Shit*, she thought, catching Mike's eye.

'Mr Barker,' she said, quite gently, 'I think you should come down to the station and talk to us, don't you?'

Barker nodded then looked up. 'But I've got a guest,' he protested.

She glanced again at Korpanski. His face, she was sure, reflected hers. Grim as a gulag.

'They'll have to stay somewhere else,' she said. 'I suggest you leave a key out and stick a note to the door.'

Barker didn't seem to realize this place would soon be crawling with police. No one would *want* to stay here. But he didn't seem to have picked up on this. He grumbled a string of complaints as he made preparations to leave Mandalay.

'How long will I be?'

This time it was the sergeant who answered. 'As long as it takes, Mr Barker.'

He was obsessional in his locking up. He left a key in an envelope and stuck it on the door with a name, Charlotte Bingley, carefully written in block capitals on the front. She must be the current occupant of the twin-bed room. Joanna wondered whether Barker spied on her too.

At the gate he asked them to stop the car and turned the *Vacancies* sign to *No Vacancies*. It seemed at once sad, poignant and a final gesture of defeat. But then he climbed back into the car and seemed settled by the action. He stared straight ahead of him, not even turning to look at his beloved lake as they passed. His mother's voice was advising him.

'Tell the truth, Horace. You must always tell the truth. And then you won't burn.'

Once in the station, Joanna cautioned him and asked him if he wanted a solicitor.

'Not for the moment,' he said comfortably. 'I'll be all right without one – for the present.'

Unfazed by the caution, the recording and the presence of the two detectives, he settled back in his chair, folded his arms and looked up. 'Now then,' he said. 'What is it you want to know?'

Well – where to begin?

'Mr Barker,' she said, 'back in July two French girls by the names of Dorothée Caron and Annabelle Bellange stayed at Mandalay, your guest house.'

'That's right,' he said, fidgeting in his chair.

'They haven't been seen since.'

'I thought you knew where they were. In London, wasn't it?'

'We're not convinced that the text message actually did come from Dorothée Caron.'

'Oh?'

'And as you know, we've found two rucksacks which we believe belong to them at your guest house.' She leaned in. *Could he not see it? Was he dense? Did he lack any insight?* 'Are you sure you don't want a solicitor to advise you?'

'It isn't necessary,' Barker replied.

'When did you last see the girls?'

'When they left,' Barker said.

'Which was?'

'On the Sunday morning. Very early. July the twenty-first, I think.'

'And you can confirm that those are their rucksacks?'

Barker nodded, his eyes now looking worried and tense as though he was catching up with the detectives' deductions.

'How come the rucksacks are still at Mandalay?'

'They just left them there.' He was looking at them as though he thought *they* were the crazy one. 'They didn't take them with them.'

'But they couldn't manage without them.'

'*I* know that, but all the same they went and their rucksacks didn't.'

'And you didn't find it strange or think to let us know?'

'I found it very strange but that is what happened.'

Joanna gave Mike an incredulous look. Was this guy for real? Apparently not.

'When I went up to clean the room a little later that day – towards evening, actually – and the rucksacks were standing in the middle of the floor, I assumed they'd be coming back for them some time but I had a family due to arrive Sunday evening and the children were going to go in the twin-bed room. I needed it and people don't like to arrive at a place when the previous occupants' belongings are still in the room. I moved them initially into my kitchen so I could give the room a thorough clean. I just thought they'd be back for them when they'd finished doing whatever it was that they were up to. But they didn't come back. They never did. I kept them in the cellar at first, out of the way, then I took them up to the kitchen. I couldn't work it out. Then those two men came and started asking questions. And then you came around, asking more questions, and the French lady, Annabelle's mother, so I had to hide them out of the way. Otherwise,' he said earnestly, 'you might have been suspicious.'

Joanna almost snorted her derision, but she had to continue with her line of questioning. 'Why didn't you let Madame Bellange know that you had her daughter's rucksack?'

'I thought it would look bad.' His logic was unarguable; his common sense completely absent. Suddenly he lost it. He sniggered. 'And what *would* you have thought,' he asked, mocking her. 'What *would* you have thought?'

I would have thought you were stark staring mad.

Then, quite suddenly, the enormity of his situation must have penetrated. It was as though he drifted in and out of comprehension. He paled, gulped, swallowed and gulped again while his eyes looked frankly terrified then calm then panicky. He pulled on his collar as though it was tightening around his neck. Joanna almost wanted to reassure him that the last hanging in Staffordshire had been a hundred years ago.

'Again I'll ask you,' she said. 'Do you want a lawyer?'

Barker screwed up his face like a small child and this time he nodded. 'Can I ask *you something*?'

'Yes.'

'The girl – the woman, Miss Bingley, who's staying there,' he said. 'What about her? What'll happen to her?'

'Your house has been sealed off,' Joanna said. 'We'll be applying for a search warrant. And advise Miss Bingley to find alternative accommodation.' She couldn't resist a swift dig at this man who had further blotted her copy book in front of the new chief superintendent. 'Under the circumstances I'm sure she'll be happy to oblige. And the other B&Bs in this area are not too busy at this time of year.'

Barker looked at the floor, seemingly more upset by the inconvenience to his beloved Mandalay than his present predicament.

The duty solicitor arrived half an hour later and to Joanna's pleasure it was her old pal, Tom Fairway, now husband of Caro, her London journalist friend and father to Luke Christopher Fairway. She gave Tom a warm smile but he, as ever, was one hundred per cent professional. He gave her a curt, slightly mischievous nod, sat down opposite Barker and introduced himself. Barker's response was to hold out a pudgy hand and thank the solicitor *'for his attendance'*, at which point Tom shrugged and gave Joanna a swift, puzzled glance.

Joanna hadn't seen him for a while. Only twice since her wedding. His hair was thinning and receding. He still wore the same glasses and was as stick thin as ever. But then Caro, a journalist who only recently left London to live in Leek, was probably no great cook.

Tom looked up at her. 'Of what is my client accused of?'

'He's just helping us with our enquiries over the disappearance of two French girls who had been staying at his bed and breakfast in July,' Joanna said. 'They haven't been seen since and we've found their rucksacks at his guest house. Tom,' she added urgently, 'can I have a word?'

'Sure.' He followed her outside.

'Mr Barker had a little peephole into the room where the girls were staying,' she said quietly. 'It's possible they found out about it and . . .'

'And you're wondering whether this was a motive for a double murder?' He pushed his heavy glasses up the bridge of his nose.

Joanna felt stung into defending her theory. 'People have been killed for less,' she said.

'Anything else?'

'On September the eleventh the mother of one of the girls received a text message from her daughter's phone. Dorothée said they were heading for London.'

'And?'

'The call originated from this area. Neither girl has been seen since Sunday morning, July twenty-first.'

'How geographically precise can you be about the location from where the text was sent?'

'We can pin it down to Rudyard,' Joanna said. 'Not to the guest house.'

Tom frowned and glanced through the round window in the door at his client, who was sitting motionless now, his eyes terrified, bulging as though he was a rabbit caught in headlights.

He re-entered the interview room. 'Right,' he said, opening up his briefcase and taking out a few sheets of paper and a biro. 'I need a bit of time alone with Mr Barker.'

Warrant in hand, Mark Fask, civilian ex-scene of crimes officer, had been summoned into Mandalay and, with his team, was making a thorough search of the place, looking for anything that might incriminate Barker or involve him further in the girls' disappearance.

'What more do you need, Fask?' he muttered and knew. Evidence of the crime.

He went from room to room testing for bloodstains and collecting hair samples. But the trouble was that many people had stayed in Mandalay since July and Barker was very thorough in his cleaning. It was possible that even if a crime had been committed here there would be little or no trace evidence. He wasn't over-hopeful.

Then he came to the twin-bed room and the Tretchikoff. He stood in front of it, his face twisting as he tried to remember where he had seen it before. Then he remembered. His grandmother had had this very print hanging over the fireplace in her lounge. Like millions of others, he suspected. It had been a very popular print in the avant-garde sixties. He stood back, hands on expanded hips, and stared. Well, who would have thought it? Here it was again and, according to his brief, Miss Wong had her beady eye on things – just like his Grandma. He put his eye to the hole but saw nothing from this side.

The adjacent room was the small box room where the rucksacks had been found. Windowless, dark, airless, claustrophobic. And the light that shone through the hole in the Chinese girl's eye almost made a camera obscura in the room. Just beneath the hole Fask noted a wooden box, probably put there for Barker to stand on and line his eye up.

It was later in the afternoon when he opened up the khaki rucksack that he found something really significant, held it in his hand and dialled the station on his own phone.

'Inspector,' he said when he was connected, 'we've found a mobile phone.'

SIXTEEN

Fask slipped the mobile phone into an evidence bag and started to charge it up, then scrolled down until he reached: *Mon numéro.*

He made a note of it then again checked with the station to find out the number of Dorothée's phone – the one that had texted her mother. It was the same one. He looked at the message history and there it was. *Maman.* Words and all: just over three weeks ago. It didn't exactly take Einstein's brain to know that things looked very black indeed for Mr Barker.

He rang the station and spoke to Korpanski. Gave him the details. 'I'll bring it back and we can check through other stuff – photos and the rest of the call record. I've found Annabelle's phone too, but the battery is taking longer to charge.'

Mike was quiet. Then he said, 'But there's no sign of the girls?'

'I've found nothing, so far, Mike. No signs of a struggle. No positive bloodstains. Nothing unusual. It's as though they just vanished into thin air.'

It wasn't quite what Korpanski wanted to hear, but still. 'OK,' he said, 'cheers.'

He related the contents of the calls to Joanna, who looked serious and thoughtful. Then she picked up the phone and dialled Fask's number herself. 'The rucksacks,' she asked. 'Were they neatly packed inside?'

Fask wasn't sure where this was leading but he answered, 'Yep. Everything folded up just so.'

'Both rucksacks?'

'Yes.'

'What about money?'

'No. No purse or credit cards.'

Joanna covered the mouthpiece with her hand and addressed Korpanski. 'Credit cards haven't been used, have they, Mike?'

Korpanski shook his head. 'Not since July.'

Joanna spoke to Fask again. 'Passports?'

'Yes. Both. In the side pockets.'

'OK, Mark. Keep looking.'

'Anything in particular?'

'No. Just use your eyes.' She was trying to work out the significance of it all. She glanced through the peephole. Tom Fairway was still asking his client questions, making notes, his face serious. She drew Mike into their office. 'Hear me out, Mike. I just want to run stuff past you before I do my usual trick of tumbling straight into something I don't understand.'

Korpanski grinned without even trying to supress his humour. He knew his colleague's impulsiveness.

'The girls' purses are missing. They have money with them and credit cards but they haven't been used.'

Korpanski blinked and said nothing.

'The mobile phone which texted Renée Caron three weeks ago is in the rucksack.'

Korpanski nodded, his dark eyes watching her slowly construct a case.

'Their passports and belongings are neatly packed.'

Korpanski held up his index finger. 'Barker,' he pointed out in a low whisper, 'is a neat and tidy man.'

Joanna nodded her agreement and ploughed on. 'I think the girls went for a short walk leaving their rucksacks, which, after all, are big, heavy things, bulky and inconvenient, in their rooms at Mandalay. Perhaps they went to say goodbye to the lake. They were big Kipling fans. Rudyard Lake was a place of pilgrimage to them.' As she spoke she wondered whether their poetry books were in the rucksacks or with them – wherever they were.

She peered through the peephole at Barker. He was speaking animatedly and from the palm-showing gesture trying to convince Tom, his solicitor, of his innocence.

But you have a lot to explain, Joanna thought.

She continued. 'I think they're somewhere in the area, Mike.'

He nodded. 'It looks like it.'

'And I think they're dead.' She needed reassurance. 'You agree with me?'

Mike nodded again and Joanna glanced at the door.

'We have a prime suspect. If Barker had nothing to do with the girls' fate why didn't he come forward and tell us he had their rucksacks?'

Korpanski waited but proffered no answer.

'I'm going to have to speak to Rush,' she said finally, 'before we continue interviewing Barker. And we're going to have to have a full-blown search of the area. Rope everyone in.'

Korpanski looked worried now. 'You're sure you want to talk to . . .' He jerked his head in the direction of Chief Superintendent Gabriel Rush's room.

'No – not sure at all, but I've got no choice now with this evidence.'

She had to hand it to Rush. He listened to her reasoning without interruption and very carefully, his face not showing emotion but his pale eyes watchful, his expression absorbed as she brought him up to date.

She had thought he might use the opportunity to score points, to tell her she should have suspected something earlier, but he didn't. He simply listened, sitting back in his chair looking thoughtful, fingers steepled, his face still expressionless. When she had finished he leaned forward, slammed his palms down on the desk, picked up his pen and started to write.

It was a list. But she couldn't read upside-down writing.

Then he looked up, his pale eyes meeting hers. 'I agree with your reasoning, Piercy,' he said, but there was no warmth in his voice, no offer of friendship or comradeship and no acknowledgement. His eyes were Arctic ice. 'You need to search the entire area. Use sniffer dogs. The weather's still warm. They'll track down putrefaction from half a mile away.'

Thanks for the graphic description. A couple of rotting women.

She knew what lay ahead – good, old-fashioned police work: gridding of the area, fingertip searches. And Rush was right – his description cruelly true. In the end it looked like this would be where the story ended and another dramatic court case would begin. Grief for the families, a sort of sad satisfaction for the force and paranoia spreading through the public so Rudyard Lake, instead of being a tribute to a great poet, would for ever be associated with murder – another famous case for Staffordshire to join Smith & Collier, William Palmer the poisoner, the Cannock Chase murders, Lesley Whittle and possibly even the final resting place of the missing child of the Moors Murderers, poor, bespectacled Keith Bennett with his chirpy grin and big teeth.

Then Rush looked at her and the corners of his mouth twitched. There was the faintest glimmer of a smile. *Rush smiling?* She looked again – and wasn't sure.

'Something's bothering you, Piercy.'

She heaved out a big sigh. 'It's this, sir. Barker isn't a complete fool. He managed Mandalay well, efficiently. He's well organized and practical. He's sorted out his own website. He's an intelligent man. If he is our man and killed the two girls . . .'

Rush shrugged but there was a gleam in his eye as he waited for her to finish the sentence.

'. . . where and how has he concealed their bodies?'

Rush interrupted. 'You haven't been looking for them.'

'No, sir,' she said earnestly. 'But it's been summer. A hot summer. There have been trippers packing around Rudyard.' She ploughed on. 'Trippers with dogs. You mentioned putrefaction. And,' she continued, finally telling him what was really bothering her, 'if he's been clever enough to murder two girls and conceal their bodies, why on earth would he keep the rucksacks?'

He thought about this one for a minute or two, then acknowledged her doubts. 'I see what you mean. Well, Piercy,' he scribbled a bit more on the pad, 'you've met this man. I haven't. You must make your own judgement and act on it.'

She was shaking her head. 'It doesn't feel quite right,' she said. 'Barker's not a fool. Even the way he spied on the room, cutting the eye out . . . It was clever and unless the girls did notice it, no one else did until the brothers saw it.'

'Killers often are fools, Piercy, even if they're not, by nature, foolish people.' Another glimmer of a smile. A slight twist of those thin lips. 'You're a long way off having a case, a long way off proving the two girls are dead and a very long way off convicting Mr Barker of murder.'

It was funny, she thought. *Mr* Barker. She'd always thought of him as simply Barker. He'd never told them his first names.

'How long do you reckon he's been spying?'

'I don't know, sir, but if anyone had noticed it they surely would have come to us?'

He gave this some thought too. 'Probably,' he said slowly.

She had her authorisation for a full search of the area. She turned to go but Rush held her back. 'Possibly,' he said very slowly and reluctantly, 'I should explain my less-than-warm welcome to you when I arrived.'

Joanna was instantly wary. 'Sir?'

'I came here aware of your reputation.' A pause. 'I knew that you were high profile and had solved some' – another pause as he picked out his word – 'difficult and unusual cases. I wanted to make it plain from the start that I know Chief Superintendent Colclough indulged you somewhat.' He smiled. A proper smile this time. 'You were both his pet and his token female senior officer.'

Joanna bowed her head, frowning. She didn't know what was coming next.

Rush drew in a harsh breath. 'I'm also aware that despite the close relationship you have with DS Korpanski you put his life in danger staking out a farm resulting in a gunshot wound to your sergeant.'

She bowed her head even lower. It hadn't exactly been the high point of her career.

Rush continued: 'I've read through the report of that incident and I think your behaviour was indefensible. Particularly as it appears DS Korpanski took a bullet that was meant for you.'

She felt a glower of anger. *Rub it in, why don't you?*

'However, on balance you *are* a good detective. More careful than I had expected and I want – I encourage – you to continue in that vein.' Then he skewered her with a stare. 'But you won't get away with anything while *I'm* in charge here. Understand?'

'Yes, sir.'

'You do understand?'

She met his eyes. 'I do, sir.'

'Right, then prove yourself to me, Inspector Piercy.'

She gave him a tight smile and left. Maybe, she thought, as she walked along the corridor, just maybe she might manage working with him. She went back in to interview Barker.

Tom met her eyes, gave a small shake of his head and looked – frankly – pissed off.

Korpanski sat at her side. Still as a sphinx but she could almost feel the electricity bounce off him. They were both tense – the sort of tension that happens when you're lifting a stone and think an adder might slither out.

'Mr Barker,' she began. 'Let's start at the beginning, shall we?'

He looked wary, but there was now an inner confidence. She wasn't frightening him any more. It was as though the worst had already happened. Surely not? But now he wasn't nervous. If anything, he was slightly truculent.

He folded his arms. 'I haven't done anything wrong.'

She decided on an oblique attack before facing him with the contents of the rucksacks and the discovery of the mobile phone. 'When did you buy the Tretchikoff?'

It did the trick. Barker looked startled. Then he did look frightened. And worried. And, more interestingly, guiltier. He had not expected this.

'Back . . .' he began, his mouth so dry she could hear his tongue sticking against his teeth.

'Mr Barker,' she prompted after a few seconds.

'In March,' he said, his eyes searching around the room for a resting place. 'She reminded me of the poem,' he said.

Joanna raised her eyebrows.

'Supi-yaw-lat.'

She stared at him. 'Explain.'

'"Mandalay",' he said. *'"There's a Burma girl a-settin' and I know she thinks of me."* Kipling,' he said, and made an attempt at a joke. 'And I don't mean the cakes.'

That was when Joanna became angry. 'We're talking about two young girls who are currently missing. Their mothers are frantic. The last place . . .' She could feel Tom's warning stare but she ignored him and carried on. 'The last place they were seen was at your bed and breakfast where you use the subterfuge of a picture to spy on your guests. The girls' luggage was there.' She kept back the fact of the text message. She would use it later – to greater effect.

'I had to let the room,' Barker insisted plaintively. 'I told you – I had a family coming. The room was booked and I couldn't let it with two big rucksacks standing in the middle, could I?'

Joanna gave Mike a swift glance. Barker just didn't get it.

He smiled again. '"*I've a neater, sweeter maiden in a cleaner, greener land!*" Now you know why I called the guest house Mandalay.' He actually looked pleased with himself.

Joanna realized she needed to try different tactics. 'Mr Barker,' she said, and felt Tom's shoulders relax, 'do you know anything about Dorothée Caron and Annabelle Bellange's whereabouts?'

'No,' he said. 'I don't.'

'When did you last see them?'

'I saw them on the Saturday night,' he said. 'They were just going out. They paid their bill and *told* me they would be leaving early on Sunday morning because they wanted to get on the road. That was the last I saw of them. I left some breakfast out for Sunday but they didn't eat it. I went out on Sunday morning to do some shopping. I needed to restock ready for my new guests. I went into Morrisons in Leek. It took me most of the morning. I arrived back at lunchtime and there was no sign of them. I assumed they'd gone early as they'd said. As I've told you, I didn't discover the rucksacks until it was almost evening.'

Korpanski interrupted. 'Did they have their keys with them?'

Barker looked annoyed. 'Yes, they did,' he said crossly. 'I had to get some new ones cut.' Now his eyes looked shifty. 'I always keep spares,' he said, his eyes sliding over the floor. 'In case,' he added with a gulping swallow, and seemed to have run out of explanations.

'Go on, Mr Barker,' Joanna said silkily, the polite voice that anyone who knew her would recognize as being her most dangerous.

Barker gave her a half smile and decided to quote Kipling again, affecting a mockney accent. *"'Er petticoat was yaller an' 'er little cap was green.'*

Joanna glanced up at the clock and then at Tom, frowning slightly. He would get the message. The police and criminal evidence clock – PACE – was ticking.

SEVENTEEN

While Joanna was interviewing Barker, trying to squeeze some truth out of him, Mark Fask and his team were searching Mandalay, starting with Barker's own rooms. The guest suites they would leave until later.

All was tidy, clean and in order – kitchen, bedroom, bathroom. Nothing remarkable here. Nothing out of place. It was as organized as a show home.

At the back of the house, on the ground floor, Barker had his own small sitting room. Rather than facing the front view, the terrace and the lawn which sloped down towards the lake, this room, darkly decorated, overlooked the back garden through French windows. It was overgrown, with rhododendrons threatening to invade the neat lawn. The scene was completed by some dark Scots pines which kept a threatening watch. There were two armchairs facing an open fire, a television – small by today's standards – and a lovely inlaid bookcase. Fask took a look at the titles and saw that Barker's interests were in this order: the novels and poems of Kipling: *The Man Who Would Be King* caught his eye, next to *The Jungle Book*, next to the *Collected Poems*. The shelf below consisted of true crime – the Moors Murderers, a biography of Harold Shipman, Donald Nielson and Dennis Nilson, while the third shelf consisted surprisingly – though it fitted with Barker's character and the ambience of Mandalay – of four or five books on art and interior design, what the Americans call home-making, cookery books, quilting and paint effects. Nothing tells us more about a person than the books on their shelves – or lack of them. And in Fask's opinion this pretty much summed up the unusual and eccentric character of Horace Gladstone Barker. She'd chuckled when she'd found this out. His mother certainly had gone for the grand old names.

But again, nothing unexpected, nothing out of place, everything as carefully set out as the stage set of a West End production.

Except. In the corner of the room stood a solid-looking 1920s oak roll top desk. It was unlocked. Fask opened it. Inside, again as expected, all was similarly neat and tidy. There was a laptop – closed – and two bundles of papers in rubber bands. At a quick glance one consisted of copies of receipts for provisions, food, cleaning materials, electricity bills and some building work – all claimable against tax. The other bundle was copies of receipts for monies received from his clients. A quick flick soon found the copy of the girls' receipt for their holiday – five nights at eighty pounds a night. Paid on arrival. Nice. Signed *Annabelle Bellange* in a flourishing script. Fask put it and the other receipts to one side. Maybe it would lead to someone else staying at Mandalay during that time?

Again everything supported the fact that Barker was an organized man. Everything was neatly pigeon-holed. Fask picked up a French dictionary. Maybe Barker had been trying to communicate with his international clients. Out fell one slightly crumpled sheet of paper.

Fask's French wasn't great. He'd failed his GCSE but knew enough to translate. And he knew exactly what it signified.

It was a transcript of the text sent to Renée Caron, Dorothée's mother. It was typed in English, with the French translation underneath. Barker had composed it, then translated it online and printed out the webpage. He slipped it into an evidence bag. The noose around Barker's fat little neck was tightening. But apart from the rucksacks this was the only other sign of Barker's involvement. Fask stared out of the sitting-room window, caught the trees waving inwards and wondered. His forensic search had uncovered the rucksacks and the phones. The police had uncovered the peeping eye of the Chinese girl. So what had he done with the girls?

He slipped the laptop into an evidence bag.

Joanna was speaking to Chief Superintendent Rush. 'We're going to have to apply for an extension, sir. I don't feel I have enough evidence to charge him. The rucksacks are circumstantial evidence – even with the geographical location of the text message. We have no bodies, sir.'

Rush nodded, his face impassive, his expression displaying neither approval nor disapproval, pleasure nor displeasure. He was as inscrutable as the face of the sphinx, as indecipherable as a book written in Sanskrit.

Joanna waited for some hint – and got nothing. She ploughed on. 'I'm going to need a full team.' She hesitated and met his eyes. She felt troubled still – something in this case was wrong. Not just not-quite-right but patently wrong. Was Rush picking up on this?

'I don't agree with you, Piercy,' he said crisply, 'but I can see your point. Charge him with involvement in the two girls' disappearance. Detain him while we make a full search of the area.'

She dipped her head, still unsure in her mind. But she was dismissed. Rush didn't want a discussion about this. He wanted an arrest.

Back in her office, she was still chewing this over when Mark Fask's call came in. She listened for a few minutes while he read out, in dreadful French, the contents of the note he had found and confirmed that the details on the printed sheet matched those on the webpage with the translator tool found in Barker's internet history. The words on the printed sheet were the same as the text. The last known sighting of the girls had been at Mandalay. Their rucksacks were there and now they had evidence that Barker had sent the text from one of the girls' phones to divert attention away from Rudyard. It was time to charge him.

The rest of the phone records were still being checked.

Tom was looking serious as she walked in. He was leaning back in his chair, as though trying to put as much distance between him and his client as was possible in the small area of the interview room. He looked at her, must have read what he saw and his expression changed to one of resignation. He knew what was coming all right. So did Barker. A small bead of sweat squeezed out of a pore on his pale forehead as she cautioned and charged him with the girls' disappearance. As she spoke she met Tom's eyes and saw, from his expression, that he knew there was every chance that this charge would be changed to one of murder.

Even Barker seemed to understand this. 'But I didn't,' he protested, without the listeners quite understanding how he could still be claiming innocence.

She leaned across the table. 'It'll go better with you, Mr Barker, if you give us the absolute truth.'

Disclosure rules meant that she had to tell Barker and his solicitor that, in the sitting room of Mandalay, in his desk, they had found a printout of the text used in the message purporting to be from Dorothée to her mother, in English with a French translation from the online translator tool he'd accessed from his laptop. 'It must have taken you a while to compose,' Joanna said.

Barker looked like a cornered rat. Eyes furtively darting around the room, hunting for an escape route, finally coming to rest, beseechingly, on his lawyer. A silent, *Get me out of this*.

Tom looked back at him steadily and then requested a private word with '*my client*'.

It would soon be time for a briefing and to assemble the team together, time to search for what Joanna was now convinced would be two bodies, but for now it was time to ring Matthew and tell him not to expect her home for tea, and forewarn him that his services may soon be needed. His response, initially, was a grunt, followed by a cheery, 'OK.' She looked at the telephone receiver in her hand, a little puzzled at this unusual truce. Normally Matthew grumbled when she was detained.

'I'll fill you in when I get home,' she added. He didn't even ask when that would be. Another departure from the norm. Perhaps he was learning about her being married to the job. She blew a kiss down the phone and, from his embarrassed chuckle, knew that his assistant would be listening on the speakerphone.

She re-entered the room and proceeded with the questioning.

'Mr Barker,' she said. 'I'll ask you again. Do you know where the girls are?'

'No,' he said flatly, and without any emotion now, as though he had schooled himself not to react. 'I don't.'

'So what explanation do you have for the rucksacks being in your house?'

'I've already told you,' he said peevishly, as if having to repeat himself. 'They just left them behind. They were in the way and I wanted to get the room ready for my next lot of visitors. They were due that evening,' he finished, 'so I moved them out the way.'

'And the text to Dorothée's mother, Mr Barker?'

'I wanted to divert any suspicion away from me and from Mandalay,' he said earnestly. 'I hated you hanging around asking questions. I knew you'd be suspicious if you saw the rucksacks.'

Too bloody right.

'But I didn't know what to do with them. You see, they might have come back for them. They'd have been angry if I'd got rid of them.'

This phrase jarred Joanna. She gave a quick glance at Korpanski who, up until then, had been as still as a statue. Even Tom Fairway looked a little startled.

Barker continued. 'So I tried to make you think they were in London.' He looked almost pleased with himself. 'And it worked. You left me alone,' he said. 'I did have to use the online translator, of course,' he finished.

Tom glanced down meaningfully at his watch. His client was due a break and Joanna decided she would use the time to return to Rudyard, see if anything else had turned up and supervise the search of the area. She was still bothered that she couldn't get a handle on Horace Barker. Some things were a little too plain and obvious – the rucksacks and even the text, while other events were subtle and clever, notably the sneaky spying through the hole in the eye of the Chinese girl, that he called Supi . . . whatever it was.

And the question remained: was it possible that Horace Gladstone Barker was telling the truth?

She sighed and minutes later turned off the Macclesfield

road to reach Rudyard, driving underneath the railway bridge just as a small train '*oooh ooh*'-ed its way across.

The lake was sparkling in the golden October sunshine; after the dry August the trees were just beginning to change colour, though a little late this year. It was so beautiful, like a vividly coloured Constable painting. England in glorious Technicolor. Yellows and reds contrasting with the green. In spite of the circumstances Joanna felt the familiar skip of autumn in her heart. She loved the month – when all the sunshine turned to gold. And the association between one of the world's great poets and this place had always made it even more special to her. From childhood she had always had an affection for it. It was, as they called it, the Staffordshire seaside, a place where the inhabitants of a landlocked county could play at being beside the seaside beside the sea. It had the lot, boats for hire, little trains, ice-cream stalls, a hot dog stand and a posh, traditional Victorian hotel. The real thing. At least a great illusion.

She turned to share this with Korpanski, who had caught up with her just as the incident van was manoeuvring into place. 'How's it going with Barker?' he asked. 'I know about the French lesson.'

'He's giving nothing away but I've bought us some more time by charging him.'

'If you've charged him why are you looking so down in the mouth?' Trust Mike to pick up on it.

'You're right,' she said, meeting his eyes with a faint smile. 'I shouldn't be, should I? I should be happy and focus on the search for the girls' bodies, but it just doesn't feel right, Mike. Unless we can link him to their murder he might slip through the net.'

'We'll get there, Jo,' DS Korpanski replied stoutly, which raised a smile from her. Oh, to be Mike, she sometimes thought – stolid and unimaginative, unlike her, who was often full of instincts (frequently misguided) and worries about arresting the wrong person.

He was waiting for her to speak. She began to revert to her original focus, of the beauty of the place, while she waited for the officers to arrive.

The briefing was a sober affair. The two girls looked so young, healthy, beautiful and fresh-faced – vibrant and alive in the photos. They were the very last people who should now be dead. But here they were all searching, searching, searching.

For two bodies which she believed they would soon find.

Besides Fask she had now three full teams – one to search the grounds of Mandalay, one to begin house-to-house enquiries in the village and the third to start on the surrounding area which was extensive and sparsely populated, consisting of isolated farms, a few cottages and a small village with a few hundred inhabitants. That and the hordes of holidaymakers who came and went. If some of the lake's visitors had seen the two French girls the search would have to be nationwide – even possibly worldwide, to reach them. But as the incident van was finally in place on the car park near the dam Joanna looked across the sparkling water and her attention was caught by the mud which rimmed the lake. The water level was still low after the extended dry season and the lake was not only a reservoir and a place of recreation but also the feeder to the Caldon Canal, popular with holidaymakers in their hired boats. Each time a lock gate opened the water level fell a little more.

There were yards of mud rimming the lake, soft and treacherous. Last year a dog had succumbed, to its owner's distress. The dog was not seen again after it sank into the mud. Since then, whenever the water level dropped, the council erected signs warning people of the danger. Mud in the dry season, bathing in the summer and thin ice in sub-zero temperatures. Rudyard Lake kept the council busy trying to keep the public safe but there were always a few, a little more reckless than the rest, who would risk it. But thankfully there were no more fatalities.

Or were there? Were the girls beneath the mud? Was it possible that Barker's claim that they intended to leave early on the Sunday morning the truth? That he had committed no worse crime than failing to report a disappearance when he discovered the rucksacks but they didn't come back? Joanna sat up instinctively, feeling that that they were getting closer to some answers. Barker had failed to report the girls' disappearance because he was anxious about Miss Wong and her dirty little secrets. So had the girls gone out by themselves and succumbed to a tragic accident? And if so, where were the bodies? Buried in the mud? Or were they at the bottom of the lake itself? If the water level dropped further would the bodies of Annabelle and Dorothée be exposed? A hand, a foot, a head? She fought back a moment of sheer exasperation. Where *were* they?

It is tempting to believe that water hides everything. But it is not so. The human body has an almost inbuilt instinct to float and show itself. Water yields its secrets. It does not hide them. She stared across the glistening surface, almost willing the lake to give up their ladies. But no. The surface remained glassy and unbroken. There was barely a ripple.

Once she'd filled her teams in on the current state of affairs she returned to the station and Barker, leaving Fask and his team to focus on the house itself. She didn't need to check up on him. He would do a thorough job without her breathing down his neck.

Alan King started setting up the computer networks. It would be his job to collate statements and information. Tall and skinny, with long, bony fingers that seemed to fly over the keys scarcely touching the keyboard, he worked quickly and efficiently.

Korpanski took Jason Spark, now a police cadet, but still as eager as a puppy, and DC Danny Hesketh-Brown who was, at last, enjoying the full fruits of parenthood, to head his team. They would search the grounds of Mandalay.

It was not as simple a job as might be imagined. Mandalay had extensive and overgrown grounds, thickly bushed with rhododendrons and a densely wooded area, tricky and sharp with brambles and nettles, fallen branches and soft soil. Like many people with a large garden, Barker appeared to have tidied up a small part of it, cultivating a neat lawn and the area surrounding it but leaving the rest to nature. As the team moved through it they realized how difficult their task would be. Near the perimeter they even found a badger set. Long holes in a soft bank. Bugger, Korpanski thought. Now they'd have to call in environmental services, even though badgers, at this very moment, were being merrily shot in some counties in a vain attempt to prevent the spread of bovine TB. But if the police barged in searching for the girls' bodies some animal rights activists would be up in arms. It was the way of things.

PC Dawn Critchlow was heading the house to house. Rudyard consisted of a string of Victorian cottages which lined the road in and a row of ex-council houses which ended in a turning area. She started at the hotel, quieter in the week but still offering fish and chips and special pensioners' rates. The barmaid today was not Sarah Gratton but another girl called Madison Grundy who proved unhelpful, though not through choice. She was dying to help. Thrilled at the thought of being near the centre of an investigation, she racked her brains for some encounter with the two girls but came up with nothing. 'Will the telly be here?' she asked, eyes wide with excitement, the vertical ponytail on top of her head waving like a spouting whale.

'Probably,' Dawn answered gloomily. While the public might be thrilled at the concept of the media, for her and her colleagues they were nothing but a nuisance – until, that is, they wanted to rope in the help of the general public. Then they were useful.

The house to house was pretty fruitless. Many people were out at work and most households did not respond to her knock. Dawn shoved a leaflet through each letterbox and wondered how many people would actually read it. In one house, right at the end, an old woman stared at her through the window but made no move to open the door. Dawn pushed a leaflet through her letterbox too.

Quite a few of the inhabitants of Rudyard village had guard dogs to keep their properties secure and as Dawn moved from house to house she was followed by a cacophony of the animals barking their warnings to keep away, each dog setting its neighbours off. It was like the Canon in D, the noise going round and round without pause. While Dawn was good at getting on with people, she had a real fear of dogs. She still had a bite mark on her plump left leg from an encounter when she'd been a child, so was wary in her visits. Once or twice the door was opened. Faces changed when they noted her uniform, but so far she hadn't met anyone who remembered the girls except Sarah Gratton, who lived in a pretty cottage converted from an unconsecrated chapel, and she was no help. While recalling the two girls she had not engaged in conversation with them; neither had she ever seen them with anyone else. 'Like I said, they were always reading their books,' she said scornfully. 'I never saw them with any blokes.'

'OK,' Dawn said, frowning. She'd seen the photographs of the two girls – seductive and with a definite 'come hither' look in their eyes. Dawn was a woman who rarely saw harm in anyone but, sure as hell, she could see that these two were trouble. Would they give the lads the *come on* only to giggle, open their books and ignore them? Such behaviour could be dangerous, in her opinion. Men didn't like to be made fools of.

Joanna left the officers to work around the lake area, returning to the station to interview Horace Barker again. She had a private word with Tom.

'He sent the text, Tom. And he knew the girls were parted from their rucksacks. At the very least he failed to alert us to their disappearance. It's a bit naive to think they would come back for them weeks later. Worst scenario is we'll have him on a double murder charge.'

Tom was silent for a moment. Then, 'What do you want me to do?'

'I need to know where the girls' bodies are,' she said. 'It'll save us time and money.'

Tom glanced back at the door to the interview room. 'It won't get him off the hook, though.'

'No. This is purely for us. If we can prove murder he'll get a mandatory life sentence and that's that but I want to know how they died sooner rather than later. I want to know what happened to them.' She appealed to him as a parent. 'I want their mothers to know their fate.'

Tom looked serious. Then he nodded. 'I'll do what I can, Jo. And if he cooperates with you?'

Joanna gave a cynical snort. 'And if this was your daughter?'

'I don't have a daughter.'

'Yet.' She continued to stare at him. 'Maybe one day.'

He moved uneasily. 'That's unfair, Joanna.'

'Life's unfair, Tom.'

He nodded grimly.

It wasn't the first time she and Tom had worked together. But fatherhood had changed him. He was different, tougher and yes, more damaged by a case such as this where a child had vanished, apparently into thin air and a mother – or in this case, two mothers – left to grieve and wonder.

And so they went through the whole thing again – and again. And Barker refused to budge an inch. He stuck to his story, that the rucksacks had been left, that he had expected the girls to return and claim them and that he had sent the text message to divert suspicion away from himself and draw the police away from Mandalay and his beloved Supi-yaw-lat. *Who was bloody Burmese anyway and not Chinese Miss Wong*, Joanna thought in frustration.

Even when she pulled the, admittedly, wild card of plea bargaining, apart from a small glint in his eye he still stuck to the same old story.

So she decided to focus on the spying through Miss Wong's eye. Which made Barker squirm. Supi, or whatever her name, was his Achilles heel.

She started at him and he dropped his eyes, searching the floor. Refused to answer her questions. It was a typically guilty attitude. Finally, he squinted across the table at her and made a confession.

EIGHTEEN

'Loo-ook,' he said, his Staffordshire pronunciation elongating the 'oo'. 'I admit it – I like to watch people.' His face looked mystified at the connection. 'It doesn't mean I killed them.' He looked at his lawyer. 'I'm not a killer,' he said simply. 'I'm not that sort of man.'

Tom put his hand on Barker's arm, trying to draw him back, but Barker took no notice. He was intent on telling his side of the story now. 'I like to watch people,' he said again, his eyes now meeting Joanna's, his head cocked on one side.

'You like to watch *women*,' Joanna said. By her side, DS Hannah Beardmore shifted slightly in her chair. A few years back her husband, Roger, had had an affair, and since then she turned prudish at any mention of sex, however tenuous the connection. Joanna had no idea how things were between Hannah and Roger these days but wondered whether this signified a happy truce between the couple or something else. She glanced at the constable. Hannah's face was pink.

Barker was obviously undecided whether to agree that yes, he liked to watch women, or confess to watching men, or at the very worst admit to spying on children, which would bring him the most terrible and dangerous accusation – of being a paedophile.

Joanna regarded him; studied his doughy face and pale complexion. Barker would do badly in jail – if that was where he was headed. There was plenty he wasn't telling them but she still wasn't convinced he had murdered two girls with such a weak motive – protection of his voyeuristic tendencies? At worst he would have faced a caution. A fine and some community service. He would be marked down as a sex offender. True, he would probably lose any recommendation for Mandalay from the tourist board and he would almost certainly have a few extra and uninvited visits from the police.

But Barker was pretty clean, really. He'd filed tax returns ever since he'd opened. His fire and food certificates were all up to date. There was nothing of any concern on his records. Joanna had watched Alan King's fingers fly across the keyboard to gain this information.

Barker was, above all, a careful man. Murder seemed too messy a business for him. Too impulsive. Too random. It struck Joanna that Barker didn't *do* random. He thought about things. He was a planner.

Except in exceptional circumstances? Was this what had happened?

Had they discovered his secret, stumbled upon the eye of Miss Wong and threatened him? Unprepared and acting on the spur of the moment, had this been the trigger which had turned Barker the voyeur into Barker the killer?

On the other hand, if Annabelle and Dorothée had meant to return to Mandalay on that Sunday morning, taking a walk before breakfast, was it possible that someone or something *else* had prevented them returning?

But what? An unexpected event such as sinking in the mud? An encounter with a killer?

In which case, Barker's behaviour was all too logical. She could picture him not knowing what to do with their luggage so hiding it – or trying to. Now that seemed in character – a stupid, panicky decision from someone with no experience of dealing with the police, one that rather than letting him off the hook pinned him firmly on it. If he was guilty, he wouldn't have been so indecisive about getting rid of the rucksacks, surely. He'd had plenty of time.

She heaved a big sigh.

She wasn't there yet and she knew it. So did Tom Fairway, apparently. He wriggled his glasses up his nose, which was always a bad sign, something he did when he wasn't quite comfortable with the situation. Added to that, he was averting his eyes from her. She and Tom had been good friends for years. Before she and Matthew had finally got together and he had found Caro she had even escorted him to the occasional party. She liked him.

'Inspector Piercy,' he said, quite gently and formally, 'you need to get your case together, don't you? Does my client get bail?'

'We'll sort that out with the magistrates,' she said crisply, standing up. In one way, Tom was right. She *did* need to get her case together. She needed time and she needed to tell Chief Superintendent Rush about finding the transcript – the proof that linked Barker with the text message made to Dorothée's mother indicating that they were decamping to London: a great city to disappear in. But as they probably hadn't vanished from London, more likely from here instead, even the wonderful Met would have a tricky job tracking them down.

As before, Rush listened without comment before saying, 'Looks like you've got a case, Piercy. Get bail set and I suggest you return to Rudyard and speak to your team.' His pale eyes met hers. 'Get the evidence.' He leaned right across the desk, his eyes burning with something. A desire to bring this case to closure? Maybe. Maybe that made Gabriel Rush tick. 'Find those bodies,' he emphasized. 'Find them. They're out there somewhere.'

She nodded, and started the process of setting bail.

Charlotte Bingley had climbed right to the top of the Winking Man and was peering down his broken, fractured nose. This – was – awesome. She was on top of the world. The exhilaration made her scoop in a great noisy rush of delight, breathing in the air, cool even on this unusually warm October day. It was always colder up here. She made her plans. She would hike along the ridge and then drop down into Tittesworth to take lunch. She took in the panorama. Miles and miles of unspoilt countryside. Pale grass, small fields, stunted bushes and grotesque, dwarfish trees, isolated sheep and one metal-grey road carving through the emptiness, all divided by rickety stone walls that crumbled if you tried to climb over them – hence the good condition of the stiles and clear signposting of the waymarked hiking trails. A buzzard hovered over her, its harsh cry echoing right down the valley. Apart from that one discordant cry it was silent up here. There was no noise pollution because there was no noise.

Except . . . one noisy motor bike thundered its way along

the A53 towards Buxton. Charlotte smiled. Why did the bikes have to make *so much* noise? It was a perfect break – apart from the forced and irritating alteration in her accommodation. It had been a nuisance to find that she had to sort out somewhere else to stay. She'd liked Mandalay and its pale, characterless cleanliness. Liked its deliberate but not overdone association with the Kipling poem. She liked its owner, too – his soft quietness. There was, in her opinion, nothing worse than an overly chatty B&B owner over breakfast. Besides, he was a great cook, really knew how to grill bacon to perfection, serve eggs with runny yolks and fry bread so it was crisp and brown and not greasy. Yes. The fact that he had abandoned her with no more than a curt note was irritating. She would write a negative review on Expedia. The alternative accommodation she'd found had not been nearly as pleasant but charged twenty pounds more a night. Ridiculous. But that was the only thing that had gone wrong on this holiday designed to escape. She glanced at the day and date on her watch. Stan and Shona would be getting married right now. This very minute, in fact, if the bride was on time. She stopped, sat down and, leaning against a cairn, drew out her flask, poured out coffee and toasted them.

Without knowing she was being watched.

One of the stones was sticking into her back. She fumbled behind her and felt a small plastic box. Someone's sandwich box. She pulled it out and opened the lid. But there were no sandwiches inside. She'd heard of letterboxes but had never actually found one. Until now. There was a book, a stamp. A list of names, people who had been here before. There was no mistaking that this was what it was.

He felt sick. It had been found now, by accident. And he knew there was something in it that would incriminate him. Link him to them. *Them.* His curse. He smiled. As he had been theirs. He shouldn't have left it on the Roaches. But something in him had felt outraged at the thought of removing it completely. It wasn't what letterboxers did. He'd watched them. They didn't take stuff away. They left stuff. So he'd hidden it carefully instead, thinking that would be enough.

But now . . . He watched her drink the coffee, wondering what or who it was that she was toasting. He studied her. She was tall and strong looking. His hand grasped a rock. She was no more than ten feet away. He could cover that ground easily . . .

Charlotte was sitting, drinking her coffee looking around her. Nothing, no one. And then she heard it: a stone, dislodged, rolling down the slope, dislodging another stone. She stood up, scanned the panorama. Empty. The rocky crags, grey stone, narrow crevices. She could see no one. And yet she felt a presence. The Winking Man appeared to close his one eye. He could feel it too. Someone was there.

She scrambled down the scree faster than she should have, tearing her trouser leg in her haste.

When she reached her car her hand was shaking so much she couldn't press the button to unlock it. Finally, sat inside, she scolded herself. If she couldn't cope with isolated places then she would have to stop climbing.

Joanna returned to Barker. Bail was set. But she didn't have to tell him – not just yet, although she knew from Tom's direct gaze that he was perfectly aware.

'OK, Mr Barker,' she said, leaning back in her chair, aware that he was less threatened now she had the much less threatening presence of PC Beardmore beside her rather than the burly Korpanski.

'Last chance to tell me exactly what happened.'

Barker glanced at Tom. 'But I already have,' he protested. 'I've already told you everything. The girls stayed. They went out for a walk, I suppose, early Sunday morning. I waited for them to come back for their breakfast, settle up and pick up their stuff but they never did.'

'But they'd already paid.'

Barker even had an answer ready for this. 'I thought maybe they'd forgotten they'd given me their credit card details. People usually come and say thank you and goodbye.' He sounded aggrieved.

Joanna moved in. 'Were you spying on them?'

Barker gave a frightened glance – not at her but curiously at Tom, as though requesting his permission to speak. He nodded.

'Yes,' he said, a sliver of shame in his tone. 'They were nice to watch. I admit I did have a little peep.'

It sounded so innocuous – a little peep. Child's talk. Nice to watch. Joanna blew out a sigh. Oh, well, let the courts put their interpretation on it.

Barker made a misguided attempt to justify his actions. 'They were very . . . attractive girls.'

'I know,' Joanna said, playing the old policeman's trick of pretending to be on his side, faking empathy. 'They were pretty, weren't they?'

Barker was nodding.

'And did they find out that you'd had *a little peep*?' Only Tom and Hannah Beardmore caught the sarcasm in her tone. Barker didn't, though he managed to look shame-faced.

'No,' he said, hanging his head. 'No. I'm pretty sure they didn't know. They never said. They never seemed embarrassed.'

Joanna nodded and pretended to swallow this. 'And did they enjoy their stay?'

'Oh, yes. They'd bring their book down and read out their poems sitting on the terrace overlooking the lake. And some-times they'd bring a bottle of wine and sit there and drink it. I'm not licensed, you see. It was lovely, their appreciating Kipling so much. It was something we could share. They'd studied him at their school, apparently. I was surprised . . .'

Perhaps he realized he was babbling. He pulled up short. 'I so enjoyed listening to them reading in their lovely accents. Then they'd go off for a walk. Goodness, one day they walked all the way into Leek and a very nice couple gave them a lift back. All the way back here. Dropped them at the door.'

'What day was that?'

'The Wednesday,' Barker said brightly. 'Market day in Leek. When I told them about it they were so excited. When I said there was a cattle market down the bottom of the town and the butter market in the square – well, they just had to go. I told them the way to walk along the little stream, through the nature reserve.' He suddenly pulled himself up short. 'I was hurt when they just left without a word.'

'You didn't think there was something odd – something a bit suspicious about it?'

'Well, yes,' he began. 'Er, no. Well, there were the rucksacks. I don't know what to say,' he finished helplessly.

'Try the truth,' Joanna said, without sympathy, her voice steely and hostile.

Barker's shoulders drooped. 'I've gone over this so many times I don't know any more what *is* the truth.'

Time for the kill. 'Do you know what has happened to the girls?'

'No.'

'Do you know where they are?'

He knew this was a trap, and almost shouted his next, '*No.*'

'Did you kill the girls, Annabelle Bellange and Dorothée Caron?'

'Oh, no. I couldn't have done. They were such lovely girls. I was really fond of them. I enjoyed having them at Mandalay.'

And suddenly Joanna had a glimmer of what just might be the truth. Had he enjoyed having them so much that he couldn't bear for them to leave? Had he felt he had to keep them there? Was that it? Such a simple explanation?

She needed evidence. She addressed her next words to Tom. 'Your client has been granted bail. He cannot leave the area and must give us his contact details. We must warn him he is still under caution.' She gathered up her papers and addressed Barker. 'If at any time,' she said, 'you feel you have more information to give us we would be very grateful if you would contact us.'

Barker met her eyes for a fleeting moment before standing up. 'Am I free to go?'

Joanna nodded and closed down the recording machines.

She returned to Rudyard and found the place bristling with police, detectives, a few media vans, the predictable ghouls at the feast and the inevitable sightseers. A few areas had been roped off with police *Do Not Cross* tape and behind them gathered the motley voyeurs.

She located Korpanski talking to some divers, but from his expression knew nothing great had been found – yet. 'We're expanding the search, Jo,' he said, 'but so far we've not found a lot. We're waiting for some environmentalists to come before we can explore the badger sets in Barker's garden. How's it going with him?'

'He's not cracking, if that's what you're asking. He still insists he has had nothing to do with the girls' disappearance.' She smiled. 'Let's go for a coffee.'

They made their way to the café and met the bright-eyed Will Murdoch again. He took their order with a round-eyed, 'What's going on?'

'We're still looking for the two French girls,' Joanna said.

'Thought they'd gone to London.'

'It appears that was a red herring,' Joanna said.

Will busied himself making the coffee with an impressive-looking espresso machine. 'Well, if you ask me,' he said, taking the money for the drinks, 'whoever it was sent that text.' His forefinger stabbed the counter. 'It was 'im what did away with them. If that's what's happened,' he added, safe-guarding his opinion.

'Put it like this,' Joanna said, 'we're looking in to it.'

Korpanski brushed away a wasp that was making a nuisance of itself. The autumn sunshine always brought this particular complication.

Joanna looked up. 'So what do you do over the winter, Will?'

'A bit of this and a bit of that. Tried a college course once but it wasn't for me.'

'Casual labour, then.'

He grinned. 'I do a bit of seasonal work. Santa Claus and all that. There's always stuff round Christmas. The ice-cream van in summer. And of course I still open here over the weekends right through the year.'

'Yeah.'

'Plus,' he said importantly, 'I'm a carer for my ma. She has mental health problems so can't leave the house.'

Joanna and Mike glanced at each other. Some kids are ambitious and others, well, they either aren't or they don't have the opportunity to be.

Will still hadn't finished. He continued with his open, frank statement. 'My dad, see. He left us a few years ago and Mum, well, she's been like that ever since he went.'

And Joanna wondered. What came first? Chicken or egg? Did his lack of ambition stem from a need to stay at home and care for his mother? Or was it the other way round? Had he once been ambitious and had to put it to one side because his mother had needed a carer?

But there is always a converse to this. Some people become dependent because they can. Had she had no willing son to care for her, might her she have been less dependent?

'Anyway,' Will said, breaking into her thoughts. 'I've got the offer of some bar work at the Rudyard Hotel through the winter. And some chef work.'

'Great,' Joanna said brightly. They huddled together in the corner of the café, aware that they would have to have a briefing later. But as much as they tried to find a way through to a solution, they made no headway. They needed to find the girls.

And the day wore on. At eight o'clock Joanna knew she was drained. Her mind was blank. She switched the computer off and drove back to Waterfall Cottage.

She arrived home mentally and physically exhausted, parked the car, pushed the cottage gate open and walked towards the front door, fumbling for her key. But Matthew must have heard her car. Before she could insert the key in the lock he opened the door to her, smiled and took her hand. 'Come,' he said.

Inside was warm and cosy. Lamps lit, the woodburner chucking out warmth and a merry glow. He handed her a glass of blood-warm red wine and she sank back on the sofa, luxuriating. 'Mmm,' she said appreciatively. 'This is nice to come home to. Maybe it was a good thing to get married after all.'

He bent over her, kissing her mouth.

'You seem different, Matt,' she said, sitting up.

'Oh?' He arched his eyebrows. 'Different? In what way?'

'Softer,' she said, still puzzling. 'More tolerant. Less angry about my working late, the bad hours, me being knackered. A bit more understanding.'

'It's called compromise,' he said, settling beside her, back against the cushions, his eyes still warm and friendly. 'You've compromised about our having a son.'

'A child,' she corrected.

He nodded, finger up, acknowledging the correction. 'A child. So I accept the sacrifice you're making.'

She raised her eyebrows. His eyes smiled briefly but behind the smile was some sadness. 'Oh, I know, Jo. It isn't what you want. For you it *is* a sacrifice. And so I must make my contribution.' He poured her another glass of wine. 'And this is it.'

In spite of the seriousness of the moment, she couldn't resist teasing him a little. 'And you think I can be so easily bought, Matthew Levin?'

He laughed then kissed her wine-stained lips and answered her question. 'I think so,' he said.

She nodded, pretended to consider his response then slipped her hand into his. He gripped it with strong fingers.

That night she threw away her packet of contraceptive pills. Might as well get it over with, Piercy, she thought. There's no going back on this one. She just hoped that Detective Sergeant Mike Korpanski was right and that the minute the child was born love would spill out of her, warm as honey. But she doubted it. Not all parents bond with their offspring.

NINETEEN

The search was necessarily extensive. With the help of the environmental services the badgers were coaxed out of the set and the soft burrows explored with the help of fibre optic cameras and sniffer dogs. It proved unfruitful. The girls weren't here. They widened the search. Barker's entire grounds were examined using heat-seeking probes. Again, nothing.

The lake was dragged. No body was found but they did bring up a soggy purse, red leather with a fifty-Euro note still inside and credit cards belonging to Dorothée Caron. DC Alan King proved to be fluent in French (an ex-girlfriend of his had been from Marseilles), and so it fell on his shoulders to keep Cécile Bellange and Renée Caron informed of the progress and tell them of this discovery. Finding the purse clinched it for Joanna. The girls were dead. They had never left this area. The text message had been a pathetic attempt by Barker to divert suspicion away from Rudyard. Joanna scanned the area and knew they were still here.

And, irrationally, she felt angry that Rudyard Lake, where she and Matthew had spent so many happy times, would somehow always be spoiled. It would always hold this memory. Defiled.

Barker's homecoming was very low key. An unmarked police car dropped him off right by his front door. He unlocked it and walked in without a backwards glance, leaving the two officers to look at each other. Was he guilty? Had he outwitted them?

PC Dawn Critchlow was spending most evenings speaking to the residents of Rudyard. Interestingly, few seemed to know Barker. Not only did he live half a mile out of the village, but he patently kept himself to himself. People knew of Mandalay but not its owner. No one had ever seen him with the girls. But then, why would they?

She'd met some strange folk during her house-to-house enquiries: a couple with a Pit Bull, a man who'd answered his door in his underpants, another elderly lady who had only spoken from behind her front door, and then there was the occupant of the end house. The woman had eyed her suspiciously from behind the curtain and Critchlow, whose husband had suffered from depression on and off ever since his garage business had failed, recognized only too well the signs of mental disturbance. She tried to coax the woman to open the door but it wasn't going to happen. Instead she was reduced to mouthing through the window. *We're looking into the disappearance of two French girls. Can you help us?*

The woman simply stared.

From her list Dawn knew that the woman's name was Wendy Murdoch and that she lived with her son, William, who worked in the village.

You had to hand it to PC Critchlow. She was persistent. She rapped on the window again and tried to look her most appealing. Mrs Murdoch's response was to draw the curtains tightly shut.

So Critchlow was reduced now to shouting through the letterbox. 'Mrs Murdoch, we need to talk to you.' She caught a movement in the hallway and continued. 'When is a good time to talk to you?'

'You'll have to wait till my boy's home.' The voice was thin and reedy, as quavering as a very old woman.

Joanna climbed the hill to speak to Mark Fask. He had spent the day combing through every inch of Mandalay and had not found anything further to link Barker with the girls' disappearance. But Barker was back now and Fask was preparing to move his van out of the drive. Job over.

'I'm sorry, Joanna,' he said, peeling off a pair of gloves, 'but I can't find evidence that the girls were killed here. There's absolutely nothing that's the least bit suspicious. No blood. No tissue. It's as clean as a new pin.'

So was that, in itself, suspicious? Joanna thought probably not. Barker was, by nature, a very clean and tidy man.

She and Fask stepped out into the garden and looked around. 'Does Mandalay have cellars?'

He shook his head. 'There's nothing there. I've looked into all that, Jo. The team have done a proper search of the place and its surrounds. They're not here. And they're not in the garden either. If you want my guess . . .' His gaze drifted across to the lake, today still and secretive, hiding her secrets in an innocence of water. Fask didn't finish his sentence but jerked his head in accusation.

'We've dragged it, Mark,' Joanna said. 'We've found nothing but Dorothée's purse. We can't drain the entire lake. Besides, the level's about as low as it gets. And their bodies would have floated.'

'Not if they were weighted down.'

She nodded, dejected. With Rush breathing down her neck she needed to find these girls and nail the killer. And not just for her reputation. Like many detectives on a murder trail, it was becoming something of a mission. She wanted answers.

But as she tramped back down the hill she had to admit that she wasn't surprised that Fask hadn't found their bodies. She'd never thought that Barker would have killed the girls and kept their bodies in Mandalay. She felt that Mandalay was, for Barker, almost a sanctified place. A shrine to the great poet where he stayed with his Supi . . . lady. As she had felt that Rudyard would always be defiled by the girls' disappearance, so Barker would have felt the same about a killing in his beloved Mandalay. Not only would it have sullied the place for ever but spoiled the memory of Kipling himself. They needed to extend the search.

She strolled back down the hill, meeting Korpanski at the bottom. She wanted a quiet word with him, not in the incident van but somewhere else, somewhere more private. The coffee shop was still open but it was a hot day and she was thirsty for an ice-cold drink. So they took a seat outside. October this year was more like August – warm and sunny, the lake innocently pretty.

The boat-hire business man, Keith Armitage, from the board, was looking glum. He strode towards Joanna, a big man with the rolling gait of a sailor. 'How long are you going to be stopping people from taking my boats out? I'm losing business here. The weather's warm. Plenty of people want to take a boat out.' His voice was accusatory.

'We won't be much longer,' Joanna tried to reassure him. 'I'm really sorry for the difficulty.'

'Oh, that's OK,' the boat owner responded grumpily. 'But you won't find them in there. Water's too clear.'

'And the mud,' Korpanski put in.

'Might take a dog,' Shannon said. 'Not a couple of girls. No way,' he said firmly before turning his back on them and stumping back to his perch on an upturned boat and lighting a cigarette, smoking it with quick, angry puffs.

Will was waiting for them in the café with a big grin. But the drinks he brought them were warm. 'Sorry,' he said. 'There's been a run on cold drinks. We didn't expect it to be so warm this time of year.'

They waited until he'd gone before Joanna spoke. 'OK, Mike,' she said. 'So what next?'

'There's still plenty of space we haven't explored, Jo.' Korpanski looked concerned. 'And maybe we should extend our search area? It's possible they left Rudyard and were heading back out towards the moors, Ramshaw Rocks, perhaps thinking of leaving another letterbox?' He too looked troubled.

'But the rucksacks? Left at the B&B when they were hitchhiking?'

'Barker said they'd walked all the way to Leek one day. Maybe that's where they went.'

'They packed up on Saturday night. Barker said they intended leaving early on the Sunday morning.'

'How much can we rely on Barker's statement?'

Joanna shrugged. 'Your guess is as good as mine, Mike. Killers have to tell lies, you know that. Horses for courses. Goes with the job.'

Both of them knew instinctively that this investigation

would take up plenty of time and use up plenty of resources before they found an answer. And sometimes – Korpanski's face looked troubled – they failed to find an explanation at all. It was possible that the girls' fate would always remain a mystery.

Just then Dawn Critchlow entered the café and, to their surprise, instead of stopping at their table, she gave them a cursory nod before walking past and heading for Will. He looked surprised too. 'Can I help you?'

'I'd like to talk to your mother, Will.'

He now looked astonished. 'My mother? Whatever for?'

'We're trying to speak to all the inhabitants of Rudyard – anyone who might have seen something of the two girls who are currently missing.'

'My mum won't be able to help you.'

'You don't know that.'

'But she's not a well lady.' He must have thought he needed to emphasize the point as he said, 'She's very ill.'

'I realize that, William.' Dawn was very good at sweetening people. 'But as she's around in the day and most of the other people in the square are out I wondered if she might have seen something.'

'I wouldn't have thought so.'

'She spends a lot of time looking through the window.'

Will frowned, and to Jo he seemed to be caught between the need to protect his mother and not getting in the way of the police investigation. His face was pink and his feet were shuffling. He gave it one last shot. 'I'd prefer you not to. You might upset her.'

'We can speak to her while you're present, in your house,' Dawn said, before twisting the thumbscrews just a little. 'It would be better than summoning her to the station, which might cause her some distress.'

He caved in at that. While Joanna and Mike watched, he capitulated. 'OK,' he said. 'I'll be home by eight. You can come by then, if you like,' he added, a little grumpily.

'Good,' Dawn said. 'It'd be much better if you're there.' She finished with a winning smile. 'See you later then. OK?'

Patently it wasn't. The normally pleasant face of Will Murdoch told as much. 'I guess so,' he said sulkily.

Joanna and Mike practically clapped. 'A lesson in getting your own way,' Joanna murmured.

Dawn then came over to the table where Korpanski and Joanna were sitting and sat down. 'What was all that about?' Joanna asked.

'We-ell,' Dawn said, hesitating, 'my team have gained access to all the properties in Rudyard except this one. Mrs Murdoch stares at me through the window but won't let me in. Her son, William, is her carer.'

'And?' Joanna was still baffled.

Dawn dropped her gaze. 'I've had a shifty round the back, Jo,' she said. 'The kitchen is small. They're all small cottages.'

'And?'

'In the lean-to in the back is a large chest freezer.'

No bodies in the lake. The lack of any traceable putrefaction in the surrounding area. Joanna drew in a sharp breath. Was this the lead they'd been looking for?

Charlotte Bingley was driving back to Rudyard still a little on edge after her trip to the rocks. Barker had rung her mobile number. 'Just to let you know,' he'd said in his slow voice, 'I'm really sorry about having to leave you in the lurch. I hope you've found somewhere else to stay.'

Charlotte was not in a particularly forgiving mood. 'I did find somewhere,' she said in a cold, clipped voice, 'but it was most inconvenient, Mr Barker. And,' she added pointedly, 'it was more expensive.'

'I had to leave due to a family bereavement,' Barker continued. 'All very tragic – and sudden. Quite unexpected, you see.' He wasn't going to tell *her* the truth.

'Oh, I'm sorry.' The words trotted out automatically, almost without any thought.' Then she did think. 'Is it possible I could come back to Mandalay then for the rest of my stay?'

The words had a ring to them, Barker realized. One he

recognized. *Come you back, you British soldier; come you back to Mandalay!*

'Of course,' he said warmly. 'You'll be *most* welcome. I was *so* sorry to inconvenience you. When would you like to return?'

'Tonight?'

TWENTY

Having made her excuses at Leek's only hotel, Charlotte Bingley arrived back at Mandalay at six p.m., just as the heat was leeching out of the day. Barker opened the door to her and they greeted each other almost as old friends.

'I'm so sorry I had to leave you in the lurch,' he said. 'I did feel really awful about it. I've never had to walk out on my guests before. But it was a quite an unexpected event. A tragic accident,' he added, to give his story extra colour.

'Oh, dear,' Charlotte responded, almost adding the dreadful cliché, *do you want to talk about it?* before telling herself not to be so stupid and replacing it with, 'So will you have to leave again to attend the funeral?'

For a moment Barker looked as though he didn't know what she was talking about. Then he remembered his little white lie and slipped straight back into it. 'Oh, yes,' he said, 'I will have to go to the funeral but only for half a day.' The lie was gaining strength and detail. 'And because they don't know *why* she died there had to be a post-mortem,' he added dramatically. 'And the coroner's involved so I'm not sure that the funeral won't be for weeks.' He gave her a reassuring smile. 'But it'll be well after you've gone, Charlotte.' He gave her a warm smile that hid a bit of a smirk.

No point in rattling the girl, was there? Telling her he had actually been with the *police*, under suspicion for liquidating two of his guests. Females, just like her. He showed his yellow teeth just as she shouldered her rucksack and headed for the stairs. 'Am I in my old room?'

Barker practically shuddered as he recalled the dreadful mess the officers had made of the wall where they had taken down his beloved Supi-yaw-lat, plastering over the hole in the wall with what had seemed to him to be malicious pleasure when he'd finally been allowed to return to Mandalay. They had taken his picture – as evidence, they'd said. She *wasn't* evidence. She was his . . .

'No, dear,' he said quickly. 'Best not go back to your old room. I've not had time to clean it.'

Charlotte was about to say that it didn't matter but Barker added quickly, 'I've put you in the grand suite.'

She was about to demur that she'd been quite happy in . . . but the words dried up in her throat. Barker was looking at her in a way that invited no protest.

Joanna and Mike had returned to Leek and were holed up in their office. 'I'm not happy about letting Barker go,' she said suddenly.

Mike pinned her with a stare. 'We couldn't keep him in custody for ever, Jo,' he pointed out. 'The evidence was kind of circumstantial and a bit flimsy and . . . well.'

They both knew they needed to find the bodies.

'We should at least be watching him.' Her face changed. 'What if he opens Mandalay up for business again?'

'He wouldn't . . .' Korpanski grinned suddenly. 'I wouldn't worry about that, Jo.' He had a mischievous twinkle in his eye. 'Phil Scott and Jason have plastered up the hole.'

She laughed. 'I hope they've made a neat job of it.'

'Not particularly.'

Then she sobered up. 'But we don't know what he's up to, Mike. By letting him go are we putting someone at risk?'

He swivelled round in his chair to face her and knew her concerns were serious. 'Well, we can always re-arrest him.'

'No, we can't really, Mike. We need that evidence. We need to find the bodies. Maybe Critchlow will have some luck with that freezer.' But Joanna was aware she sounded pessimistic. She really couldn't see Will or his ill mother having anything to do with the girls' disappearance.

PC Dawn Critchlow was standing outside number eight on The Crescent. The property was not so much neglected – the garden was quite neat and the white paintwork in good condition – as unloved. The house was a little spoiled by the dingy pebble dash, probably applied in the fifties when there had

been a fashion for it. No. Number eight was simply uncared
for. A place of residence that had received no affection. It
was a sad, bland little house. As she pushed the garden gate
open she was aware of the strange woman staring at her
through the window and behind her the boy from the café,
Will.

It was he who let her in, clearly unhappy about the disturbance. 'I don't know why . . .'

In answer, Dawn addressed his mother directly. 'Mrs
Murdoch,' she said. The woman was dressed in a tartan pleated
skirt that was mid-calf length, thick brown tights and pink
slippers. She wore a dark red cardigan that was wrongly
buttoned up. There are few more obvious visible clues that
hint at mental health issues than the combination of well-worn
slippers with a wrongly buttoned up cardigan. Will clearly felt
the need to be protective of her, though his glance at his mother
also held some exasperation.

Dawn was surprised when the woman's steady brown eyes
fixed on her. 'Yes?'

'I'm hoping you can help me.'

'Yes?' she said again.

'Back in July . . .'

The woman interrupted her. 'I don't have a good memory,
you know. And it's Wendy. You can call me Wendy.'

Dawn continued: 'Back in July two French girls were staying
at Mandalay – the . . .'

'Mandalay,' Mrs Murdoch cackled, 'Mandalay, did you say?
Barker's place?'

'Yes.' PC Critchlow couldn't hide her surprise. 'Do you
know him?'

'Years ago, I did,' Wendy Murdoch said. 'More years ago
than I care to recall.'

'Oh?' Dawn Critchlow was flummoxed.

'We were – for a while – you might say we were sweet-
hearts.' She cackled again.

'No. Really?'

Wendy Murdoch looked mischievous. 'We were,' she
insisted. 'Indeed we were. Years ago. But, well, he had to
look after his old mum.' She looked up, directly at Will.

'Just like you do, William, you could say. And then . . . we sort of drifted apart really. Maybe neither of us was a passionate creature. And then I met Ian.' She smiled to herself. 'But he took off not long after young Will here was born. And then, well . . .' She looked up. 'Life goes on, doesn't it?'

'Yeah. I suppose so.'

During the exchange Will had hovered nervously in the doorway, hopping from foot to foot in a little tapping dance. Dawn looked across the room at him and wondered. She never quite trusted obedient sons. Maybe because she didn't have one – not a son or a daughter.

She returned to her original question. 'So did you see the girls, Wendy?'

'What did they look like?'

Dawn produced the photograph. Wendy Murdoch stared at it for a while then commented, 'Pretty, aren't they?'

It was not an answer but Dawn agreed. Thoughts were crossing her mind.

'They look flirty, don't they?'

Dawn frowned. She puzzled over this for a while. They did look flirty, inviting in the picture but in real life it had seemed they were more engrossed in their poetry book. So what, she wondered, was the truth?

Wendy hadn't finished. 'Just the sort of girls men would like.' She looked at Will.

'So, do you remember seeing them?'

Wendy Murdoch folded her arms tightly and bunched in her lips. 'No, I do not.' She was almost shouting. 'I did not.'

Will put his hand on her arm. 'Mum,' he said.

It was just one word, but it stopped her dead in her tracks.

'We're searching all the properties in Rudyard just in case, you know.'

'They're not here.'

'Do you mind if I just take a look around?'

Wendy Murdoch shrugged. 'Help yourself,' she said.

The house was a small two-bedroomed cottage. Dawn even managed to take a peek into the tiny loft space, which was hardly big enough for two bodies. Then she went into the shed. The chest freezer practically filled the space. Why such an enormous freezer for just two people? Dawn wondered. No, something wasn't right . . . She lifted the lid.

TWENTY-ONE

Later, when she related her encounter during the briefing, Joanna asked her what her private thoughts were. Did this mother and son relationship have any bearing on their case?

'I don't know, Joanna,' Dawn said, frowning. 'I don't know. But I feel there's something strange about the place, about the relationship between William and his mother. He plays the protective son looking after his frail mother but it all seems a bit plastic. A bit staged. Put on for my benefit, almost. But there's no doubt he has her where he wants her. He gets the carer's allowance and a certain amount of freedom, somewhere to live and the upper hand.'

'You saw nothing in the house? Nothing of any interest in the freezer?'

'No. The house is too small to conceal anything. Besides, with Wendy Murdoch there all the time I don't see how two girls could possibly have been killed and their bodies concealed without her knowing something about it.' She gave a shame-faced grin at the memory. 'I got excited when I saw the chest freezer in the garage but it was full of ice cream. Will was obviously holding stock for the van. Or he'd pinched it,' she added.

'Hmm, shame that. Wouldn't it have been nice—' She stopped herself. What was she saying? Nice if they'd found two preserved bodies? 'It was always a long shot. Why would he have any designs on the two girls? He doesn't look like a sex fiend to me and we've no evidence they encountered each other.'

DC Alan King stepped forward. 'No, Joanna,' he agreed. 'We have nothing to connect him to the girls. No sightings, no contacts. No one ever saw them together.'

'But he probably did meet up with them at some point,' Joanna said, thinking. 'He was selling ice creams, remember? And serving coffee and sandwiches in café. Perfect opportunity

for an introduction, maybe? A little light banter?' She looked
around the room. 'Anyone got anything more?'

Jason Spark put his hand up. 'I've been manning the phone
lines,' he said. 'We have a member of the public who says he
thought he saw two French girls talking to two men back in
July.'

'Where was this?'

'On Ramshaw Rocks. One of the climbs on the Roaches.'

'Ah – the place where the girls planted the letterbox.'
Privately her heart was sinking. If they had to widen the search
for the missing girls to the entire Staffordshire and Derbyshire
moorlands they might never find them. The area was simply
too vast.

'Do we know when?'

He was on holiday in the middle of July.'

The right time period.

'Was he able to give a description of the two men?'

Spark shook his head and looked a little crestfallen.
'Apparently they had their hoods pulled down over their faces.
It was one of those rainy days. He wasn't even absolutely
certain it was two girls and two men but he thought he heard
someone speaking French.'

'You've got his name and number?'

Spark nodded.

'Is he local?'

'He's from Macclesfield.'

'OK. Tomorrow, show him the pictures. And we need to
rope the media in too. We need all the help we can get. In the
meantime we'll spread our search to encompass the area right
around the lake.' She crossed the board to a large map of
the area. The north side of the lake was less popular than the
south. One had to walk quite a distance to encompass the area
and round the top of the water. On one side were a few cottages
and holiday lets, and on the other the terminal of the small
railway and the end of the cycle track. Heavily wooded,
sparsely populated, largely farmland. If a body – or in this
case two bodies – had been hidden here, it was less likely
they would be found quickly.

It was as the officers dispersed that Joanna recalled

something the Stuart brothers had said and suddenly knew why she had not fixed on Barker one hundred per cent.

'*We often go there.*'

They'd been there before. Of course they'd been there before. She practically slapped her forehead. The Roaches was a favourite challenge to climbers. A chance to hone their skills with so many different climbs, some easy, some hard and all the intermediates. The place swarmed with climbers who arrived well equipped with ropes and crampons. She and Matthew had seen them many times right through the summer: healthy, happy climbers, just like James and Martin, standing at the bottom looking up to the challenge, swapping stories of near misses and information about their equipment. The question was when had they been there before? July, maybe? And rather than in September had they found the letterbox then and maybe met up with them? They were a good-looking pair of guys. Fit and healthy. This seemed a much more plausible explanation for an involvement than either Barker or Will Murdoch. Two girls, two guys. That was a bit easier. But why had they come back, searching for them?

And so, as the search continued for the two girls, Joanna prepared to revisit the brothers.

But for now she needed to get home.

Unusually she was back at Waterfall Cottage by seven, a little *before* Matthew. And to add to the gold star which should be pinned on her apron, by the time he came in the spaghetti bolognese was almost ready for a sprinkle of *parmigiano*.

'Hey,' he said, putting his arms around her. 'What's this? Domestication.' He planted a smacker of a kiss on her lips. 'At last? I like it,' he said with gusto.

She laughed with him. This happy détente could last, she thought. And how great it would be if it did. 'Well, there's nothing pressing at the moment and I seemed to remember it was my turn to cook tea, so I thought I'd crack on.'

'Lovely,' he said. And then his face changed, became abstracted. She turned around. There was something in his voice. Some doubt.

'Matt,' she said, concerned. 'What is it?'

'Eloise,' he said simply. She might have guessed. 'Jane rang me at work. She says Eloise is not eating properly.'

'I thought she looked a bit . . .'

'We should have her round a bit more,' he said firmly. 'I'm the one who lives near. Jane's miles away. Eloise elected to come here, to Keele, to be near me.'

Or to annoy me. To get in the way.

'I shouldn't neglect her,' Matthew went on, oblivious to her private thoughts. 'I should talk to her. I mean, Jane's miles away,' he repeated limply.

Suddenly Joanna felt awash with guilt. Whose fault was it that Matthew and Jane had initially separated then divorced? Whose fault was it that Jane now lived in York and, yes, she was miles away from her daughter?

Wait a minute, she thought as she dropped the pasta on to the plate then spooned the meat sauce over it. It's not entirely mine. But still.

'OK by me, Matt.' She reached across and touched his hand, but her husband was still preoccupied, worrying about his daughter.

She was racked with guilt. And she knew, like oil floating on water, that that guilt would always be there. No amount of detergent would ever wash it away.

They ate in silence, which he broke as they were sipping wine, glancing up at one another but not quite finding the right words to continue the conversation.

Matthew looked up brightly, attempting at a grin which was only half successful. 'How's your case going?' It was a valiant attempt at breaking the subject.

'The girls are dead, Matt,' she said. 'I'm sure of it. We have to find their bodies.'

Matthew watched her.

'They're here somewhere,' she said, 'somewhere not too far from the lake itself. When or if we do find them we may have trouble proving the cause of death. It might be difficult to get trace evidence of their attacker. We've found nothing so far at the home of the chief suspect and Fask is bloody scrupulous. Their bodies will almost certainly be decomposed.'

'That doesn't bother me.' Matthew sounded almost cheerful.

'I've done it before. I can handle a bit of putrefaction, a few bluebottles buzzing around.'

She almost threw the pepper pot at him.

'So you think they died somewhere in the vicinity?'

She nodded. 'I'm sure of it, Matt, unless – well, I'm just hoping we don't have to widen the search to encompass the moorlands too.'

'What makes you so certain they're dead?'

'Everything points to it. Nothing points to them being alive.'

Matthew waited.

'Barker has to be our main suspect, but I haven't ruled out the two Stuart brothers – the letterboxers. We'll bring them in for questioning. The real question is where are the bodies? And why haven't we found them?'

Matthew grinned. 'I'm not teaching you to suck eggs, Joanna, but . . .'

Again she reached across and touched his hand. 'No,' she said, studying his face and reading his mind. 'They're not at the bottom of the lake. We've checked.'

They ate in silence, the dual subject of Eloise and the missing girls temporarily dropped as they talked a little about their next holiday.

When they'd finished and the dishes were loaded into the dishwasher, Matthew looked meaningfully at the open doorway. 'Ah,' he said, eyeing the sofa. He pulled her to him. 'You've changed,' he said, 'and I like it. I like the married you, Joanna Piercy.'

'I haven't really changed.' She was anxious for him not to be misled by her small spurt of domestication. 'I'm the same,' she said, wanting to be honest. But she would realize that Matthew liked to believe things that were not necessarily true. He would believe what he wanted to believe.

He was nodding, his green eyes alight with merriment and happiness at having found her – or what he believed was her. 'Oh,' he said, his mouth inches from her own, 'yes, you have changed. And what's more I like it. In fact,' he said with a burst of confidence, 'I love it.'

She wasn't going to argue.

*   *   *

Barker was hovering at the bottom of the staircase when she descended. 'Did you sleep well, my dear?'

In actual fact, she hadn't. She had become acutely aware of the quiet of the house, and that there were only two people in it – herself and Barker. At one point she'd even fancied she'd heard him breathing outside her door. Unnerved, she had softly risen from the bed, tiptoed to the door, gently turned the key and pushed the bolt across.

And yet, she would not have said she was a fanciful woman. So what did that mean? Was she right? She studied Barker's pale face. There was something twitchy about it. Something nervous, almost rodent-like.

Only two more days to go.

'Yes,' she said. 'I did sleep well. Thank you.'

'Good. I'm glad of that.' His hands were moving, fingers twining and loosening. 'And what would you like for breakfast this morning? Full English?'

Charlotte felt vaguely nauseous. 'Could I just have a little scrambled egg?'

'Of course, my dear. Whatever you like.' Barker moved softly, a slight waddle in his gait as he exited the room. She heard the sharp metallic clatter of pots and pans being moved in the kitchen and chided herself for being silly. But as she poured her coffee, something else registered.

Something was wrong with him. Mr Barker was afraid of something.

Had he been anyone else she might have asked if he was all right. Perhaps he was still upset at the death of his . . . what was the family member? He hadn't said. So she didn't ask anything, simply sat down and waited, listening to him humming in the kitchen. And eventually he reappeared with perfectly cooked scrambled eggs on toast.

Whatever else he might be, Mr Barker was a fantastic cook.

James and Martin were less than enthusiastic to meet up with the police again. James huffed and puffed when Joanna rang their home number. 'You can either come here or to the station,' she said, 'or we can come to your flat. This morning?' she added. 'But we do need to talk to you.'

In the meantime, the search for the missing girls continued. Divers searched the lake. Sniffer dogs were brought in, trained to recognize the scent of putrefaction and primed with the scent of the girls taken from clothes removed from their rucksacks. Houses, the woods, all areas came under scrutiny. Gradually they were covering the area around the lake. They only had the northern end to complete. Then they must decide where to extend the search which had so far turned up nothing except Dorothée's purse. A briefing was set for 8.30 a.m., which Korpanski would take.

Joanna took DC Alan King with her down to the brothers' flat in Birmingham. His powers of observation plus his knowledge of IT could prove useful.

The brothers obviously weren't short of a bob or two. Their flat turned out to be in a smart area in Edgbaston, on the third floor, with a nice view of the university and Big Joe, the clock tower.

The brothers let them in warily, perched on the edge of the sofa and waited.

'We'll come straight to the point,' Joanna said. 'Obviously we know that you were at the Roaches a couple of weeks ago, but you were also there earlier in the summer, weren't you?'

They glanced at each other, shocked into silence by the statement. Joanna held her breath. She hardly dared look at DC King.

There was a silence, then James said, 'How did you know?'

'I just guessed,' she said. 'And you were seen. You met the girls then, didn't you? Spent some time with them. And then came back six weeks later. Why?'

Had it been, she wondered, *because they'd been worried they'd left some clue? Had they pretended to be looking for the girls in case anyone saw them, when it had actually been to replace the girls' picture in the box planted at Ramshaw Rocks?*

James became the spokesman. 'We did meet them at the Roaches back in July.' He smiled. 'But there's really nothing sinister in it. It was a really shitty day – heavy rain – and the rocks were slippery. The girls were trying to have a go at climbing the spout but they were useless. Annabelle slipped and we sheltered under the Tor and shared our flask of coffee and sandwiches with them. It was us who told them about letterboxing. It all seemed such a laugh. We spent the afternoon with them and then met up the following day. At the time, when I met Annabelle, I was in a relationship. I'd thought Kay and I would be getting engaged and probably marry, but she dumped me in August, just after Martin and I got back from our trip. Then I started thinking about Annabelle. I knew she wasn't in a relationship because she'd told me so. I hadn't taken her mobile number because of Kay, but when Kay dropped me I started thinking about her. I remembered telling her about the letterbox and how you could use it to communicate. So we went back, and, sure enough, found the box with the photo and the message. So we retraced the girls' steps and realized . . .' He looked helplessly at his brother.

'Why didn't you alert the police that the girls appeared to be missing?'

'There was nothing to alarm us. Barker was strange but we didn't seriously think there was anything in it. It could simply have been that Annabelle hadn't been quite as keen as I'd thought.

'But I did I want to meet up with her again,' James continued. 'Even if it didn't lead to anything. She's a really nice girl and there's just a chance that my firm will send me to Paris for a couple of years. My French is, well, OK.'

Joanna caught a look of doubt creeping along Alan King's face. She met his eyes with a question of her own. The story held water.

The brothers looked at each other. 'We couldn't seem to track them down,' Martin continued the story. 'They hadn't left a phone number with the note, so we decided to play detective. We went back to Mandalay and retraced their steps. And then we did get a bit rattled.'

His brother nodded, his shoulders slumped. 'I suppose I just assumed it had been a bit of a flirtation and she hadn't meant it when she'd said that she'd like to see me again. I thought maybe the language barrier . . . maybe I'd just misunderstood. Maybe . . .' He shrugged. '*C'est la vie.*' Then he said frankly, 'When you started asking questions we did

wonder what on earth had happened. Then when the news-
papers ran the story that the girls were missing I thought we'd
better keep schtum. When I realized they hadn't been seen
since the weekend after we'd met up with them I got really
worried.' He glanced at his brother. 'We both did. Maybe
someone *had* seen us talking to them. It could look bad for
us. We thought they'd gone back to Europe after their stay at
Mandalay. But they hadn't, had they? And their mothers didn't
know where they were.'

His brother was nodding his agreement with vigour. Joanna
was thinking, trying to reason it through. If James and Martin
had had something to do with the girls' disappearance why
would they return to the area, risking that they might be
recognized, publicly ask questions and draw attention to
themselves?

The story not only held water but, in her mind, it pointed
towards their innocence.

TWENTY-TWO

In the end it was DC Danny Hesketh-Brown who made the discovery. At the northern end of the lake was a small cluster of cottages, usually rented out to holidaymakers, reached by a single track road that was little used. One of the cottages had not been let all summer. In fact it was, as the brochures would have put it, in need of some tender loving care. Plus new electrics, new plumbing – the lot. It was a wreck and hadn't actually been let for the last seven summers. Also, it was built partly of asbestos and the fence around it, topped with razor wire, warned people to keep out. Summerland, optimistically named, belonged to a local farmer who hadn't yet decided whether he wanted to renovate the cottage, knock it down and return the plot to grazing land, or sell it to a speculator who had intimated he might just want to put a caravan park there. Every week Joseph Shannon came up with a different idea. But he wasn't particularly materialistic and was content with his lot in life. As he would put it in broad Staffordshire, when pestered, 'I inna bothered.'

Needless to say, Hesketh-Brown and his team had no intention of obeying the notice and keeping out. In fact, the minute he saw the sad little place the DC's pulse quickened. If he had had a couple of bodies to dump this would be just the sort of place he'd choose.

They knew to whom Summerland belonged. Shannon was a Staffordshire farmer. And while no one was beyond suspicion, Shannon was about as far away from a killer as could be imagined. He was as stolid as a Staffordshire potato and about as unimaginative too. His family had farmed the few acres just the other side of Horton for generations. He had been married and had one son who, true to form, also farmed the land. The son was unmarried, and Shannon was himself a widower, his wife succumbing to a cruel from of breast cancer when the boy had been a teenager. Father and son farmed together and, on occasion, kept sheep in the neglected cottage and garden, the sheep using the garage for shelter. It was, like Summerland, also made of asbestos. Maybe sheep just weren't as affected. Or maybe they just didn't live long enough for them to develop mesotheliomas. Or maybe no one really cared. Currently, with the sheep being back out in the fields the place was so obviously deserted that Danny wondered when it had last been used. Once it must have been a pretty, idyllic little cottage. Now, like a woman ruined of her beauty, it stared defiantly back through panes cataract-milky with age and neglect. One could date it from the green and cream décor which was around in the forties. It hadn't been touched since.

Only a local would know this place, tucked away behind the trees, and there was no sign of recent habitation or visitation. It certainly didn't invite attention. In fact, it didn't invite anything – it repelled. DC Hesketh-Brown pushed open the gate, letting it sink off the hinges set into wood so rotten it was as soft as sponge. The front door was locked and the back door too, but underneath a flower pot, unimaginative and common, was a large rusting key.

A bit of WD40 and it turned the lock. Inside was cobwebbed and fusty. Nobody except the Adams Family would consider coming here for a holiday. If a killer wanted to conceal a body he would be safe from attention. It couldn't have been used as a holiday let for years. In fact, Hesketh-Brown reflected, looking at the respectable size of the plot, when farmer Shannon finally made up his mind and sold it, if it wasn't to the caravan park prospector it would probably be knocked down and an idyllic, modern, eco-friendly little cottage would be built here instead. Actually, he thought, as he and his team moved from room to room, he wouldn't mind living here himself. Lovely location. Spot of fishing in the lake, barbecues in the summer, log fire through the winter – could grow a few vegetables too. The kids would love it. He could buy a dinghy and teach Tom to sail. And Betsy? Ah. Thereby hung his problem. Betsy, Mrs Hesketh-Brown, was a teacher in Tunstall, and somehow he couldn't imagine her getting to work each day from here.

Hesketh-Brown tucked away the happy little dream. He stood on the doorstep. Whatever his instincts the house inside was clean – at least, in the police sense. There was nothing here. Certainly no bodies. No smell.

The lock on the garage did not respond to his can of WD40 and none of his skeleton keys fitted it. There was only one thing for it: break the padlock, or at least the fastenings on the door. It wasn't hugely secure anyway, he reasoned, and gave the door a mighty kick.

The minute he was inside, he knew.

DC King and Joanna were just on their way back from Birmingham. Their visit hadn't really told them anything but it had made the girls more real than Madame Bellange could ever have done. Mothers never quite see their daughters realistically for one reason or another. They invariably typecast them, either seeing them in their own image – a sort of mini-me, or as sweet, innocent little girls who never hit puberty. And then there is the mother who perceives her daughter as a siren – a temptress. A rival. None of these images is quite the real thing because the female of the species is far too complex to typecast.

But the image of the two girls sheltering in the cave with the Stuart brothers, drinking their coffee and gently flirting while sheltering from the rain, was a pleasant one. Poignant when you speculated on their fate but still pleasant for all that. And talking to the brothers again, Joanna had almost seen them, the elusive Annabelle Bellange and Dorothée Caron. Two young girls with a sense of adventure strong enough to carry them to the land of a poet they had been studying at school.

'I don't think it was them,' Joanna commented as she pulled out into the fast lane and zipped past a couple of mid-laners. 'But they did lie. They did know the girls.'

King grunted. 'Yeah,' he said. 'They knew them all right, but what motive could they have had for killing them, for hiding their bodies then coming back. Why would they do that?'

'Why would anyone?' Joanna responded grumpily. This case was not going smoothly. Irrational or not, she was beginning to see the two French girls as something of a tease.

Peeping from behind trees or boats or even peeping through the eye of a painting, giggling to themselves.

Danny was in the garage, which wasn't really big enough to be a garage anyway – only a SMART car would have fitted in it. At the back was a large chest freezer. Rusting, dirty, dusty. And unplugged. Hesketh-Brown looked at it balefully. Then he slipped on a pair of gloves and a face mask, and lifted the lid.

'Oh, shit.' He was beyond the stage of vomiting. He'd half expected something like this anyway. He dropped the lid and met his colleague's eyes. He had no mobile signal down here and the phone wasn't connected, so he left Hannah Beardmore to stand guard while he took the path which climbed the small hill. As soon as he got a couple of bars on his mobile he rang the station.

In less than half an hour, the wheels were in motion. Matthew Levin, Rush and Joanna had all been contacted. She took the call on the car phone just as they passed junction fourteen – the Eccleshall/Stafford north turnoff – and she felt a strange mixture of exhilaration and depression. No mystery here. They would find no teasing, giggling, sheepish girls ready to be scolded by their mothers and returned, tail between their legs, to France. Nothing but a couple of corpses to be identified, too rotten for that to be done by their loving parents, but by dental records and belongings. And DNA. There would be no kiss goodbye.

Yet at the same time, now they had their bodies, Joanna's blood was up. They could begin to find their killer. King glanced across and she filled him in, and saw her emotions mirrored in the DC's grey eyes. He knew who would be setting up the cross referencing, the computer links, searching databases. Joanna drew in a deep breath.

Now the work could really begin.

While she covered the miles between herself and the crime scene, the first rule of order was already being carried out. Isolate the area and clear a forensic corridor to gain access without compromising the scene.

The home office pathologist, i.e. her very own Matthew Levin, had an important job. Stupid as it might seem when two girls were so obviously dead and just as obviously had been dead for a number of weeks, it was still mandatory for them to be certified officially dead by a doctor and the coroner contacted before removal from the crime scene could be permitted.

Rush rang her just as they were passing Lime Kiln Bank on the Leek road through Hanley. There was no blue light on this squad car and its use wouldn't have been justified anyway. There was no hurry – not now. Even so, Joanna, inside, was in a tearing hurry. There was no time to lose, she felt. And no car, helicopter or police motorbike could be fast enough to satisfy her impatience.

'Sir.'

'I'm sure you're heading straight for Rudyard.' It was a statement. He obviously also knew of her impatient streak.

'Yes, sir.'

'I'd like to meet up with you – perhaps tomorrow?' Now that *was* a question.

'Yes, sir.'

'In the morning.' And that was an order. 'I take it these are the missing girls?'

'Almost certainly, sir, but of course we'll be making sure.'

'And an arrest?'

Again something warned her, but she spoke the words anyway. 'We'll be bringing Barker in for questioning shortly,' she said.

He rung off.

No one within a mile of Rudyard Lake could possibly mistake the fact that something dramatic was happening. There was almost a traffic jam at the far end of the lake as cars, vans and lorries jostled for access along the narrow track. And that, Joanna thought gloomily, was before the press homed in on their little drama.

The entire area was now taped off with only police personnel and people associated with the case allowed access. She was donning her forensic suit when Matthew's BMW swung in next to her squad car. There is always an added dimension to seeing someone in your personal life arrive in your work mode. She smirked at him, enjoying the sight of the long legs threading into a similar suit and the blond hair disappearing in the J-cloth headgear.

'Shall we?' he said as though inviting her for a dance rather than to view a couple of rotting corpses in a seedy garage.

Her response would have justified an invitation to a Viennese Waltz. 'Why not?' And they walked inside.

The scene was already well lit and a health and safety check carried out in view of the asbestos. As long as no one cut into it they were safe – for now.

The lid was still down on the freezer. Matthew lifted it and peered inside, the pair of them trying to ignore the stink of putrefaction, a stench strong enough to draw predators from miles around. In this case the freezer lid had provided an effective seal until raised.

The girls had been thrown in. In death, their limbs were tangled. They were wearing shorts and T-shirts. The shorts were damp, growing some fungus. Putrefaction begins at the caecum and progresses through the body, and the leakage had stained their clothes. Because they had been sealed inside the freezer there was no insect degradation. Joanna studied not the girls but her husband's face. Matthew's face was a mixture. Gentle, strong and determined. As he lifted the girls' limbs he seemed oblivious to the smell and seemed to see only what he needed to. Finally he closed the lid of the freezer and looked at her. 'They've been dead a few weeks,' he said. 'Probably around the day they went missing.' Then he addressed the watching officers. 'We need to get them out of the freezer and down to the mortuary so I can establish the cause of death.' Then he looked back at her and his green eyes initially softened. He addressed his next words to her very softly. 'And will you be attending the post-mortem, Inspector?'

She nodded, still tasting the putrefaction in her mouth, sensing it in her nose, feeling it crawl along her skin like an invasion of worms.

'It'll have to be in the afternoon,' he said. 'I'm lecturing in the morning.'

Again she nodded. The police photographer was busy recording the scene and an hour later the mortuary van arrived to take the two girls, separate now for the first time in weeks.

Now the real work began. The area would be scrutinized, combed and re-combed. And somewhere they would surely find something that would help them find the killer.

Now it was no longer a missing person's investigation but a murder hunt. And someone needed to inform the families.

Joanna glanced at King and he nodded. He knew what was expected of him.

'I'll go and make the call now,' he said.

The forensic van moved to the top of the lane and connected with the phone lines and broadband. King disappeared inside and she heard the sound of his fluent French, clipped yet sympathetic. She caught a few words. *Je regrette, non, madame.* We are investigating. *Mais oui.* He put down the phone, picked it up again and presumably spoke to the other mother. Joanna heard almost the same phrases being spoken and then King emerged from the van. 'They're coming over,' he said glumly.

Joanna's response was brisk. 'Well, we expected that. We'd better find somewhere for them to stay,' she said. 'And not Mandalay.'

Mandalay.

TWENTY-THREE

She filled Rush in as best she could.

'The post-mortem's later this afternoon,' she said. 'We'll be checking the DNA and dental records to be absolutely sure they are the missing girls but they fit the description as far as age and appearance goes. There's little doubt that they are Annabelle and Dorothée.' She met his eyes boldly. *What other two young women are missing in this area?*

Rush's mouth tightened and his eyes seem to shrink and bore into hers. She flinched from the gingery lashes, noted the receding hairline and weak chin which reminded her of President Assad of Syria, who was also not her favourite man. His voice, when he spoke, was clipped and uncompromising. 'I take it you'll be attending the PM.'

She nodded. It wasn't something she looked forward to, but she had a duty.

Rush nodded his head. In approval? 'I'll speak to you later.'

She was dismissed.

She spent the morning with Mike at Rudyard Lake, sifting through the mass of evidence that had been raked in: everything from ice-cream wrappers to a grubby thong which had been found under a bush. Some story there. Between ninety-eight and a hundred per cent of their trophies would prove to have no bearing on the case at all. But one had to try everything. One crucial piece of evidence, no matter how small, could be the one that solved their case.

After a couple of hours deciding which articles were for DNA testing and which could simply be stored under *Evidence*, she recorded an appeal for help from the general public. She'd drafted her statement out very carefully. The points to empha-size in this were the time frames, the descriptions, clothing and general appearance. What they couldn't cope with were thousands of rogue calls that led them in the wrong direction, or sightings of girls other than their two. Irrelevancies and red herrings which, like the assortment of bits and pieces in their bin bags, would still have to be sifted through. She made the appeal as clear and concise as she could, for local and national broadcast, and hoped that the post-mortem would guide them towards some answers. Then she drove into Newcastle-under-Lyme and the mortuary.

Matthew was already garbed up in green scrubs, waiting for her, a slight smile on his face. However much she might deny it, she could not hide her squeamishness from him, and he knew it. She handed him the two photographs. 'This is Annabelle Bellange. And this,' she said, handing him the second one, 'is Dorothée Caron.'

He took a cursory glance at the two pictures and then, without sentiment, crossed the room and pinned them to a board. The two girls, still in the clothes they had been found in – shorts and T-shirts, were lying on the mortuary slabs no more than four feet apart. Matthew looked from one to the other. He would treat these two as a single performance.

Joanna noticed that Annabelle was wearing one sneaker, while the other foot was bare. She indicated to the police photographer, who was faithfully recording the entire procedure to take a close up of the shoe, and indicated that this should be bagged up. If they found its partner it might help them discover where the two girls had died. Frequently X-rays or even CT scans were taken to record in minutiae the severity and extent of any assault.

'OK,' Matthew said, more to Paul, his assistant, than to her, 'let's get going.' He pulled his mask up over his nose and mouth.

Once the initial weights and measurements were done they began the serious stuff. Joanna had never been able to watch the initial stages of a PM when the Stryker saw carved through the cranium and the face was peeled down to expose the brain and underlying facial injuries. Still a little squeamish even after so many years' experience, she kept her eyes firmly fixed on a mark on the wall instead of on Matthew and the mortuary assistant's busy little hands, probing here and there. But even she, with her weak stomach and lack of medical knowledge, could see that that when he pressed on the lungs a certain amount of frothing appeared at the mouth. She knew the significance of this too. As he worked he muttered to himself, occasionally recording his comments and methodically taking samples. She watched him, her husband, in his own world.

An hour later he finally looked up. 'Annabelle drowned,' he said, confirming her suspicion. 'There's no sign of any other injury. I've got some samples to look for diatoms but my guess is that she drowned in the lake. It would make sense.'

She shook her head. No, it wouldn't. How could a drowning in the lake fit in with a body concealed in the deep freeze of a derelict house at least four hundred yards from the shore?

She looked sharply at him. 'There's no sign of any other injury, you say?'

Slowly Matthew shook his head. 'No,' he said firmly. 'She drowned.'

Joanna was thoughtful. If both girls had simply drowned, why hide the bodies? And who had? Was it the same person who had hidden the rucksacks so ineffectually – Barker? 'Matthew,' she said hesitantly, 'are you able to tell me whether she was placed in the freezer soon after drowning, or did someone find her body and hide it at a later date?' For God knows what reason, she puzzled silently.

'She was placed in the freezer within a couple of hours of her dying,' he said. 'I don't want to go into detail, though I will in court – either the coroner's or crown court. But in general it's to do with lividity or blood pooling.'

Joanna nodded. She knew enough about post-mortem changes to understand what Matthew was talking about.

She gestured towards the second girl, Dorothée. While her friend's face looked as though it had melted, discoloured flesh fallen away from facial bones, Dorothée's was almost unrecognizable as a face at all. Misshapen.

Matthew followed her gaze. 'I'm going to do an X-ray,' he said. 'It looks to me as though there's been quite an assault on her face. We're going to have to rely on underlying tissue and bone to be sure,' he said, 'but . . .' His voice trailed away and Joanna knew why. Matthew *hated* to guess or even to make any statement he could not back up with scientific fact. He looked at her and the skin around his eyes crinkled, looking suddenly soft and warm, his eyes a friendly, mossy green. When someone is wearing a face mask over their nose and mouth you can still tell when they are smiling by the movement of paper and eyes. They are your clue.

She smiled back at him and he bent over the second corpse, repeating the actions of the first.

It took him a little longer this time and she soon saw why. It was the cranium that was the problem. It was split, pieces pushed into the brain, which Matthew carefully removed using his fingertips and forceps to collect them into a small dish. Joanna looked. Some of the splinters were not of bone. They looked like . . . wood? She moved back. This girl had not died of drowning. Even she could see that. Again Matthew was quiet as he worked, apart from a few soft observations made into the tape recorder as an aide memoir. This time the mortuary assistant was using a ruler and the photographer was taking numerous pictures from all angles. There were other injuries too. Matthew spent time on the hands and forearms and she watched, fascinated, as he exposed a break in the right wrist, the bones splintering through the skin.

Unlike her friend, Dorothée had not drowned. Her lungs were clear. Matthew's concluding words were no surprise to her.

'Dorothée,' he said, confirming her own observation, 'did not drown. She was hit repeatedly on and around the head. The marks on her forearms, wrist and hands are defensive wounds. She was fighting her attacker off. Put up a pretty good fight, I'd say.' There was pity in his voice as he looked down at the body.

'But not quite good enough,' Joanna said.

'No. Not good enough.' Joanna stared at him as, momentarily, he seemed to struggle to keep his composure. 'She lost. She had numerous skull fractures, which probably caused her death. They are extensive. Some of those were done post-mortem, as though her killer wanted to be absolutely sure that she really was dead.'

'Any idea what she was hit with?'

'Well, it wasn't anything sharp. There are no incisions. I

would have thought something wide and flat like a shovel.'
Matthew frowned. 'But that's metal and in that case I would
have expected more contusion around the edges. Maybe some
cuts. There is a bit of a clue, though.' He fished around in the
shallow bowl and brought out—

'Is that a splinter of . . .?'

'Wood,' he said. 'So I think something shovel-shaped with
a wide edge. Maybe . . .' He half turned back towards the
table, '. . . possibly – no, probably – made of wood or partially
made of wood. There were a few splinters embedded in the
skull. So something broad and flat and made of wood.' He
hesitated, his eyes clouding. 'That's not all.'

Joanna waited.

'She was sexually assaulted. Her clothes were torn. Here
. . .' He crossed the room and showed Joanna the shorts
Dorothée had been wearing when found. The button and the
zip had been torn apart. Matthew returned to the girl on the
slab. 'There is bruising around her vagina. But no penetration
and certainly no ejaculation took place. I've taken swabs and
samples but I don't think we'll get any DNA evidence from
that.' He cleared his throat; a sure sign that he was affected
by the procedure and the conjecture. 'I haven't found any
pubic hair or anything else, for that matter.'

He was watching her, knowing that she would already be
trying to work out the sequence of events.

And she was. So now she had her scenario. One drowned,
the other assaulted. She looked at her husband hopefully. 'Any
idea in what order the girls were killed?'

'I can't say who died first,' he said. 'They've both been
dead for around ten to twelve weeks.' He made an attempt to
lighten her mood. 'You know the old adage for working out
the time of death,' he said, smiling now. 'They died sometime
after they were last seen alive and before their bodies were
found.'

She managed the weakest of smiles, which made him
apologize.

'Sorry, Jo. Couldn't resist.'

'We're bringing the families over from Europe,' she mused.
Involuntarily they both looked at the bodies on the slabs.

The mortuary attendant was doing a good job of putting the girls back together again. Yet . . .

'It's out of the question,' Matthew said. 'You must dissuade them from viewing them.' He practically shuddered. 'Would you want to see a child of yours in this state?' His face was screwed up in pain. 'I don't think so.'

'No. You're right.' She moved towards the door. 'Well, I suppose that's it.'

'Sorry, Jo,' he said. 'I'd better get on now. I really should get my notes down as quickly as possible, before I forget anything.' He gave her one of his wide grins and a wink before gently brushing her cheek with his lips. 'I'll see you later,' he said. Then, green eyes alight, he added, 'Or much later?'

She nodded, managed a weak smile in return, and left.

First she went to Leek station and reported back to CS Gabriel Rush, who listened with what she was now understanding to be his habitual intensity. 'So Annabelle drowned,' he said thoughtfully, his bony fingers tapping the desk, 'and Dorothée . . .'

'Multiple traumatic head injuries, sir.' Goodness, she was picking up on Matthew-speak.

'Did Levin have any idea what the weapon used would have been?'

'Only something broad and flat and made of wood. And she'd been sexually assaulted.'

She picked up on his interest. Sexual assault usually meant . . .

'No, sir. No ejaculation so no DNA.'

'Aah.' Rush was thoughtful. 'And any idea in what order they died?'

'He didn't know, sir.'

'I didn't mean Doctor Levin,' he said, carefully picking out his words like debris from between his teeth. 'I meant *you.* Have *you* any idea in which order they died?'

She was a little startled. 'No, sir.'

'Have you formed any *theory* as to the sequence of events?'

'I haven't had a lot of time to think about it,' she said, needled into defending herself. 'I've come straight from the mortuary.' Then, slowly, her brain began to unravel. 'If Annabelle drowned and the diatoms indicate she drowned in the lake she wasn't swimming, sir. She was fully dressed.'

Rush didn't encourage her with words but with a dip of his chin and a swift, curious glance from under those sandy lashes.

'She must have been in a boat,' she said, seeing the light as though an electric current was pulsing through her head. 'And the injury to Dorothée Matthew thinks was done with something flat, probably wooden. An oar or a paddle?' She didn't go any further but she was getting nearer. She sensed it.

'Good,' he said and then, quite abruptly, he changed tack. 'The girls' relatives?'

'Both mothers are flying over, together with Monsieur Bellange. DC Alan King is booking them into a hotel in Leek. Then he'll liaise with them. His French is good and—'

'All right,' Rush said, suddenly impatient. 'All right. That's enough for now. I don't need all the details. Keep me informed and let me know before your budget hits the stratosphere.'

As always, the mention of budgets put Joanna into a cold sweat and made her feel that she was overspending before she'd really started. Riding on that was a feeling of guilt that she should have looked harder into the text message which might have solved the case sooner. She should have suspected something. Found the girls weeks ago, et cetera.

'Do you think you have any significant DNA evidence off the clothes?'

'Not from Annabelle's,' she said carefully. 'Not after the immersion in water. Perhaps Dorothée's, though I didn't see anything obvious. There was a great deal of staining and degradation on both their clothes. They've gone to the lab to be looked at but I'm not hugely hopeful. Annabelle was only wearing one shoe, so if we can find the other we might possibly get some idea of where they died but again, I'm not optimistic, sir. Dorothée's shorts were torn but I didn't see anything. Anyway, the lab will take a good look.'

'Yes.' His face tightened with momentary disgust, as though he saw the garments himself. 'Well. Use the media to its maximum effect. Bit of free advertising, eh?' His face twisted into an even more bizarre grimace which showed small, neat, predatory teeth. It was only as Joanna left the room that she realized: Rush had been making a joke. Or at least, his idea of a joke.

TWENTY-FOUR

As she drove back to Rudyard she began to work out what might have happened. And by the time she reached the turn-off to Rudyard she was beginning to see clearly. Various images were swimming into her brain. First there was a boat. And an oar. Two girls and a man. He tries to have sex with one girl and when she resists he hits her with the oar. The other girl, terrified, swims away. But she can't swim. She drowns. There had not been a mark on Annabelle. And then the man – or men – panic. He or they continue hitting Dorothée until she too is dead. And now there are two corpses to dispose of.

But who? And when? Rudyard Lake was busy from early morning to late night, particularly in shorts and T-shirt weather. The scenario she had imagined, an attempted rape and a girl drowning, would surely have attracted attention? The lake wasn't that big. Even at the far end, surely someone would have noticed?

The image in her mind was quickly replaced by reality. Drawn up on the shore of the lake were small rowing boats and the sign, 'For Hire, £5 an hour' on a board leaning up against an upturned boat. Sitting on the upturned boat was the disgruntled boat-hire man, Keith Armitage, his eyes boiling in resentment at his lack of earnings on such promising weather. Beside the boats was a rack of wooden oars, upright as trees. Was the murder weapon amongst them?

She could see it all in her mind's eye, but she still couldn't make sense of it. There were still pieces of the jigsaw missing.

She parked her car next to the other police vehicles. Korpanski was watching her from the window of the briefing room. She filled him in on the results of the pos-mortem and then pooled her ideas with his. Like her, he could not make sense of events.

She called a briefing right away. She needed the officers to understand it all. She always hoped that one of them would come up with an idea. She watched their faces, grim and determined, and searched for a spark when one of them had an idea. But this time, no. They looked to her for an explanation and she had none. They dispersed.

Then things went into overdrive. The area around the boats down to the shore was cordoned off and the craft and paddles subjected to scrutiny. At least now they had a focus. A nucleus for their activity.

DC King had gone to meet the family members at Manchester airport. Joanna would have to speak to them later and discourage them from viewing the girls. In the meantime . . .

She looked across the water, sullen and stormy today, in a sulk − perhaps for the part it had played in the tragedy. She let her gaze slide over it, swim beneath it and finally surface. What secrets were hidden down there? Not the bodies, but was there something else down there apart from the pathetic, sodden red purse? Was there something down there which would lead them to the killer? Who was he? How had he done it? Was her theory right? What was his motive? Was it simply sexual lust? Had rape been his reason for taking the girls out on the lake? Hiding the bodies was the easy part to understand. Killers hide bodies in the hope of evading discovery.

Keith Armitage got up from the boat and walked towards them, scowling. 'How long are you going to be here?'

'As long as it takes, Mr Armitage.'

Like many police officers, she had little sympathy for the people caught up in the investigation of a crime. Her focus and pity was all for the victims and their families.

Armitage lost his temper then. 'How am I supposed to make a livin' 'ere with you lot buzzin' around like bees round a honey pot?'

'That isn't my concern, Mr Armitage,' Joanna said, her eyes narrowing. He had a nasty temper. He also had access to boats − and oars. Something in her mind clicked. Was his temper nasty enough to murder? Armitage's gaze wandered resentfully around the white-suited figures as he blew out an angry breath. 'I'm not going to be able to do much business with them lot hanging around,' he said grumpily. 'So I may as well . . .' He stomped back off to his perch on the boat and regarded the scene with frank hostility, every now and then clearing his throat with an angry rasp or lighting another cigarette.

Joanna watched him for a minute or two, pondering, then went to find Korpanski. He was directing the operations with all the panache of a Hollywood movie mogul organizing a crowd scene, pointing people in various directions. She watched him for a minute. Mike Korpanski was enjoying himself. She approached him. 'Can I have a word?'

They headed back to the studio they'd been using as a briefing room over the coffee shop. Joanna indicated the boat owner through the window. 'What do you make of him, Mike?'

'Pretty bloody cross.'

'Mmm. Shall we get him in and have a chat?'

Mike went to get him. Through the window Joanna saw Armitage glance up then throw his cigarette away and follow the sergeant.

His mood had improved. While his resentment hadn't exactly melted away, he did look resigned to spending a while 'helping the police with their enquiries'.

Concisely, Joanna explained exactly who she was and what they were doing there. She described to him the manner of the girls' deaths. 'So you see, Mr Armitage,' she continued smoothly, 'we're very anxious to know who did this. And we feel it probable that the assault on the girls happened when they were in a boat.' She watched his eyes narrow. He looked puzzled. Still angry, but also confused.

'I don't get it,' he said, resentment still boiling in his voice. 'What are you saying? What exactly are you suggesting? You think I had . . .' Behind the bluster Joanna read an element of fright. This guy, whatever he might appear, was nervous. 'Are you thinking *I* had something to do with it?'

'We're suggesting nothing of the sort, Mr Armitage,' she said, making a mental note to look into the guy's past. There *was* something he was uneasy about. But then killers often acted in an unpredictable way.

She pressed on. 'Do you remember two French girls hiring a boat back in July?'

'I don't know,' he said, blustering again. 'How can you

expect me to remember that far back? It's ages ago. Have you
any idea how many people hire my boats out? Sometimes I've
twenty or more out at the same time. That's hordes of people.'
And then, quite cleverly, he picked up on the very obstacle
that was bothering Joanna. 'How the heck do you think nobody
saw anything?'

She couldn't answer that one. So she moved on, flipping
the photographs on to the table. 'These girls,' she said,
watching for his reaction very carefully. 'They're very attractive, aren't they?'

'Yeah,' Armitage said uncomfortably. 'Yeah. I suppose they
are. Quite.' He leaned forward in his chair to emphasize his
next point. 'If they're your sort.'

'So do you remember them?'

'I don't know,' he said. 'I think . . . No.' He frowned. Then
his face cleared. 'Hang on a minute,' he said. 'Hang on. Were
they wearing shorts? Nice legs?' He appeared unabashed.

'You know what?' The light Joanna had been searching for
had switched on in his face. I did see them,' he said and
pointed towards the officers. 'They were having ice creams,'
he said, 'and sitting over there. They were wearing shorts.'

'Who were they with?'

Armitage looked puzzled. 'They weren't with anyone,' he
said. 'They were on their own. They weren't talking to anyone.
They were simply looking out across the water, eating ice
cream.'

TWENTY-FIVE

She had nothing to hold Armitage for, and yet she didn't want to let him go either. But she had no right to detain him and so reluctantly she released him and watched him through the window as he crossed the car park with thumping, heavy steps and returned to his perch on the top of one of his beloved boats, throwing a hostile glance back in their direction.

Mike was downstairs, still directing operations. 'The three French parents have arrived,' he said. 'They want to talk to you.' His dark eyes rested on her. 'As senior investigating officer . . .' he said, unmistakably dumping the responsibility on her.

'OK.' She felt her shoulders slump. This was an unenviable job but Mike was right. As SIO it *was* her responsibility.

'There is one thing that's been unearthed,' he said, like her, looking out of the window at Armitage's rigidly resentful form. 'Five years ago there was a charge against him of raping a young woman. He worked as a taxi driver then and was taking her home. She was fairly drunk and said that when she came to in the back of the cab he was on top of her.'

Joanna frowned. 'She was on her own?'

'Yeah. The allegations were later dropped.' Korpanski shifted so he faced the lake rather than her. 'The cab company obviously wouldn't employ him after that, and that was when he started this boat business. He's done well,' he added. 'Giving sailing lessons, boat hire. Seasonal stuff through the winter – he serves mulled wine and mince pies and stuff, and organizes a Christmas Fair. He's quite enterprising. Probably did him a favour not being able to be a taxi driver any more.'

'Yeah. I see,' Joanna said, and knew that theoretically she did now have enough to detain him. But . . . She went outside just as DC Alan King turned up.

He was to act as translator – if needed. They had commandeered the small wildlife centre as a private interview room. Joanna shook hands with them each in turn. Madame Bellange looked straight at her, saying nothing but she was in tight control. Armand Bellange was a small, neat man, with quick dark eyes black as currants. He looked shaken. He too shook hands and stood back. Renée Caron appeared the most upset. She held a small cotton handkerchief to her eyes which were reddened and a little swollen. She sniffed. They all sat down.

Joanna began. 'First of all,' she said, 'I must say how very sorry I am about what happened to your daughters. I also want to assure you that we will do absolutely everything we can to bring the perpetrator to justice.'

Armand Bellange spoke. 'Can we see our daughters?' He spoke for all of them.

Reluctantly Joanna shook her head. 'It really isn't a good idea. The girls have been dead for weeks. Probably since they were last seen in July.' She met their eyes and hoped they would understand without her having to go into graphic description. 'Remember them as they were,' she urged.

Their faces changed. They had, indeed, read between the lines. They'd drawn mental pictures and it had compounded their grief. Renée Caron dropped her head. '*Mon dieu*,' she said. '*Mon dieu*.'

Armand's voice shook with anger as he spoke in careful English. 'Do you have any idea who committed this crime?'

'We have leads,' Joanna said. 'When we're sure of our facts we will make an arrest.'

They were silent now, the shock permeating through them. She continued, 'Do you want to talk to me separately?'

Cécile Bellange spoke up. '*Non*,' she said quickly. '*Mais non*. Our girls were great friends. They played together as small children. They grew up together. They died together. They will be buried together. There will be no secrets between us.'

'How did our daughters die?' Armand's voice again, pushing for the truth.

'Annabelle drowned,' Joanna said.

Cécile's face crumpled. 'She had a fear of water, always,' she said. 'She never learned to swim. She had lessons as a child but . . .' she paused, 'water terrified her. It is,' she finished, with dignity, 'an irony.'

Cécile Bellange's eyes wandered through the window on to the glassy surface of the lake. Inviting, deceitful, guilelessly innocent. 'Was it there?' she asked.

'We don't know for sure,' Joanna said tentatively, 'but there is a test we can do. When we have the result we will know for certain. But it was almost certainly on the lake.'

Renée Caron spoke. 'And Dorothée?'

This was more difficult. 'She was hit over the head.' Joanna hesitated.

Renée Caron scrutinized her. 'And?'

Joanna's silence spoke volumes.

Renée Caron's voice was breaking. 'She was raped?'

'There was an attempt. No full penetration.'

The words provoked an outburst of weeping. This was only adding to their unhappiness. Joanna would have loved to have kept this last cruel fact back, but there was a demand for the full truth, unembellished, to be given to the relatives. It only made things worse if they found out something later and particularly if it was from another, unofficial source such as the press.

She tried to bring this dreadful interview to a close, but first she had to ask: 'Tell me,' she said. 'Were the girls virgins?'

Armand gave a wonderfully expressive Gallic shrug. 'Who can know,' he said. 'What man – or woman – truthfully knows that about their daughter?'

Neither woman added to this. Joanna had to be content with that.

'DC King will take you to a hotel,' she said. 'Naturally Staffordshire police will pick up the bill. We will keep you informed of any progress.'

Armand stood up and put his arm around his ex-wife. Then he extended a hand to Renée Caron. 'Come,' he said. 'We take some rest now.'

Cécile Bellange's shoulders were still straight and proud but Renée Caron was destroyed.

DC King held the car doors open and minutes later they were gone.

Joanna found Mike back at the incident room. 'Let's do a recap,' she said. 'Barker.'

'Has to be a possibility,' Korpanski agreed, 'but he's looking a bit less likely. I can't see him taking the girls out on a boat and then hammering one of them over the head with the oar while watching the other one drown.'

'OK. What about the Stuart brothers?'

Korpanski screwed up his face. 'I can't see it somehow,' he said. 'I mean, why would they? They could have had their pick of girls. The two barmaids at the Rudyard Hotel were practically gagging for them.'

'I know that. But . . .' Joanna crossed the room and pointed to the board. 'Time frame,' she said. 'Saturday *night*, twentieth of July. Mike, it had to be at night. That's why no one saw or heard anything. The hotel runs a music karaoke on a Saturday. It would have been noisy. James and Martin invite the girls out for a moonlight cruise. They try to have sex with them. Dorothée struggles. Annabelle, terrified, jumps overboard and drowns?'

'It's certainly a *potential s*cenario,' Korpanski said. But Joanna had picked up on the dubious note in his voice. 'But?' she challenged.

'I'm just not sure it's the truth.'

'OK.' Joanna stood up. Truth was she shared Korpanski's doubts.

'Let's go and see how things are progressing,' she said.

The water's edge was still a hive of activity. If anything, it was even busier. A television crew had arrived and were filming a reporter at the water's edge – or as near as they could get with the police tape strung across, preventing access. There were quite a few voyeurs pretending not to be looking but admiring the scene, though some were craning their necks to see everything.

Joanna moved in. Jason Spark was examining an oar which was splintered. 'I think this might be it,' he said, excited, as Joanna approached. She studied it. It was certainly damaged. But even if it was the murder weapon six weeks' immersion in and out of the water would surely have washed any forensic evidence away. However, Matthew had collected some splinters. 'Bag it up,' she said. It was silly to be pleased about what was a potential find but Jason had started life as a 'special' constable and had shown enthusiasm, promise and a certain inspiration that inspired his colleagues. That was why they called him Jason Bright Spark. When he had finally been accepted as a full-time constable she had been pleased. And now here he was, making what was probably a significant find.

Armitage was eyeing them balefully from his perch.

Joanna glanced across at him, then turned her attention back to the oar. If this was it, it was hard evidence. They could match up the wood with the splinters Matthew had removed from Dorothée Caron's brain. She nodded approval at Jason, who couldn't contain his excitement at having possibly found something which would prove crucial in the investigation. He was almost jumping up and down. She put a hand on his shoulder.

It was Mark Fask who made the next discovery.

One of the boats had a broken seat and had been pulled away from the other boats for hire.

She looked at it first, wondering. Then she approached Armitage. 'When was this boat taken out of service?'

He looked mystified. 'I don't know,' he began. 'Sometime . . . back in the summer.' He looked pained. 'I can't remember exactly when but I've been busy. I usually get around to repairs and things over the winter.' He appeared to hesitate after speaking, his eyes watching her as though he was evaluating whether she believed him.

'And when you realized the seat was broken did you take it straight out of service?'

Armitage snorted. '''Course I did,' he said. 'Think anyone would hire a boat with a seat broke?' His eyes twinkled. 'And that's quite apart from health and safety.'

It made sense. She watched him for a further minute more then turned on her heel and left.

It was time to return to Mandalay and her original suspect – Horace Gladstone Barker. He looked less than pleased to see her but tried his best to smile. 'Inspector,' he said in his soft flat voice. 'What a pleasure.'

'Indeed.'

'I heard on the . . .' His voice died away as Korpanski stepped forward. Barker seemed to shrink into a pale and slack-skinned amorphous heap.

'Tell me, Mr Barker,' Joanna began briskly. 'Have *you* ever taken a boat out on the lake?'

Barker swivelled his head to look at her, apparently baffled by the question, so Joanna repeated it. Then he snorted. It was a mocking, incredulous sound. 'Me? Take a boat out on the lake? I'm as likely to book a trip to Burma. I have a fear of water. I like *looking* at it,' he said creepily. 'Not being *on* it. And certainly not being *in* it. And definitely not *under* it. I couldn't handle a boat.'

'You mean you've never taken a boat out on the lake?'

Barker turned his attention to the burly sergeant. 'I haven't even been on the pleasure cruise, Sergeant,' he said with a certain amount of dignity which vanished when he added, 'not even on the Treasure Island pirate's cruise.'

Joanna raised her eyebrows at Mike, who was doing his best not to smile. 'Mr Barker,' she said, deciding to put her theory to the test. 'Is it possible the girls left on Saturday night rather than on Sunday morning?'

He thought about it for a while. 'I last saw them on the Saturday night,' he said slowly. 'They were on their way out. I told them to make sure they had their keys with them.'

'Did you hear them come in?'

'I'm a heavy sleeper,' Barker said.

'Had their beds been slept in?'

'They always made them so I wouldn't have been able to tell.'

'Did you hear them go out on the Sunday morning?'

'I did not,' Barker said.

Joanna gave Mike a sharp quick look. It shifted the emphasis, made the scenario so much more plausible.

She studied Barker's bland face and he stared back at her. But there was something defiant in his manner now. He was almost challenging her to re-arrest him. It was she who dropped her eyes first. Whatever the explanation, she decided, it might not lie here.

She left Mandalay despondent, still feeling they were fumbling in the dark.

There was, however, one beautiful, glistening ray of hope. Matthew rang to say the analysis of the diatoms had come through. They confirmed that Annabelle Bellange had died in the lake, and also that microscope examination of the splinters taken from the oar earlier that day matched the splinters removed from Dorothée Caron's skull.

She almost did a high-five with Mike. They had their murder weapon and they knew where Annabelle Bellange had drowned. If the boat with the broken seat provided a speck of blood they also had the scene of Dorothée's murder too. As suspected, both had died at Rudyard Lake, the place they had come to on a pilgrimage. Ironic, or perhaps a fitting tribute? The two girls' names would now be forever linked with the name of Rudyard. To the great man. Author and poet.

It was a stroke of luck that the boat had been taken straight out of service.

But while Joanna felt instinctively that she understood the sequence of events, they still didn't know who was behind them. She could only hope that their killer had obeyed Locard's exchange principle – that he had both taken something *from* and left something *at* the scene of the crime.

'It must have happened at night, Mike,' she said. 'It was the height of summer. There were plenty of people here then.' She screwed up her face. 'We need a weather report. School holidays had just begun. It was a Saturday night. The lake isn't that big. Someone would have seen or heard something. It was risky but we're assuming this was a spur-of-the-moment action.'

Korpanski nodded and went on the computer to check the weather report.

She rang Matthew next. 'Matt,' she said, 'this attempted rape on Dorothée. Is it possible . . . the bruising and marks. Could they have been done with an object rather than . . .?'

'You mean rather than attempted intercourse?'

Delicately put, she thought, mentally slapping her husband on the back. 'Yes.'

'Ye-es,' he said, and she sensed the impending 'but'. She was right. 'Bu-ut,' he said, drawing out the objection, 'there was no debris. No glass or wood. No plastic. And the abrasions . . .'

Every now and then their working relationship and personal relationship collided. This was just such an occasion.

'An erect penis is a rounded object,' Matthew said awkwardly. She could sense his embarrassment right down the phone line. 'It leaves certain marks,' he continued, just as embarrassed. 'I don't think it was a hard object. I think it was attempted penetration.'

She disconnected. Mike Korpanski was keeping his eye on her, watching her and smirking.

'I wonder,' she said, 'if it wasn't even as planned as we'd thought. I wonder if, it being a nice evening, the girls packed up on the Saturday night ready to leave early on the Sunday morning, then went out to take a last look at the lake. What was the weather like that night?'

Korpanski crossed to his computer and tapped on a few keys. 'Full moon,' he said. 'The lake must have looked bewitching. And it was a warm night, hence the shorts.'

'Opportunist,' she said, pressing her hands to her forehead.

'Right. Let's go back.'

Armitage made no attempt to hide his dislike of them and his mistrust at their return. His eyes wandered around the swarm of officers scrutinizing the area and then turned heavenwards in exasperation. After his last encounter with the police his mistrust of them was as obvious as the glowing sun in the sky.

He didn't stop fiddling with the boat repairs until they were right up to him. And even then, he kept his back turned on them in contempt and hostility.

'Tell me,' Joanna asked softly, ignoring his poor manners. 'What time do you close in the summer?'

'Eight o'clock.'

'And your boats? How do you keep them safe?'

'They're locked up,' he said.

'Then who has a key, Mr Armitage?'

The look he gave them was defiant.

Joanna continued, 'When your boat seat was broken, had

you had a break in?' She looked innocently at Korpanski. 'We
didn't get a report of a break-in here, at the boatyard, back in
July, did we, Mike?'

Neither of them had checked. It was an inspired guess. In
reality, Joanna didn't have a clue, but Mike played along
beautifully.

'No,' Armitage said grumpily.

'So, does anybody take your boats out at night?'

Armitage was no fool. His sharp eyes showed he knew
exactly what they were asking. He licked his lips. Dry and
cracked, his tongue seemed to stick.

Joanna had to repeat the question. 'Well, Mr Armitage?'

'They're locked up,' he said.

'Then *who* has a key, Mr Armitage?'

Joanna glanced at Mike. Who was he shielding? And why?
Were the pair of them allying themselves against the police
because Armitage had previous form?

'Who has access to your craft when you're closed, Mr
Armitage?' She felt her face harden. He needed the thumbscrews turning. 'Or was it you who took them out – to show
them the lake – and like the allegation made against you before,
you attempted to have sex with one of them?'

'I know what you'll do,' he said. 'Just like before, you'll
try to pin something on me. Well, you can't this time because
the weekend those two girls were last seen I was at an eightieth
birthday party on the Saturday night. From eight o'clock,' he
finished triumphantly.

She still needed to push. 'Two girls are dead, Mr Armitage.
Their parents haven't even been allowed to see their bodies
because they've been hidden for almost twelve weeks. They've
decomposed to a disgusting degree.' She took a step closer.
'Their mothers and father can't even kiss their little girls
goodbye.'

Armitage blinked.

She continued: 'These were two lovely girls who were bright
and adventurous. They'd travelled from Europe to make a
pilgrimage to Rudyard Kipling. That's why they came to this
particular little corner of Staffordshire instead of staying in
London or Stratford or one of the other more popular tourist

hotspots. They should have brought their parents joy, married, had children, careers. Instead . . .'

Armitage held up his hand as a 'stop' sign. 'They're locked up,' he protested, still stubborn, but his voice sound weaker now, almost resigned. They were almost there.

'Then who has a key, Mr Armitage?'

TWENTY-SIX

Just like Joanna thought, Armitage finally caved in. 'Young Will,' he said in a voice hoarse with shame. 'He's fond of sailing. I don't mind him takin' a boat out. He's careful and always puts it back ship shape. He has a key,' he said. 'He helps me every now and again – does a bit of everything round the lake, you know. The van, the café . . . I think he sometimes takes a boat out on the lake.' And then he damned him. 'I think he had the boat out the night the seat was broken,' he said.

Joanna looked at Mike, her face reflecting shock. Fresh-faced Will? The boy whose face was lit with innocence? Will, the carer for his mother? Will the ice-cream and café boy?

Joanna looked at Mike and they both shrugged, palms out. *Will?*

They found him standing in the empty café. Mid-week, October, children back at school. It was a disconsolate scene, from the cakes which looked dry and stale to the coffee machine bubbling away quite merrily to the cups lined up, waiting to be filled.

He eyed them as they walked in and his shoulders drooped. His chin dropped, his eyes regarding them warily. He gave it one last try. 'Coffee, Inspector?'

And instinctively, Joanna knew that he was their guilty man. She could see it as clearly as though she had been a witness.

She saw no point in doing anything but charging him with the murder of the two girls, cautioning him and taking him back to the police station.

On the way there she rang DC King. The girls' parents were in her mind and she didn't want the news that they'd made an arrest to leak out. Not just yet.

When charged with a serious offence people react in different ways. Some people bluster, others vigorously deny it. Some admit their crime – too quickly in the eyes of their barristers – as though once confessed they were relieved of their secret burden of guilt.

Will was of the startled, rabbit-caught-in-car-headlights variety. He blinked and looked bemused, confused even. Startled and uncomprehending. 'But,' he said, shaking his head. It was the nearest he would ever get to a denial.

Joanna had decided to confront him with her version of events.

'You got friendly with the two French girls, Annabelle and Dorothée,' she said.

Will stared, his blue eyes so guileless Joanna wondered how he could look so innocent and yet be so guilty.

Will smiled at her. It was friendly and open. 'That's right,' he said. He could have been admitting to serving them with a ninety-nine.

'When did you meet them?'

'Not long after they arrived,' he said. 'I like to go walking and was out on the moors one day when I found one of them letterboxes. It said they were in Rudyard and to look them up.' He suddenly sounded aggrieved. 'They shouldn't have led me on. They shouldn't have done that. They made me think they wanted me. *Wanted me*,' he repeated. 'It isn't fair what they did.'

An interesting perspective that attempted rape and murder is fair whereas flirting is not, Joanna mused.

'You know you have the right to a lawyer?'

'I don't need no lawyer,' Will said disdainfully. 'Why would I want a lawyer?'

Joanna lifted her eyebrows at Mike, who gave her a lopsided grin and an *is-this-guy-for-real* scowl simultaneously. 'We need you to explain more, Will,' she said. 'Did they know you? Had they met you before?'

'Yeah. I knew they were staying at Barker's – we'd chatted when they came to the café or bought an ice cream. We'd got along all right. When I saw the picture in the letterbox I knew who they were even if they didn't know me.'

Joanna gave Mike another look and shrugged.

Will continued his protestations. 'They was leadin' me on.

They were all right when they were gettin' a free trip on the boat. And when I tried to . . .' That was when words failed him. 'When I . . .' He simply couldn't find the right phrases. 'They started . . .'

'You tried to have sex with Dorothée, didn't you?'

Will leaned forward. 'They weren't taking me seriously. It was just to stop her laughing at me, you see.'

It was an explanation – of sorts. 'Then I hit her. And then.' He cleared his throat with an explosive cough. 'The other one. She was screamin' and all sorts. She jumped overboard.' A look of disdain fleeted across his face. 'It were obvious she couldn't swim but her friend shouted at her to get help.'

'The other one,' Joanna said coldly, 'was called Annabelle Bellange.'

Give her the dignity of her name. 'The girl you tried to have sex with and, failing that, hit with the oar, was called Dorothée Caron.'

How many killers, she wondered, know the names of their victims? Not all – not until or unless they come to court. Then they know and remember those names all right.

'Nothing but a pair of cockteasers,' Will said contemptuously. Then something happened to him and his attitude changed. 'Will my mum have to know?'

Mike and Joanna exchanged another incredulous look. People were so unpredictable and this one more than most.

'What'll happen to her now?' he asked. 'Who'll look after her?'

Surely the question he should be asking was, *What will happen to me now?*

Korpanski's gaze said it all. What will happen to your mum? That, my lad, is the least of your worries.

TWENTY-SEVEN

I t was eleven o'clock when she finally arrived home. Will Murdoch had been charged and she had had the pleasure of telling her new chief superintendent that he had confessed to the murder of Dorothée Caron but had insisted that Annabelle Bellange had dived out of the boat and drowned and he *'wasn't going to swing for that one too'*.

No one had pointed out that the last hanging in the United Kingdom had been in 1964.

When asked if he had tried to save her for the first time, his angelic features had coloured.

Oh no, Joanna had thought. *You couldn't and wouldn't have been able to save her because you were too busy murdering her best friend.*

When she had finished questioning Will she had the difficult job of speaking to the Bellanges and Renée Caron. The three of them had looked stunned that such a thing could happen and Joanna knew that as her vision of Rudyard Lake had been spoiled for ever, so had their vision of 'Merry England' – not only the country but the poet, too, had been tainted for their entire lives. As gently as she could she had explained the circumstances of their daughters' deaths and the British legal process of charging, remand and the judiciary system. She'd added that a life sentence was mandatory for murder and that they would be pushing that he serve no less than twenty-five years. This had made all three of them look weary. Not grieved, simply exhausted. Another young life ruined.

At the same time, Joanna had advised them to be prepared for a manslaughter charge as there had been no obvious premeditation for murder. And then she'd had to explain that there might be a plea that the balance of his mind was unsound and that the lawyers may well make much of the fact that William Murdoch was his mother's sole carer. That had meant, in turn, that he'd had limited, if any, opportunities to socialize with his peers. He was isolated, frustrated and dangerously clueless when it came to girls.

'Tell me,' Madame Bellange said, tears in her eyes now, as though her iron self-control had exploded. 'Would it have made any difference if we had disbelieved the text message?'

'No.'

'Or raised the alarm that they were missing sooner?'

'No.'

She'd left them then, talking in French. King had gone home for the night.

She let herself into the cottage, weary but exultant. Matthew greeted her at the doorway and without a word gave her a hug. 'Well done,' he said, leading her into the sitting room and handing her a glass of wine. 'Well done. Thank God you've found out who did it.'

She gave a watery smile. 'We still have to get him behind bars, Matt.'

He patted her arm. 'True. But I have good vibes about the months ahead,' he said, brushing her mouth with his fingers. 'Good vibes. This is the beginning. I suppose he'll say he has a personality disorder.'

She dropped on to the sofa. 'Now that's an interesting observation,' she said. 'Hannah Beardmore, bless her, rang Andrea Newton at social services about Will Murdoch's mother as she was going to be left all alone. Do you know what she said?'

Matthew shrugged and she took a deep draft of wine before answering her own question. 'She said that she'd always wondered who was the vulnerable adult and who was the carer, so that tells you something. She said she thought it would do Mrs Murdoch good to be on her own and not mollycoddled by her son. Then she said she'd always thought there was something a bit strange about Will.'

'Well, well, well,' he said.

'And what about Eloise?' she asked, aware that there seemed to be no cloud handing over Matthew tonight.

'It's OK,' he said, his voice still bright.

She stared at him, bemused. 'But I thought . . .'

'I had a word with her,' he said happily. 'She was just

anxious about the exams.' He laughed. 'You know what a
perfectionist she is.'

'Yes,' she said quietly. 'I know. So all that anxiety?'

'She's promised to behave herself in future. But I meant
what I said. We must keep an eye on her.'

Three months later

They had a date for the court case. Murdoch was in a remand
centre and yes, his brief was banging on about responsibilities
to his mother and his balance of mind, but Joanna felt little
sympathy.

Her period came late, heavier than usual and accompanied
by stomach cramps that seemed worse than the norm. Bugger,
she thought. Double bugger. And then, riding on the shoulders
of the angry double bugger, rode fear. Matthew had married
her because he wanted a legitimate child. Correction. Not a
legitimate child. A legal son who'd bear the name Levin of
which he was so proud. His forebears, such as his great-
grandfather Jakob, had travelled from Russia in the late-nine-
teenth century to escape the progroms against Jews. Her one
accidental and unplanned pregnancy three years ago had
resulted in a spontaneous miscarriage. What if she couldn't
keep her side of the bargain? She felt sick. What then?

One of the long-standing bones of contention in his and
Jane's marriage had been her refusal to have another child.
Eloise had been a 'mistake', she'd said, and following on from
that she had no intention of going through 'all that' again.
And yet Jane had managed to give her next husband twin sons,
an event that had hurt Matthew more than he could ever say.
She had seen the lines of pain wash over his features like
waves on the lake. And she knew she had to do this for him
whatever her own personal prejudices.

So creeping in now was fear. Having not wanted a child
she had never ever considered this scenario – that she might
not actually be able to bear one.

And what then, Piercy? What then?